Execution, Texas:

1987

Stonewall Inn Editions

Keith Kahla, General Editor

Execution, Texas:

1987

D. Travers Scott

St. Martin's Press ⚏ New York

Excerpts from and material related to this book have appeared previously in *Convolvulus, Mysterious Wysteria, Pink Pages, Pucker Up, Random St. Magazine, Slur, Talking Raven Quarterly, Visions of Death in 1987,* and *WhiteWalls.*

"Cake" (page 40): Words and music by J. Keith Strickland, Cynthia Wilson, and Ricky Helton Wilson © 1989 EMI Blackwood Music, Inc., Boo Fant Tunes, Inc., and Ricky Wilson Designee. All rights for Boo Fant Tunes, Inc., controlled and administrated by EMI Blackwood Music, Inc. All rights reserved. International copyright secured. Used by permission.

"The Black Wedding" ("La Boda Negra," page 211) sung and arranged by Lydia Mendoza, translation by Guillermo Hernández and Yolanda Zepeda. From Lydia Mendoza's CD *Mal Hombre*, Arhoolie/Folklyric CD 7002, 10341 San Pablo Ave., El Cerrito, CA 94530. All rights reserved. Used by permission.

Library of Congress Cataloging-in-Publication Data

Scott, D. Travers.
    Execution, Texas: 1987 / D. Travers Scott.—1st Stonewall Inn
ed.
        p. cm.
    ISBN 0-312-19878-7
    1. Young men—Texas—Fiction. 2. Texas—Fiction. I. Title.
[PS3569.C614E97   1997]
813'.54—dc21   98-51317
                                                                                    CIP

First Stonewall Inn Edition: March 1999

10 9 8 7 6 5 4 3 2 1

for Sherry Harper

acknowledgments

Heartfelt thanks to the following for encouragement, assistance, and support: 848 Community Space (San Francisco), Marc Almond, Ellen Blum, Bill Brent, Andy Byrum, Amelia Copeland, Club Lower Links (Chicago), Carole DeSanti, Jennifer Natalya Fink, Michael Thomas Ford, Karen Green, Scott Heim, Lin Hixson, Dan Jackson, Brian Keith Jackson, Keith Kahla, Kevin Killian, Michael Lowenthal, Michelle Manes, John Edward McGrath, James McManus, The Metropolitan Arts Commission of Portland, Oregon; Edward Ash Milby, Iris Moore, Tommy Mueller, Achy Obejas, Scott O'Hara, *P-form* magazine, Teresa Powell, Carol A. Queen, Vanessa Renwick, Thomas Roche, Rexall Rose (Portland Oregon), Doug Sadownick, Lawrence Schimel, David Sedaris, Matthew Stadler, Tristan Taormino, Ken Thompson, Selene Wacker, Mikel Wadewitz, Jan Wallace, all the publications in which elements of this book have appeared, all my teachers, and all my parents and family. Love and boundless appreciation to David Eckard, for being beside me every step of the way.

Execution, Texas:

1987

My family has a story:

After her young husband's death, my great-grandmother moved to Texas to teach school in the small town of Execution. The town's name unnerved her, but like midnight coyote wails and many other things Western, it also reassured. A town named for strong-armed law must be a safe place for a widow to raise her son. The sheriff would be a good role model, and she would have less to fear from amorous strangers.

The week she arrived in Execution, she took her boy to the public hanging of a murderer. She wanted him to see the town live up to its name.

My grandfather's eyes gleamed as he passed on this heirloom memory. Certain details focused his mind, pulled him from his cloud of drink and prescriptions. He turned sharp and coherent, as if the past helped him engage the present.

"And as the killer's body was hanging from the noose, the widow of the man who'd been murdered, she brought herself forward for collecting her due. She waited till the body quit dancing, then real slow, real proper and ladylike, she pulled this long beaded pin from out her mourning veil. She stuck that pin deep into the murderer's body, again and again and again. Everybody there at the town square—the sheriff, the preacher, his daughter (who'd someday be your Meemaw)—everybody started clapping their hands for the widow. My mother, she being a widow, too, started clapping. So did I."

Texas claimed my family. After telling stories, my grandfather would play old 78s. I'd watch him sip brown bottles, and we'd listen to Hank Williams' forlorn wail: "I Can't Escape from You" and "Why Should We Try Anymore?" The cowboy banshee would rise from the black grooves like a ghost, "Our story, so old, again has been told. . . ."

april, 1987

Seeger King Has a Vision Before Prom

"I thought I'd die when my son turned twenty-five," his father said.

Seeger spied on his parents finishing dinner with their neighbors. His stepmother, Rhonda, rose from behind the fridge, mason jar in one hand and box of wine in the other. Cicadas' alien yowl underscored the evening like a constant passing plane. The neighbors' son and dog shouted from the alley. Nightbreeze rustled lace curtains. Carly Simon's "Coming Around Again" warbled from the stereo, soothing.

"Well?" Rhonda said, carrying the jar and wine box to the table.

"Well, what?" Abraham answered, arms across chest. Seeger adjusted the hall door's shutters for a better view.

"What makes you think you're going to go off and die so soon?" Rhonda tweaked the plastic tap, dribbling Gallo Ripe Burgundy into neighbor Bill's jar.

"Came out when Joan and I split," Abraham said. "We did this exercise—you know, in therapy?"

Seeger rolled his eyes at Abe's showing off.

"Well now, we did this here exercise where you imagined what the rest of your life would be like. Want to top me off, too?"

Seeger noticed that Abraham didn't hold out his jar for Rhonda. His father realigned his fork, spoon, and knife till parallel. He passed his palm absently across the top of his salt-and-pepper crewcut and watched his wife pour the wine.

"Oh, fudge," Rhonda sighed, shaking the box as the ruby trickle dwindled. "That's the last of it, 'less anyone feels like driving into Dallas."

"Ain't living in a dry county a bitch?" said Pam, Bill's wife.

"Anyhow," Abraham went on, "when I got to imagining Seeger at twenty-five, I couldn't think of anything, 'cause I'd be dead by then. My parents died when I was twenty-five; my father's dad died when he was roundabout twenty-five. I expected there'd be a pattern, *subconsciously.*"

Seeger's right eyelid twitched.

"That's not very positive thinking, Abraham," Rhonda said. She put the empty wine box beside the trashcan. "Prayer shapes reality."

God, she's gonna sing one of those Christian motivational songs, Seeger thought. Dinner's chides about his hair, which was lacquered into a dramatic swoop over one eye, had frayed his patience.

Abraham cleared his throat. "Yeah, I know. I been praying for years no one would buy this house just so I could be stuck here teaching redneck bastards rest my life."

"Abe, it's not just a religious issue." Rhonda bent over, cooling her face in the oscillating fan on the kitchen counter. "Bill Cosby said pretty near the same thing in that *Fatherhood* book of his." Her voice vibrated like a ghost as it passed through the fan's blades.

"Oh now, and I can guess who he went praying to, all those years kicking back around the *Playboy* mansion."

Rhonda diplomatically folded her arms. "Seeger, hon," she called, "you want some pie?"

Seeger slid back down the hall, not wanting them to know he'd been watching. "Sure," he replied with calculated languor. He could put up with them a while longer for strawberry-rhubarb.

Seeger gave his prom ensemble a final appraisal in the hall mirror. The Vavoom Megagel kept his long, coal-black hair securely in place without darkening the blond streak at his right temple (like his favorite singer, Marc Almond, on the cover of his "Love Letter" 10" single, the one featuring the limited-edition Cabaret Voltaire remix and the a cappella version with the Westminster City School Choir). His black full-dress tails, regrettably rental, fit fine. He had a real collapsible top hat. He and his girlfriend, Cordelia, had found it in Dallas at this place called Millennium, across from State Fair Park. You couldn't even tell where he and Cordelia had patched the lining with material from one of her camisoles. His cuff links gleamed: chrome circles embossed with the Cyrillic initials of the Soviet space agency, an Ides of March present from Cordelia. Her inspiration had also wrought the crimson lamé cummerbund and coordinating handkerchief square. Finally, his mail-order black PVC loafers with triple chrome buckles and thick rubber soles squeaked pleasingly as he stretched up on his tiptoes. Abraham called them his "disco moon booties."

Seeger felt satisfied, tentatively. He closed his eyes and visualized his aura as an icy cyan. His real mother, Joan, had told him blue was the color of self-confidence. He opened his eyes.

Hope Cordelia doesn't show during dessert. Want to take off soon as she gets here, none of that picture-taking, oohing-aahing, reminiscing shit.

"You think you're really gonna go and die when he's twenty-five?" Pam asked.

"Course I don't believe in it." Abraham aimed his fork at Seeger as he crept into the room. A smidge of golden fat dangled from the tip. "So don't be getting your hopes up, Plastic-hair." Seeger ignored him and sat down.

"Twenty-five's a right good time for an inheritance," Bill said brightly. "House downpayment, honeymoon—"

"He's *not* getting married anytime before he's thirty," Rhonda announced. She waited beside the humming radar range, hand on hip, the other holding a knife. The kitchen light flickered from the old range's powersurge. "He's learned all about youth's foolishness from us," she said with a frank smile. Seeger looked away.

"And not that I wouldn't give my blessing to my dear son's each and every whim," Abraham said, "but might I please request that if you and Miss Cordelia do start shacking up—"

"Abe!"

"Y'all will keep that sister of hers—"

"Stepsister—" Seeger corrected.

"Stepsister."

"And cousin."

"Whatever the damn girl is, can you just try keeping Vikki at arm's length from this family?"

"Don't worry," Seeger muttered.

"Cordelia I can deal with, but that sister of hers! Having Vikki in class this year has been enough to damn near—"

"Oooh!" Rhonda interrupted, swooping down on the table with a steaming pie. "Can you make a spot for this, hon?"

Seeger pushed away dinner's aluminum baking pan. Pork drippings sloshed toward him. Recalling the pinkish gray meat he'd eaten earlier pricked him with nausea. Abe had been so proud of the new find from his show-off-for-the-neighbors yuppie grocery store in Dallas. But what *was* pork tenderloin, anyway? Seeger's mouth oozed saliva; his tongue felt thick and limp. Exactly where on the pig did that thick meat log come from? Was it a large, full-body muscle? Marrow from inside the spine? Did butchers core it out, like geologists taking a soil sample, boring into layers of flesh with a tubular razor? Gross.

The pie's crust collapsed as Rhonda set it down, red lumps oozing out. " 'Fraid it's more of a cobbler," she apologized.

Abraham jabbed the pile, studying a steaming rhubarb lump.

"Go on, now, taste it," Rhonda said.

Seeger remembered his mother saying, "Taste it," to him during a visit last year:

Seeger had taken the mug from Joan's hands.

"What is it?" He had eyed the thin, niveous liquid.

"Leche de madre."

Seeger had looked past her into the living room. Her roommate had lounged on the futon, naked breasts and full belly a planet and two moons against a swirling, violet galaxy of paisley batik. Some New Age blips and whooshes had trickled out of the stereo.

Seeger had looked at the milk, queasy. Did this count as a "bodily fluid?" Well, *duh,* it was a fluid from the body, but that *Time* magazine article hadn't said anything about breast milk.

"Go on," Joan had said, flicking stray black bangs off her forehead. "None of your high school buds ever get to taste this ambrosia of life."

How much of an AIDS risk could a monogamous, artifically inseminated lesbian be, anyway? Certainly not more than Jésus. You weren't the first guy he ever had sex with, and he did come in your mouth that first time.

"Sandra and I are going to eat the placenta," the roommate had announced. "She got a recipe from the Wimmins' Center based on an ancient Mayan ritual."

He had breathed in deep, deciding it definitely was not safe, but Joan wouldn't accept that. She would just think he was being delicate. The hand-thrown ceramic had pressed lumpily against Seeger's lips like a blistered kiss, and he'd swallowed.

Seeger watched his father swallow the pie.

"You get yourself a big inheritance when your folks passed?" Pam asked greedily.

"My inheritance," Abraham said, "pretty much ended up paying for the divorce."

Seeger glared sullenly. Abraham stabbed another morsel. "This ain't bad." Rhonda smiled.

Brakes squealed outside. Seeger twitched. His mind buzzed, slackened. He felt his eyes unfocus like when he sank into a daydream or a deep memory, but much faster. Something was yanking him deep underwater. The floor gave way.

Headlights flashed. Seeger saw Rhonda's head snap away from her headrest amid a shimmering school of glass shards. Liquid vinyl masked Abe's face like a caul. The passenger side ballooned inward. The truck spun and flipped on its side, Abraham's arm hanging from his shoulder harness like an abandoned marionette. Rhonda fell atop him, spine wrapping around skull. His parents pressed together, bloody eye socket and broken tooth against spongy red nose. Bullets of molten glass and plastic tore their skin. Seeger watched them melt and cauterize together inside a vast explosion, so bright he felt as if he was staring into the sun.

"Hel-lo!" sang out his girlfriend, waltzing in. Seeger shuddered, blinked. Holy fuck, what was that? He looked around the table.

"Girl, look at you!" Pam crowed.

Seeger wiped his sweaty palms on his slacks. Never had a . . . a *vision* like that before, only fuzzy mental-image shit. He could still smell acrid burning rubber. Maybe it's some sort of adolescent-hormone psychic-burst thing, like poltergeists around girls with their periods. Maybe symbolic, some sort of rebellious, anti-authority thing, yeah. Got to tell Joan. See if she can translate . . .

"If you must," Cordelia sighed, fluttering her eyelashes and gazing heavenward. Seeger lost his train of thought, Cordelia's stunning pose distracting him. She froze with one hand touching her chest and the other grasping air above. Her dress, prize of their truant expeditions to Dallas's wholesale outlets, combined prom formal with flamenco passion. Formfitting ruby fabric flared out midcalf and, on the chest, red brocade laced across flesh-colored silk so it appeared her breasts were bared.

"Well." Rhonda composed herself. "You like some pie, Cordelia?"

"No, thank you!" She pulled a chair between Abraham and Seeger. "I had Tater Tot Casserole at the Student Union after work. I'm sure it's a delicious pie, though." She touched her curly bronze hair and flashed Rhonda a smile of apology.

"Not near as delicious as Tater Tot Casserole," Abraham said dryly, cleaning his thick glasses with lenstissue and returning both to his chest pocket.

"Actually, it was quite the scandalous casserole." Cordelia kissed Seeger's cheek and squeezed his leg under the table. "That's why I'm so late; I had to drive all the way home from Denton to change, then when I got there, Mother bet me five dollars I couldn't find my rosary, so I had to prove her wrong."

"Why'd your mom want you to find your rosary?" Seeger spoke with intentional blasé, his vision's urgency fading while he fell in love with Cordelia's bewildering everyone again. He pressed his knee against her leg.

"Because of the Tater Tot Casserole," she exclaimed. "As if making me live at home weren't enough, Unclefred is now forcing us to have Family Dinner once a week. It's stupid enough in and of itself, with two teenage daughters and a working wife, but he scheduled it for Saturday nights, no less! Tonight everyone was actually home because Vikki is grounded and Mom worked lunch at the Broken Spoke, so it was this huge family scene that I was not joining them to break bread."

She rolled her eyes. "Mom said I didn't care about Family and I said I did and she said real melodramatically, like she'd pulled one over on me, 'Honor thy mother and father!' and I said right back in her face, '*I love Jesus!*' and then she bet me five dollars I couldn't even find my rosary."

"Did you, now?" Seeger nibbled his crust, egging her on.

"You bet. Of course, Unclefred still said, 'You have no respect for anything,' because I came in wearing it as a headband and singing, 'Jésus Christo, Estrella-Supérior.' But he's one to talk, he can't even take communion because they're living in a state of venial, if not mortal, sin for his having had an affair with his brother's wife until they divorced and she married him."

The table silenced. She and Seeger exchanged sly looks of accomplishment.

"Why aren't y'all eating at prom?" Pam asked.

"Ugh," Cordelia groaned. "It's going to be some horrid chicken cordon faux. We'll probably just have drinks and dessert."

"They can't be serving at prom," Abe barked.

"Aaaabe, c'mon," Seeger said. "Nonalcoholic, you know, bubbly white grape juice."

"I should hope so." Rhonda tucked her auburn, shoulder-length bob behind one ear and gave Seeger a pointed look. Seeger pressed down gently on Cordelia's foot with his own.

Abraham glanced from Cordelia to his son. "Well. Suppose we should do pictures before y'all take off." He pushed from the table.

"They'll have a photographer there," Seeger snapped. He took his plate to the sink.

"Oh. Don't y'all need a check or something?"

"We'll pay for it at school." Seeger brushed past him into the hall. He held open the screendoor for Cordelia. She rose from the table, turned, and bent slightly to wave goodbye to the adults. She smiled and stepped backward out the door, pushing her skirt against Seeger's crotch. Seeger bent and turned slightly to hide his tenting pants. He gave the kitchen a quick last glance and, seeing no traces of automobile wreckage, shot his folks a final scowl. "See y'all."

The aluminum screendoor slapped shut, rubber flap dragging thickly across the floor. Abraham centered his pie plate before him.

Seeger and Cordelia After Prom

"You like it?" Cordelia squeezed his hand, moist in hers.

"Fantastic!" Seeger nodded rapidly, eyes darting around Uz, a new club in Dallas's sprawling industrial zone. Clove cigarettes soaked the air in treacly honey-smoke. Scrap auto parts dangled from the warehouse ceiling high above. Seeger's eyes followed their wires up into darkness, a starless sky of rusted metal.

"I can't believe we got in!"

"I bit the doorman's arm last week when Vikki took me here and he likes me now. I couldn't wait to show you."

"You never get carded. You can just laugh and they'll let you in anywhere. People just want you in their club things. Just like Edie Sedgwick."

Her face lit up. They lunged into a kiss, tongues caressing soft inner lips, each other's sweet-spit tastes swirling about their brains dizzyingly. Seeger jerked away, hearing the intro synthchimes of that new song about touching roses. Cordelia held herself, poised, waiting. The music's bells stuttered, multiplied. Remix, Seeger thought. Worth buying.

"You want to dance?" he asked her.

"Oh no I don't want to let go of you." She squeezed his hands and pulled him closer.

Seeger nodded and pulled her toward the dancefloor's periphery. He scanned the club again, comparing himself with the Dallas crowd: SMU coeds' padded shoulders nudged slumming execs who loosened ties and anxiously sipped glowing drinks. Adventuresome jocks scanned the crowd for a challenge. Deathrockers picked their ratted black hair, some looking very hardcore Goth, others dressed casual in gray T-shirts with bangle jewelry and heavy black eyeliner (kind of like Marc Almond on the first two Soft Cell albums). Seeger smirked, remembering when he used to be into that. He noted that new geek look was getting a foothold: wan young men in 1950s shirts and ratty cardigans. Maybe I should get some of those at the First Baptist bazaar. It wouldn't be near as picked over as the thrift stores these Dallas kids have to use. But, God, don't I already look fucking geekish enough? Cordelia seems to think those boys're cute, though.

"What a festive soirée," Cordelia sighed dreamily, leaning into him. She ran fingertips up Seeger's arm, circled his face, and turned him to face her. She traced emerging cheek and jawbones, detected hints of stubble. Her touch blew away Seeger's insecurity. A new surge of euphoria shot through him.

"Oh my God," Cordelia gasped, "your pupils are so huge!"

Seeger tossed his hair, inhaling to fill his lungs. Cordelia's smile hit him, brilliant as a klieg light. "X is so definitely worth twenty-five dollars," he enthused.

She touched his hair. He blinked and breathed rapidly through his mouth. The air filled with snapping, clapping, and gasping from that weird new "Close to Me."

"You want to dance?" he said again.

"No." She shook her head firmly. "Everyone's dancing alone."

"I know. That's fine. That's great."

"Let's not let go of each other's hands all night." She grabbed Seeger's hands, and he squeezed hers back, feeling her palms' softness, the smooth hardness of her nails.

"Oh!" she said. "There's something else to show you." She grinned conspiratorially. "Come on."

She pulled him forward, dodging twisting dancers, veering through curving hallways. An aluminum stormdoor encrusted with barn-red paint swung open into a small, graffiti-covered room, drenched in black-light. Cordelia watched Seeger as he surveyed the cartoons dancing atop an airbrushed Camaro, a rainbow spiral sucking up the floor. Anarchy, ankhs, tags, Egyptian eyes, a beatific Bob Dobbs chewing his pipe. *Come inside, my little fishes! Tom Landry is an alien invader.* Beside *Dare I eat a peach?* someone had added, *Fucking poseur!* Seeger smiled at the Eliot reference; he'd studied that first semester.

Cordelia nudged him. "Isn't it great? It's like a little private room. Look at this." In the cold blacklight, Cordelia scampered up a wooden scaffold. Her nails dug into Felix the Cat. Lizard-tongued putti licked Seeger's palms.

They settled into each other's arms.

"I hope our clothes are safe in the Datsun," he chirped, again spot-checking his post-prom ensemble: a billowy white dress shirt (like Marc on the *Stories of Johnny* 10"), baggy black trousers tight-rolled at the ankle and belted with his black-vinyl-and-chrome backpack strap. Same shoes. He hoped he looked OK for this place.

"Oh I'm sure," Cordelia said. "Who'd steal a tuxedo, flamenco gown, and Brussels Mint Distinctive Cookies?"

Seeger smiled. He was more than OK anytime he was with her. "Well, it is Flamenco Gown Fabulous."

"To go with Tuxedo Fabulous! I didn't notice any other collapsible top hats at your prom."

"And all those *Miami Vice* pastel tuxes! And I can't believe Allison Oakley wore a hoop skirt."

"With matching peach lace parasol!" Cordelia squealed. "Not Parasol Fabulous."

"There was definitely no flamenco besides you."

Cordelia nodded. "Although Sam kept staring at my chest all night."

She hissed out her ex-boyfriend's name. She pressed down her opalescent bubble skirt, face clouding. "He still always wants to have sex with me," she exclaimed with venom. "He says so when he calls, no matter what I tell him."

She set her jaw. Her eyes watered. "I do love Sam, as a friend, but I never want to have sex with him again! I can't believe I did for so long." She stuck out her tongue like a baby tasting a foul new food. "He can't seem to understand that just because I'm trying to be his friend it doesn't mean I'll still have sex with him." She scowled, biting her lower lip. Her breath came in quick explosions. Her eyes darted about, and lips parted, but no words came, as if her mind was outracing her speech. Seeger squeezed her hand helplessly. His euphoria staggered, swayed like an unsteady drunk. He monitored Cordelia for symptoms of a major crash. He braced himself.

"It's OK," he said desperately. "Really it's OK." He bit his lip. Don't let her get mental. Oh, God, please keep this fun. Don't bring us down yet.

"Even when we did, he *never* gave me oral sex," she said, holding out a finger as if enumerating the first in a long list of grievances. Seeger swallowed and tried to keep his face expressionless. The few times he and Cordelia had had sex, he'd never done *that*. Despite their constant tactile affection and flirtation, their sex had been too infrequent, he worried. A host of inconveniences and interruptions always seemed to get in the way. He'd told himself she really wanted affection more than sex, especially after Sam. Affection was more important, anyway, more real. Although Seeger had desperately wanted to have sex with Sam since fifth grade.

"He said he couldn't stand it!" she fumed. "Like it was dirty or something. He's so selfish, didn't care at all about how I felt—"

Fuck, don't do this now! Seeger sweated, hot and constricted. He wanted to run away, to dive into the pool of smiling dancers, to be ecstatic and high and loved all night. Goddammit, why does she always do this?

Cordelia curled her finger into a fist and kissed the knuckle. With a fiendish smile, she disarmed Seeger completely.

"From now on, it's a prerequisite for my boyfriends to perform two hours of meaningful conversation before any sexual activity," she informed him. She tossed her head back. Seeger's chest unclenched.

"I've decided," she said, "that they also have to be bisexual, make

14

martinis, and tie their own bow ties." She crossed her arms firmly, pearl bracelets clicking. "You've got most of those points covered."

Seeger smiled. It's OK, it's great, it's always OK. He cranked up his Texan drawl: "Well, now, Ah certainly aim to please ya there, Miss Cordeel-yuh."

"Good." She nodded authoritatively. "We can work on the other points." She slid her hand between his legs. Her pearls glinted against his black pants. Seeger shuddered as a drug wave raced through him. His thighs flexed, toes curled. He leaned back stiffly and closed his eyes. He smelled Cordelia's perfume, Poison. The first fragrance he'd learned to recognize since Jésus' Drakkar Noir. Jésus. Seeger felt an overwhelming rush of love and forgiveness, and missed his boyfriend of just over a year ago.

"Jésus couldn't make two hours of meaningful conversation."

"I know," she consoled.

"We still don't talk to each other at school; we still act like we hate each other, and I don't. I really totally forgive him and love him as a person."

"I know. Men are shits." She patted his leg. "Thank God, you're not."

Seeger flashed on someone else, someone new, someone Cordelia didn't know about: Kent Lozone. He wanted to continue this confessional rush, expanding and wallowing in intimacy by telling Cordelia all about Kent, this boy at school. Kent, this sophomore wrestler who made Seeger's brain lock up, his mouth disconnect, his world fall apart and explode. Kent, Kent Lozone, a weird Yankee transplant like Cordelia. She'd like him, yeah, Kent—Oh shit! Seeger realized he hadn't even told her about his intense vision-thing at dinner. His mind raced, clicking together connections and associations, linking frameworks. God, I love this drug! he thought. How can I explain the whole story to her, how everything connects? He bolted upright.

"OK um you know—" He snapped his hands in the air before him.

"Is this a long story?" Cordelia asked.

"Yeah, is that OK?"

"Yes, oh yes. Perfect! I love when we tell each other long stories. I love talking to you and how you listen to me." She settled back against his chest.

"Me too! OK OK I um. Did I ever tell you how Joan had this boyfriend once who used to be gay? It was like this phase he'd gone through but he got over it because he said it was a dead end?"

"How rude!"

"Well, maybe it was a dead end for him."

"Maybe he didn't explore it far enough," she pointed out.

"Anyway he was also a psychic and all this other shit. He'd worked for the FBI. He'd been in a Mexican prison. He was a macrobiotic. He was old too. Sort of like this New Age Jason Robards–type guy. He lived in a mobile home with his mother.

"Joan told me all about Willie one Thanksgiving after she picked me up at the airport in Corpus Christi. We were gonna stay with him. He had a studio he'd built next to his mom's trailer. We were going to stay there. Joan raved all about his psychic ability and how much he'd already taught her. I was suspicious. Even though I was just thirteen, it was totally obvious to me she was bouncing back from Eddie." Seeger caught his breath. Cordelia nodded in encouragement.

"Eddie was this scruffy young boyfriend she'd had the summer before in Killeen. She seemed happy now because Eddie had been kind of a rapscallion she'd had to mother. Willie sounded like more of a mentor. But I was loyal to Eddie. Eddie had taken us to go see *Texas Chainsaw Massacre* at the drive-in. He rode a motorcycle. He acted all like a big brother to me." Seeger looked at Cordelia and made a quick, stuttering laugh. "He was really cute."

"The truth comes out." Cordelia smiled.

"But Joan was living in Fulton then, this fishing village on the South Gulf Coast. It had snowbird bungalows on the main streets painted all turquoise and salmon and yellow. They had stuff in their yards like colored Coke-bottle trees, lawn balls, and those plastic sunflowers with the spinning petals. When you got farther into town it was all old wooden and stucco cottages with rusty pickups in the driveway and drainage ditches with kids catching crawdads. They all had these wild yards: big, unmowed patches of Saint Augustine grass, that all thick and fleshy kind? It just spilled down into the oystershell roads and driveways 'cause there were no sidewalks. The grass grew out in long veins till cars ran them over or till kids ripped them up. Why do kids do violent shit like that for no reason?"

Seeger stared at his fingers twitching in midair, remembering child prisoners of late summer vacation, trudging home from the Mavrik Market in torn flip-flops, sucking on cerulean Fla-Vor-Ice sticks with bitter, unfocused disappointment. The blue stickiness bled down their skinny arms and dripped onto the pages of *USA Today:* Karen Carpenter's death and the space shuttle *Challenger*'s maiden flight crumpled up in the dirty roadside.

Cordelia kissed his neck, nuzzling beneath his jawbone. Seeger snapped out of it.

"Anyway Joan told me that Willie 'had been gay for a while.' I acted all mellow but I didn't want Willie sensing that I was bisexual so I breathed deep and visualized the Tower of Light around my mind and my heart. That's this psychic self-defense Joan taught me: you imagine this pearly blue column surrounding you and rising up into heaven. It's a psychic barrier but it's not aggressive or hostile. No one can tell you're putting one up. All they read is a blank static."

Cordelia brushed aside his long hair, kissed his forehead. She stretched up and gently pressed his head against her collarbone. Seeger continued his story resting under her chin.

"Willie's mom's trailer was surrounded by all these creepy mesquite trees. They didn't have any fronds, just these spindly branches with wrinkly, brown-red beans. The branches all clawed away from the water like they were black, muscley arms with thorns all over them. They had, like, poor posture from all the years of the wind's pressure. They were all stooped and bent over like old women who didn't get enough calcium. When there were hurricanes they'd finally snap and break.

"We didn't go in and meet his mother. We just went straight into the studio. He smiled at me a lot. He shook my hand and acted all like I was an adult. He offered me a beer but I said no thanks. I wanted to keep my psychic barriers strong.

"We lay down on sleeping bags. He turned on the radio: it was that Rita Coolidge James Bond song, "All Time High"? I put on my Walkman. We said goodnights and I rolled away not wanting to see them like three feet away from me. I remember staring at the red power light on my Walkman. I had a hundred-and-twenty-minute tape and I had the volume real loud. I knew they'd think it was all normal for a thirteen-year-old to fall asleep with his Walkman blasting. But it wasn't loud enough to drown them out. I heard Joan say, 'It's so hard not to yell out but it almost makes it more intense.' Willie said, 'I've been able to focus my concentration so that I can experience orgasm but not ejaculate.' "

Cordelia lifted her fingers from Seeger's hair and held them motionless in the air, splayed apart and aiming skyward like a dead horse's legs.

"Willie came the next day to Thanksgiving dinner with us and Meemaw at the Holiday Inn buffet. After we decided to go to the beach. But Fulton didn't really have a beach. There was just this long strip of concrete chunks and rusty iron rods all bent and twisted and piled up as a breakwater. It was all crawling with fiddler crabs and silverfish and waterbugs. There were screaming seagulls everywhere. There were these ruined old beach cottages on stilts and their rickety piers creeping out into deep water. Every fourth one or so was all collapsed and rotten, just a skeleton of pilings. After they get battered by a hurricane, people just abandon them. They never get repaired or taken down or anything. Squished between the concrete chunks were rusty cans of Big Red and paper grocery bags from H.E.B. with hurricane maps on them? You ever seen those? Down on the Coast, they always do that in late summer and fall. It's kind of a hobby for South Texas kids to track when disasters are coming, not be surprised when everything gets destroyed."

Cordelia squeezed close, resting her hand in his lap. "Is Joan bringing a boyfriend when you two go to Mexico?"

"Not that I know of. Maybe she will but she hasn't told me. I usually don't find out about things till I'm down there. I don't even know where all we're going or what we'll be doing. It'll be spontaneous, I guess. She just sold one of her rental trailers so she's got all this cash and wants to take me to Mexico. God I'm talking so much. I don't know why."

She kissed his neck. "It's fine. You know I know what you're saying. We don't even have to talk to understand each other."

He gasped and breathed in another wash of her fragrance, its multiple layers of musk shimmering in his head. The music changed key in the background, and he surfed the crest of a higher euphoric swell. Infinitely secure, he felt confident that their lives and emotions would soon align when he graduated and they both moved to New York. Without Execution and their fucked-up families stressing them out, they'd be free and encouraged to grow creatively. They'd find friends like themselves; everyone would be bisexual; they'd have sex all the time.

"I'm always so happy with you," he chattered. "I don't know what I'd do without someone else who sees all the bizarreness and beautifulness in everything, who feels the same"—searching for the word, he jerked his arms in the air as if being adjusted by an invisible chiropractor—"*detachedness* from everything. You're the only other person who isn't all wrapped up in everything. You can see how crazy the world is without being a part of it too."

"Yes! And we're going to escape together to the craziest place on earth: New York City! Chelsea Hotel, here we come!"

"I know. Can you even imagine what all it'll be like?" He sat up and turned to look at her.

"Oh yes!" she gasped. She glanced down.

"Look." She touched his chest. "The blacklight shows all this junk on your shirt."

He squinted, looking at her closely for the first time since they'd been in the psychedelic alcove. Gritty specks surrounded her eyes. "Your makeup's different."

Cordelia sat up. "Really?" She stared at her nails, black with blue-cream swirls.

He pointed at her blouse. "Oh yuk. There's chipped paint all over everything." They craned to inspect their backs. They stopped, eyes locking. They grabbed hands and leapt off the scaffold onto blunt, cold cement.

Cordelia scowled, picking at the wall. "Ugh! They just slapped this Day-Glo paint on top all these other layers! No wonder it's all flaky and chipped."

"God," Seeger said through locked teeth, "my mouth is so dry and my jaws keep clenching."

She faced him, eyes wide. "You've already peaked?" Her face twitched, startled, with a hint of anger.

Seeger felt a gap tear open in his euphoria, the start of coming down. The elevator beneath his feet vanished, leaving him dangling in midair. He wasn't getting depressed, but for the first time in the trip, he wasn't getting higher. He nodded. "Vitamin C," he said.

She nodded once, decisively. "Grapefruit juice." She pushed open the door. The natural spectrum gushed in, washing away alien cobalts. He slid his arm around her waist, and they worked their way to the bar.

Seeger Dreams After Prom

Mom's right index fingertip presses firmly against Seeger's asshole, circling slowly across creased sphincter crinkles, sparking off slickly lubricated anus sensations, his cremaster flexing and elevating testicles, prostate instinctively anticipating massage. Seminal vesicles and Cowper's glands shudder with stage fright on their tight-butt debut.

Mom swirls antiseptic creme round and round in concentric running circles, healing the rash and protecting bouncing-baby-boy-bottom. S.W.A.K. "Is Seeger ready?" calls tiny tyke friend through the open screendoor. "He'll be there in a minute!" Mom yelps nervously, yanking up the trousers so sonster can walk to first grade with his fast friend. Mom makes him walk to school with someone since there's safety in numbers. Buddy-pal, in lieu of brother, will keep progeny close, steered clear of leering, clutching molesters and pervs. She pats his medicated butt bounding off to school.

School Lunch

LaTonia Freeman bolted ahead of Seeger, slicing through the air with her lunch tray to lay claim on the Curse's only free table. "Sorry, Troy," she sighed as she slid into the blue-and-gray bench. Troy and Seeger nodded; they were distant stepcousins of some sort through Joan's side of the family. Troy skulked away, Seeger settled across from his best friend.

The Curse was the fast-food property directly across the expressway from Execution High School's front steps, on the terminal end of an L-shaped stripmall that also housed the Beauty Barn, Karla's Kuntry Krullers, and Fashion Fantasy. Seeger and Cordelia called it Alliteration Alley. Despite the school's constant customer base, businesses that moved into the Curse inevitably failed. The property changed hands annually. An ex–football player's entrepreneurial venture marked its current incarnation: Tony Hill's Cowboy Catfish. Last year it had been Char-Dog, sophomore year it had been Wok 'n' Roll, and Seeger's freshman year it had been Fatburger. Execution kids measured their lives in food from the Curse.

"Too hot to eat this shit outside." LaTonia scowled and stuck out her tongue. Seeger nodded, grimacing as he spit a scalding hush puppy into his palm. LaTonia shook her head. "Boy ain't got no home training a-tall."

Seeger's savior and co-conspirator in Honor Society, LaTonia had found the other "gifted" students as hopelessly inane as Seeger did. Together, they'd endured advanced placement classes and associated activities she'd deemed essential to becoming her family's first powerlawyer. Seeger held no such aspirations, but since his father was a teacher and Seeger's aptitude percentiles high, he'd always been placed in the AP classes and honorary clubs. He'd tried to make the best of them. LaTonia and Seeger's study sessions usually devolved into scheming for parties only their circle of half a dozen friends would enjoy: a seventies Groove-a-Thon, replete with Pam Grier videos, Curtis Mayfield albums, and compulsory, marathon rounds of the *Mod Squad* board game. Going out with Cordelia had cut down on evening party-planning sessions, but since Cordelia spent her days at nearby North Texas State University, LaTonia and Seeger had plenty of time together at school.

"So," she said, snapping her paper napkin in the air and draping it across her lap, "what'd I miss at prom?"

Seeger swished Pineapple Crush around his mouth. He shrugged. "The VFW looking like it does for every other dance. Waiting in line for pictures: it was a fairy tale theme, you know? Prom Committee didn't want us art fags involved, so they did the set themselves. They built this backdrop that was all curled-paper spires for castles and shit. It looked like where the trolley goes in *Mister Rogers' Neighborhood*."

"Meow-meow prom?" LaTonia purred in a feline singsong, imitating the kids'-show puppet. "Meow corsage? Meow-meow Everclear? Meow-meow rape?"

Seeger slapped his forehead. "Rape! I knew I forgot something, we were so busy with the rubber chicken—"

"What you doing with a rubber chicken?"

"The food—"

"I thought y'all weren't going to eat?"

"I was still hungry."

LaTonia shook her head. "One day your metabolism's going to crash and you'll end up looking like me."

"Is *that* how you become Negro?"

LaTonia pelted him with a catfish plank.

"Oh!" he said. "The big deal was that Student Council brought in this DJ from Dallas who spins at Klub Sprx."

"OOOOH," LaTonia gasped, eyes wide.

"*Supposedly.* But he played total crap, worse than they play there, so it didn't make any difference at all. He played 'Hot for Teacher!' " Seeger shuddered. "Anyway, we just ate, got pictures, and then took off for Dallas; Cordelia got us in to Uz!"

"How was the X?"

Seeger scrunched up his face in recall, chewing a hush puppy. "Mmmm . . . It was really wavy, and not that speedy, so that was nice, but coming down seemed scratchier than usual. I ended up with a stomachache from all the grapefruit juice. I had real trippy dreams."

Seeger frowned, remembering the pre-X truck-wreck vision at dinner. He wasn't sure it had really happened. Here and now, at a fast-food hut across from school, gossiping with his best friend, surrounded by the jerks he'd sat in classes with all his life, the collision seemed ephemeral and vaguely ridiculous, like his post-X dreams of getting sexy with his mother. Eech. He shook his head.

LaTonia peered out through the grime-streaked glass. "Ashton used to go to Uz a lot with his ex; she was a real X-girl."

"Y'all should meet us there sometime! I can't believe you're still hiding him from all us," Seeger slouched into his bench, sulking.

LaTonia rolled her eyes. "Remember? He doesn't know I'm in high school, OK?" She knocked knees with him under the table. "Maybe I'll tell him this summer, after graduation. 'Sides, you're one to talk about keeping secrets, when you've got a fantastic girlfriend already."

Seeger sat up. "What?"

LaTonia cleared her throat. "Kent Lozone?"

"Oh." Seeger looked around the restaurant. His voice dropped. "Nothing's happened between Kent and me. We hardly even know each other." Seeger forked coleslaw into his mouth, scowling.

"Yeah," LaTonia said, eyeing him, "but you're in love with him."

Mouth full of mayonnaise and cabbage, Seeger nodded glumly.

Kent Approaches

Seeger struggled not to keep staring at the center of the universe. He tried to listen to his high school principal:

"I know these last few weeks of the year are hard to get through,"

Principal Foote warned them solemnly, "but there are still finals and a lot of important things to get taken care of. Even you seniors; don't think y'all can just kick back. I'm expecting each and every one of you to set an example for the underclassmen. Continue the fine tradition of the sixty-two classes that have come before you."

Seeger paid no attention. His Outstanding Achievement in Art certificate limply absorbed his palm's sweat. None of this shit mattered.

Principal Foote spread his arms wide. "Y'all are the best of this school. You've proven yourselves to be exemplary students all through this year, and that's why we're giving you these here little tokens of recognition right now. The other students all look up to you; y'all're this school's leaders. And I expect y'all to lead us through these last few weeks without any screwups."

Seeger focused on the center of the universe. It lay squarely in northeast Texas, forty-five miles of spaghettibowl expressway loops outside Dallas, in Execution's aged red-brick high school, in the front entrance hall near the auditorium and across from the principal's office, among a baker's dozen of antsy students pulled from class for an awkward pat on the back, in the very front of the group, only three bodies across from Seeger, sporting red horn-rim glasses and a yellow polo shirt with collar upturned.

"We just want to make you proud, Larry!" Kent Lozone piped up, his nasal Yankee accent dripping disrespect, his lips deliciously exposing the gap between his front teeth. The circle of students shifted weight, tittered.

LaTonia smiled broadly. She turned to Seeger, eyes narrowing and lips curling down sourly around clenched teeth.

Seeger stared past her. None of this matters, he told himself. This is all such bullshit, such fantasy; absolutely none of this is real. Only Kent Lozone—taut neck tendons—crevice below Adam's apple—bulldog shoulders—jaws clenched behind smile—only Kent was real.

"Verdict's still out on you, Lozone," Principal Foote said with a tight smile, mispronouncing his name as *Lozoney*. "Don't forget, now: it's 'Principal Foote' for two more years, OK? And two more months, still, for y'all seniors." He clomped back to his office on shiny snakeskin boots.

Kent turned to a lanky and glum sophomore comrade. Jealousy stabbed Seeger—what was that guy's name? Isaac something? The boys nodded; his friend meandered down the hall without Kent. Kent shot Seeger a look of invitation. Seeger flinched. Kent advanced over.

"So! Guess I'll, ah, see you around," Kent said.

"Yeah." Christ, my voice sounds all tight and whiny. Seeger jerked his head away nonchalantly. No, look at him! Seeger twisted back around to face the younger boy. Seeger's head bobbed nervously. He pictured himself as a fifties ceramic poodle, head bouncing merrily atop a spring-loaded neck. Control yourself, dammit! Seeger stared. Kent's brown eyes burned steady and insistent, like rocket boosters after liftoff. "Beware of love and of dark-eyed men," Marc Almond sang in "The River."

LaTonia appraised the two boys, lips pursed. She exhaled a quick puff of air through her nose and turned to the skinny girl beside her. "Come on, Vikki," she huffed with a raised eyebrow, "let's get ourselves on to class and leave these two be." LaTonia's broad frame cut through the crowd with her usual authority. Vikki flitted beside her like a hummingbird.

"Damn," Kent said, eyeing the girls amble away, "good thing La Tonia's in Honor Society and not Wrestling. She'd whip my ass."

Seeger stared at him. Late afternoon sun filtered through the skylight's wire-reinforced glass, illuminating hairs on the cusp of Kent's jug ears. Seeger felt dumbly certain the constellation of each and every element of Kent's physique and persona had never before occurred in this world. "Yeah, um, she could."

"You're in Honor Soc with her, right?" Kent asked, pronouncing the abbreviation *sock*. "Or are you here for Artsy Fartsy Club today?"

"Uh, I'm both," Seeger confessed, blushing. He hiccuped a laugh and buried hands in pockets.

Kent whistled. "Big Stud on Campus you are."

Seeger rolled his eyes and looked away. "Yeah, right." He twisted out a quick, fractured grin. Without thinking, he stepped backward down the emptying hall. Kent opened his mouth.

Seeger's chin hit his chest. He scowled at the pen in his hand. Its inscription read, "Awarded by your Principal, Lawrence Foote, for 'Outstanding Contribution' to Execution High School!" Shit, no, look back up! He looked. Kent had retreated to his friend, jabbing the tall morose guy with his pen. Seeger watched as they sauntered past the Wall of Fame, thirty-seven laminated rectangles arranged like bricks and taped to the wall. The adjacent football trophy cases dwarfed them.

The two boys disappeared into the side hall, and Seeger stared at the

Wall of Fame. SEEGER KING, TRI-REGION ART FEST abutted KENT LO-
ZONE, DISTRICT 3A WRESTLING. Seeger imagined their bodies equally
close: curving chest flush against arched back, nipples tickling shoulder
blades, forearms clamped around torso, guts squeezed, the piercing from
a bullet-shaped dick—

In a shower!

Yeah, Seeger thought, his daydream blossoming. He imagined the
two of them in a big communal shower with evenly spaced chrome
showerheads jutting from white ceramic-tile walls. Scalding water
would shoot out in great arcs, giving off thunderclouds of steam.

It'd be easier to breathe underneath all the steam, with my face
pressed down against the floor, which would be all covered in the same
tiles. It'd still be hard to see: water would get in my eyes and nose and
mouth. Thick clumps of hair would tangle in my eyelashes. Actually,
one eye would be squinched completely shut, pressed against the floor.
With the other I'd see every detail of the bone-white squares, their
moldy black grout and the steady flow gushing toward a dull silver
drain.

Oh, that's just great, he thought, shoving his pen into his pocket and
storming off to his locker. Too bad your *girlfriend* can't fuck you like
that.

Chaos in Abraham's Class

With an exasperated flourish, Seeger's U.S. History teacher, who was
also his father, whipped off his blue-jean jacket and killed *The Last of the
Mohicans.*

"Heads up, kids," Abraham announced. "Y'all owe me one. I have
decided that the class of eighty-seven Execution High seniors shall be relieved of cramming Mr. James Fenimore Cooper into the final days of
the year. We're just too far behind now for y'all to get any pleasure,
much less any useful insight into the cross-fertilization of history and literature, from that annual ordeal."

Seeger shoved his hair out of his eye and gauged responses around the
room. He always wondered what his peers thought of his dad, especially when Abe pulled this more-burned-out-than-thou act. Senior

Class President Tate Kistwell made a face of exaggerated relief and shot a thumbs-up to anyone looking his way. Seeger knew he was desperate to regain popularity lost from skipping rodeo team regionals to take his wife and son on a honeymoon.

"Anyhow, after twelve years in the Texas Public Football System, further Wild West propaganda is the last thing any of y'all need. Instead, please choose from this list, now being passed around, your very own moderately-significant-but-mighty-easy-to-swallow historical event, and submit a standard report."

LaTonia formed a gun with her thumb and forefinger—her and Seeger's joke of expecting his father to flip out one day and go on a shooting rampage. Seeger smiled grimly. He wondered what his family and life would've been like if, instead of becoming a teacher, Abraham had remained a newscaster at that Dallas UHF channel. Seeger had been too young to remember those days, when his dad had been something of a celebrity, driving long hours into Dallas and everyone from Execution First Baptist would ooh and aah over their pastor's son reading the news on TV. Father and son, both preaching their form of truth. He wondered if Abe would be so burned out now, or maybe worse, if he'd stayed in TV. They'd certainly have had more money. He would've eventually moved them into Dallas for sure, not stayed in bumfuck Execution. TV had been their potential escape hatch, but for some reason it had closed.

Abraham slapped the blackboard. "Today we'll continue working on research finals. For those of y'all writing on Kennedy, my personal materials on the family are on the back table. Remember: this man changed my life—any damage to them elicits a merciless beating. Cultural Literacy terms are on the board, and today's Current Event topic is 'The Fall of the Illustrious Reverend Jim Bakker and his dear wife, Tammy Faye.' "

Vikki, Cordelia's stepsister and cousin, dropped her forehead to her desk with a thud.

Seeger sighed. At least I followed that vibe not to buy a copy of *Mohicans*. Wish Abe'd break his work/home separation deal and actually tell me this shit beforehand sometimes. He looked down at his desk. A carved marijuana leaf glared back. He traced his fingertip along the leaf, wrinkling his nose at the artist's juvenile line, his lack of confident gesture. Next to it, a cartoon freak brandished his doobage proudly.

Seeger remembered times he'd sniffed pot-sweet air as a child.

Once, he'd been perched on a futon and terrified. Joan and her friends from the Historical Society had been disco-dancing downstairs. The noise had swelled—"Body! Body!"—when Joan had opened the door and mounted the stairs up to the bedroom.

"Seeg, hon?" she'd called up. "What you want to talk about? Still not freaked out about Three Mile Island, are you?"

"Um . . . no." Out the window Seeger had glimpsed another Skylab party. A model of the crashing spacestation dangled from a wrought-iron balcony railing, fluttering against the gray Humble sky. The man on their NASA tour had promised them no one would get hit by Skylab. Seeger had decided to become an artist and not an astronaut.

"I just . . . I think that . . . that maybe"—sand grains seeped from his sneakers onto the futon—"you drink and smoke dope a little too much." He'd winced once the words fell from his mouth, as if afraid she'd raise a fist. Joan had laughed at him.

A shriek cut short his flashback. Seeger turned to see Vikki and her desk fall over.

"Miss Herodotus! Are you all right?"

"Ye—yes," Vikki giggled on the floor. Execution High's chair-desks were a single unit: chair, desktop, and armrest joined and wrapped around the student as one. Access was only via wriggling around the desktop while simultaneously tucking knees under and feet back. They were a tight fit; LaTonia could barely squeeze into one. Vikki and her desk had fallen to the left, with the floor now blocking her open side. The class cheered on Vikki's paroxysms; her Outstanding Contribution pen rolled across the gray and red-flecked tiles.

Seeger cringed but offered no help. Vikki falling over drunk was a familiar sight. Doing so in first period was a new twist, but he'd distanced himself from Vikki to try to sustain Abe's approval of Cordelia.

"Someone give Miss Herodotus a hand, now." Mr. King seated himself.

Tate sprung to Vikki's rescue. Her squeals hit a new pitch as his arm descended into her desk.

LaTonia tipped her hand back like a bottle. Seeger nodded. He turned around to see his dad looking squarely at him, eyebrow raised. Mr. King turned to LaTonia, shook his head. He gazed up at his poster of Bruce Springsteen's blue-jean butt. He breathed deep, as if for strength. Seeger and LaTonia checked each other. She shrugged. Seeger removed himself from the whole situation, writing a note to his girlfriend.

> *Coredie Sedgwick,*
> *Your stepsister/cousin fell over in class today. Perhaps you two should save happy hour until after school. Hope you arrived at NTSU in one piece. By the way, please conserve the blue curaçao for this weekend—*

Seeger paused, remembering his introduction to the blue liqueur just over a year ago, when he'd been recently dumped by one boy and was wallowing in unrequited love for another:

"Ain't this awesome?" Sam had said, wiping his palms on the steering wheel of his cramped Pinto hatchback. Seeger had slumped forward against the front-seat headrest. "Mm-hm," he'd murmured listlessly.

"Seeg!" Sam had huffed. "You got to least try getting over this Jésus thing." He'd shoved Seeger off the seat edge. "He dumped you 'cause he's too chickenshit his family'd find out he's a fag. Of course they'd find out, with the tongues in this town? Can't believe yours haven't. But if he didn't have the *eggs* to go through with it, then fuck him! I caught a ton of shit when Pastor Hank found out Molly and I were screwing, and I took it like a man. Jésus was a fucking wuss, you're a great guy, and I'm taking you out tonight with my new girlfriend. What more you want?"

Sam had grinned, eyebrow cocked. Seeger had eyed his cheek stubble, a virile smudge darkened in the orange streetlights of the expressway junction parking lot.

Seeger had fallen into the backseat. "How about being out with just you?"

Sam had shrugged this off as a minor, technical detail they'd been over hundreds of times. "Seeg, you know if I ever decide to check it out, you're my man." Seeger had blushed.

"Hey—she's coming." Sam had turned around and stared, agape, out the passenger window. "God, she's such a fucking babe. Totally blows all the Executed chicks to hell. Wish she'd moved here sooner for sure."

Seeger had looked across the lot at Cordelia sauntering out of New Peking Fast Go, proudly holding aloft a paper bag. A scarlet paisley bow had tied up her ginger curls, thick strands corkscrewing down across her left eyebrow. An extra-large T-shirt for their school's paper, the *Execution Journal,* had billowed in the arid night breeze, flapping their school colors of red and black around her thighs' snug maroon floral-print pedal pushers. Tiny black socks had peeked above her scuffed red pumps. Pulsing in the wind, she'd sailed across the lot, a vision of sensuous blood tones, a ruddy heart beating its way through the sterile cement terrain.

"Mission accomplished, boys!" She'd reached into the bag. "It's Sun Country Coolers' Black Cherry Chablis."

She'd crinkled her face, and Seeger had noticed, in the oblique light, her freckled nose and cheeks were glittery—not big chunks like actual glitter, but a sheer dusting of golden powder. No wonder Sam's so worked up, he'd thought. She really is, God, subtle but really, um, glamorous. Never see other girls at school like that.

Cordelia had smiled, shrugged. "At least my womanly wiles procured us something." She'd glared at them both. "The man in there loves me. His name's Chow. He's sweet, but he has a terrible selection. There was a blueberry flavor, but it wasn't blue, so I didn't get it."

Sam had listened to Cordelia with some affected expression of studly nonchalance. God, Seeger had realized, he really has no clue what she's about.

"Oh, God, blue would've been so great," Seeger had said.

"Mm-hm!" Cordelia had purred. "I love blue drinks!" Blue drinks. The very concept had entranced Seeger.

"Blueberry'd taste like shit," Sam had objected. "We could've just gotten Coronas."

Seeger and Cordelia had groaned in unison. "No way, Sam," Seeger had explained. "Not blue*berry,* just blue, the *color.* And it'd have to be a mixed drink; you couldn't have blue beer."

"Yes, they have these fabulous blue curaçao maragaritas at Pancho's Buffet in Grand Prairie."

"Wish we could get blue drinks to go," Seeger had sighed.

"Well," Cordelia had said in a mischievous singsong, "if my stepsister/cousin is working—you know Vikki, right?—she might be able to sneak us some in take-out cups."

Seeger had clapped. "Yes! Blue drinks to go!"

"Blue drinks to go!"

"Fucking A!" Sam had joined in, starting the engine. Marc Almond's overwrought "Love and Little White Lies," Seeger's pointed-yet-unacknowledged-by-Sam selection, had blared from the cassette.

"Pancho's cattycorner Sound Warehouse?" Sam had asked.

"Yes," she'd said, opening a cooler with a single, decisive twist and handing it to Seeger. "At Pancho's Buffet, home of Psychotic Chefs Anonymous, we shall find the rapture that is: Blue Drinks To Go!"

Seeger had sipped his cooler, mesmerized. Her words had sprayed through the nightair, a heady and delicious perfume like mist from a tangerine rind. "Ecstasy shall be ours," he'd murmured.

"Yes!" she'd cackled, gleefully returning his smile in the rearview. She'd cocked her head, eyes maintaining a lock with Seeger. "Oh, Sam, I *like* your friend. Vikki told me you two were fun, but you never know, with her judgment." She'd settled into her seat and instructed them, "Let's have a wonderful time tonight."

Seeger recalled the warm mix of sexual currents he'd felt with Sam and Cordelia. Being around them had been an intoxicating triangle, until Sam had fled the mounting emotional intensity and left Cordelia and Seeger to each other's devices. Cordelia had known full well Seeger liked guys. Their shared infatuation with and subsequent resentment toward Sam had been one of their first major bonds. But in the six months she and Seeger had been going out, he'd never been attracted to any other guy enough to act. He let Cordelia think, and tried to convince himself, that his bisexuality could remain merely a chic accessory. It had been easily confined to hours with International Male's *Undergear* catalog and fistfuls of any viscous bathroom liquid. No testosterone bundle had ever come close to eclipsing her stunning persona until now, until Kent. Seeger looked at his note to Cordelia. What if I get all drunk and stupid and start babbling to Cordelia about Kent, like I almost did on the X? Not that there's really anything to hide; nothing's happened.

Kent. Kent was definitely something new—a magnetic sophomore class clown and cocky athlete. He was smart, too. Honor Roll, Beta Club. He didn't act the part, though. He wrote sarcastic letters to the school paper about cafeteria elimination of chartreuse gravy and enlightened his English class as to Whitman's sexual preference. They would say "hey" passing in the halls, and Seeger would go to his next class stupefied, staring at his desk, the walls, out the window, thinking of nothing else. Kent had the amazing ability to, for short periods of time, short-circuit Seeger's continually churning brain, halt the relentless parade of memories, worries, pop culture flotsam, and emotional waves. Kent was two classrooms down in sophomore English. Seeger got hard.

Seeger approached his father's desk, nervously humming Marc Almond's cover of *"You Only Live Twice (007 Theme)"*—the B-side to the U.S. *Soul Inside* EP Marc recorded when he was with Soft Cell. Not to be confused with plain old *"007 Theme"* on the U.K. *Soul Inside* EP, which was totally different, the instrumental Bond theme from *Thunderball*. This was from a different movie altogether, and even though Marc hadn't written the lyrics, they were so intense that he could have. Seeger had drawn them in calligraphy on his binder. Eyes lowered, he snagged the bathroom pass from the vertical file labeled BATHROOM PASSES and went to go jack off.

Lunch Date

LaTonia extracted shriveled jalapeño skins from her cornbread. "Damn, I'm glad it's almost our last lunch here."

Seeger nodded. "It'll change by fall, anyway. The Curse."

"Yeah, but it always changes into something worse."

"Fatburger was good," Seeger said judiciously. "I liked Fatburger. Pizza puffs and BBQ roll-ups."

"Speaking of pizza puffs." LaTonia nodded.

Seeger looked over his shoulder.

"Hey," Kent shouted, walking over. "I didn't know all the cool kids ate here!" He stood beside their booth and peered into the basket on his tray. "Are catfish like smelt?" he asked.

"Here," LaTonia said, rising, "take my seat." Seeger shot her a wide-eyed *What are you doing?!* She smiled back and indicated her seat to Kent like a game-show hostess.

Kent plopped down. The boys stared up at LaTonia. "I've got to call a friend before class. Cordelia Herodotus. You know her, Kent?"

Seeger's face reddened. He attacked his hush puppies, staring down at the table.

"Un-uh," Kent said. "Don't think so."

"Mm. She graduated last year." LaTonia stepped away. "Ask Seeger," she said. "See ya."

Kent looked at Seeger. Seeger washed down the greasy bread with coke, a cold citrusy lump sludging down his throat. His stomach churned.

"What's up?" Kent said. Seeger stared back at him, speechless.

"I'm so fucked with exams," Kent sighed. "I took World History instead of World Geography and I think it was a big mistake. Coach Verbal . . ."

Seeger nodded and let the boy talk, submerging himself in the waves of Kent's banter like a warm bath.

A Vision at Work

"We're closing soon, Mrs. Remington." Seeger smiled apologetically at the store's only customer. Eva's Craft Cottage sat on the corner of Execution's newest glassed-in strip mall. The wall opposite Seeger and behind his customer afforded a panoramic view of the freeway offramp leading into Execution. Past Mrs. Remington's shoulders, Seeger watched red taillights glide in and out of town.

"Oh, Seeger honey," she sighed. "Don't y'all have those new puffy paints? The Day-Glo ones with glitter?"

Seeger checked the digital clock under the counter: 5:55. "Just what you see out there," he said. "If you want, I can ask Eva to order some."

"Oh, no, don't go to no trouble. Let me piddle around a sec more and I'll pick something out."

Seeger shrugged and picked up the list he'd worked out on a pad of *Eva's Craft Cottage* stationery. Bonnet-wearing geese marched above two columns labeled Yes and No.

All break he talked to me. Seeger checked the Yes column.

He invited me and LaTonia over for lunch since his older sister and parents were all in Dallas at her pre-grad luncheon thing at private school: Yes.

He nuked us pizza and Spaghettio's: Doesn't mean anything, but sure was cute.

He imitated the Dallas policemen arresting AIDS protesters, complete with trout-shaped oven mitts for surgical gloves: Big Yes.

Persistent eye contact: Scary Yes.

Seeger examined the empty No column.

OK, he's dated Francie, Lori, and that Band girl who got kicked in the face by a horse. A No for each?

I've dated Cordelia six months, he thought guiltily.

Let's just say, No for *Excessive Heterosexuality.*

What about how he listens to rap music all the time?

Mrs. Remington sniffed. Seeger looked up, startled. "Studying?" she asked. Seeger nodded. "Still got time to teach ceramics Thursday? We're always plumb tickled having a young person there."

Seeger nodded, blushing, and crammed the list under the counter. He rang up Mrs. Remington. Holding out her change, he leaned forward and smiled habitually.

"Shit!" Seeger shouted.

Outside, Abe's red pickup careened down the offramp, brakes screeching. The truck showed no sign of slowing. It flew off the asphalt and into the air above the parking lot like a plane taking off. The street-lamps silhouetted two figures in the front cab, tiny black torsos bathed in gold. Gold engulfed them as the truck exploded in midair, dazzling yellow light spraying from inside the cab and flooding the store with scorching rays.

"Young man! Hush up that tongue, now." Mrs. Remington snatched the change from Seeger's hand and huffed out of the store.

Nothing in the parking lot. Crickets. Seeger leaned over to lock the door and sat himself down in the empty store.

may, 1987

The End of School

"Kiss that shit goodbye," LaTonia shouted. She and Seeger exited the climate-controlled corridors of mandatory education forever. Afternoon heat crashed down around them like a blanket soaked in hot soup. Their arms chicken-skinned. Steaming grass, dirt, and asphalt filled their lungs. Wading into the chrome reflections that ricocheted across the parking lot, Seeger scanned the crowd for Kent.

LaTonia shimmied down the steps, shaking her briefcase and singing, "Ain't no stoppin' us now—"

"Oh, you be so illing," Seeger said. "The sistah—"

A sweaty male mass landed on Seeger's back. Arms around his neck, light tan with pale, tickling hairs, a scattering of those dizzying freckles, swelling forearms, deodorized sweat, nails bitten to the fingertips, scar on right index knuckle . . .

"Hey, you fuck!" Kent shouted.

Spectacular, Seeger thought. Exactly how the last day of high school should be. "Look, 'Tonia," he said, "It's that Kent Lasagna. He's just now becoming a *junior*."

LaTonia curled her lip. "High school fool," she growled. "Triple-processed Bootney Farnsworth."

Kent's brows knitted for half a second as he glanced at LaTonia. He shook his head, tossing his carroty bleached bangs, and grinned brilliantly at Seeger. "Don't give me that 'just a junior' shit, studmonger; you're only a year older than me."

A house key, dangling from his neck on a dirty shoelace, bounced against his "EHS Wrestling" T-shirt's muscular horned toad. His glasses reflected the merciless North Texas sun, harsh flares obscuring luxurious sorrel eyes.

"Yeah, but I'm a graduate now, that's all that counts."

"Yeah yeah yeah," Kent said, "Big Dick on Campus skipped third grade. Rah rah rah. You giving me a ride or what?"

Can't believe this guy likes me, Seeger thought. I'm such a skinny, faggy twerp, and this guy actually likes me. "Ask Ms. Freeman. I didn't drive today."

The boys sat books atop LaTonia's blue Cutlass. She clicked open her attaché and pulled out keys. "Why don't you go ride with Isaac, Bootney?" She slammed her case. "He lives right next to you."

"I don't think so." Kent swayed shoulders petulantly. "I need to go straight to work. The Oshman's Sporting Goods off Arapaho."

LaTonia shot Seeger a grave look.

Kent stood outside the car door. "I want front," he pouted.

"Sit in my lap," Seeger suggested.

LaTonia leaned across the seat. "Backseat, Kent," she ordered. Despite Cordelia's commandeering Seeger's free time, LaTonia adored Cordelia. Her loyalty to Seeger extended to only humoring his obsession with Kent.

Seeger spun the radio to the Fresh Rock channel. "Damn music," LaTonia muttered. "Cockatoo-headed crackers—"

"Just deal, OK?" Seeger rolled his eyes.

"Look what I got for my locker next year," Kent said, holding up a *Teen Beat* centerfold of Judd Nelson. "My sister, Saint Cecilia of Brainhood, has always been too good for this kind of thing, so her poor deprived little brother has to fend for himself."

"Then why'd you pick that big butthole?" asked LaTonia, appraising Kent in the rearview. She threw on brakes and they all jerked forward, back. A handsome student with pensive eyes and a trumpet had run in front of them. He jumped, peered in LaTonia's car.

Seeger and Jésus met eyes through the windshield.

Parked behind Bowie Middle School, he and Jésus had jammed themselves behind the steering wheel of Jésus' puke-green '74 Buick Regal. Their lips had pressed together while a boombox had poured out Marc Almond and Jimmy Sommerville's euphoric cover of that old Donna Summer song, "I Feel Love." Jimmy's tremulous falsetto and

Marc's writhing tenor had swirled about his and Jésus' passionate wrestling. Seeger had thrown his head back, gasping as Jésus sucked his dick.

"Not so loud," Jésus had giggled, lifting his head up from Seeger's lap. Seeger had stared out the window, steam diffusing the mammoth December moon into a silver aura enveloping the car. Seeger had basked in body heat, love, his possession of openly gay pop music, and relief over finally turning sixteen. According to Bronksi Beat's *The Age of Consent* album inner sleeve, Seeger had come of legal age to have sex with men in Denmark, France, Holland, Hungary, Italy, Norway, Portugal, Poland, and Switzerland. Even though sodomy was illegal at any age in Texas, 1986 nevertheless had blossomed before him like a glistening, mercury magnolia, full of infinite potential.

"You sure I should come in?" Jésus had asked later, under the emergency-red glare of the Kings' porchlight. He'd smoothed his hair and denim shirt.

"Yeah, why not?" Seeger had wiped his mouth on his hand. "God, my hand smells like your dick."

"I wonder why?" Jésus had snickered, looking around the gravel-filled yard. He'd nodded toward a clump of pricklypear cactus under the master bedroom window. "You can eat those, you know."

"Yeah, I know, you've told me." Seeger had pulled out his house key but hesitated. "What's bugging you?"

"I don't know, your mom just seems all weird around me."

Seeger had sighed. "That's just because you're Mexican. She doesn't know you're my boyfriend." He'd spread his arms for inspection. "Spot check?" Jésus had studied him. "Shirt tucked in? No come stains on pants?"

"You're fine. Me?"

"Yeah."

Seeger had breathed deep, smelling frost's clean promise in the cold air, seasoned with the musky sex remnants around his lips. Perfect, Seeger had thought. Back in the car, that was an absolutely perfect moment. This is a perfect night. I'll keep it locked in memory for the rest of my life.

"Thanks for the birthday present," he'd said, voice cracking and unsteady. He'd lunged forward and embraced Jésus, feeling as if he'd cry. The pressure of another cock against his had, again, astounded him.

"Hey!" Jésus had jerked away.

"No one's watching," Seeger had said darkly and shoved open the door.

"LaTonia and Cordelia came by looking for you," Abe had announced as they'd entered.

"Come see what they brought!" Rhonda had sung out from the kitchen.

A small grocery-store cake had graced the center of the table, with sixteen candles and "Sweet Sixteen" scripted across an idyllic green pasture of icing. Plastic cows and candy boulders had accessorized the corners.

"Oh God!" Seeger had gasped.

"Lord's name," Rhonda had warned.

"Sorry." He'd stuck his finger in the icing. "That's so sweet of them."

"They said they had to get ready for Sam's New Year's party and didn't want to leave it there 'cause everyone would eat it," Rhonda had explained. "They said they'd just meet y'all at Sam's house later. Y'all want some cokes? Dr Pepper's got NutraSweet now."

The boys had shaken their heads. "No, thanks, ma'am," Jésus had said.

Seeger had beamed, happily snug at the center of attention.

"Look!" he'd said, cutting through the sweet, buttery meadow, "It's a 'chocolate . . . devil's food . . . cake.' " He'd enunciated the words seductively, imitating the B-52s' song "Cake."

Jésus had smiled and continued the quote. " 'Nothing like a chocolate . . . devil's food . . . cake.' "

" 'Cinnamon. Sugar.' "

" 'Mm-hm. I swear.' "

"I'd say it's a pretty weird cake for a guy," Abraham had grumbled.

Seeger and Jésus had shared a look of disbelief at Abraham's obliviousness to their musical reference.

"But that's your friends," Abraham had continued, "—weird."

"There's not going to be any drinking or *wildness* at this party tonight, is there?" Rhonda had asked. "Y'all aren't going all the ways into Dallas, now, are you?"

"No," Seeger had muttered around a chocolate mouthful.

"Well, now. We're letting you stay out late since it's New Year's and your birthday, but you still need to be home by one. You get drunks on the road even this far outside Dallas. So drive real careful." Rhonda had given Jésus a sharp glance.

"Hadn't y'all better get a move on?" Abraham had said. "Don't want to keep y'all's dates waiting."

"Aaaabe," Seeger had groaned, "they aren't our dates! Cordelia goes out with Sam and LaTonia and me—"

"LaTonia and I."

"We're all just friends." Jésus had shifted uncomfortably.

"Yeah, right," Abraham had said, nodding knowingly. "Just have fun and be careful."

"Yeah yeah yeah, OK." Seeger had thrown on his trenchcoat, scowling. You don't know shit, he'd thought and ushered Jésus to the door.

"Hey, son—one more thing."

"What?!"

"Happy birthday."

"Thanks," he'd muttered between his teeth and yanked open the door for Jésus.

"Damn, it was Fuckpig Jésus," LaTonia said, wincing from where the steering wheel had jabbed her chest. "Shit, Seeg, if I'd had my eyes open, I could've iced your ex, and it would've been an accident."

LaTonia blared her horn. Jésus scurried away.

Seeger held his breath and, with a purposefully blank face, checked the rearview. Had Kent heard that? Had he understood about him and Jésus?

Kent smiled. "Ain't Judd Nelson a hot pup? He's a Saggitarius."

Seeger exhaled slowly. "Um . . . my moon's in Sag," he sputtered, trying to anchor onto a new subject.

"Libra. And my name is Charles," LaTonia said with caustic suaveness, eyeing Kent. "That crap's only good for picking up stupid men."

"Are you into it?" Kent asked Seeger dubiously.

Seeger blinked. Great, now I sound like some New Age freak. "Oh," he said, rolling his eyes and shaking his head, "my real mom is. She had my chart done a few years back."

"I don't know my sign." Kent frowned at the centerfold. "It says Judd likes Scorpios." His face lit up with an exaggerated, vacuous grin. "And blondes!"

Seeger snatched the picture. "I don't think that's suitable material for such an innocent mind." Kent grabbed his wrist; Seeger pushed his face. Judd fell to the floorboards. They scuffled for several blocks.

"King station." LaTonia jerked to a stop in front of the Kings' sandstone, pumice, and cactus yard. Seeger clambered out of the car, legs tangling in the seatbelt while he struggled not to spill his books. Kent jumped out easily behind him.

"So," Seeger said. What do I say? Ask him out, like on a date? What are you supposed—

"Kent, come on, boy, get back in," LaTonia barked. "I got to get to work."

"Call me, OK?" Seeger blurted out as Kent slid back into the car. Oh, fuck, that sounded really desperate. He felt sick. Don't jump all over him, keep in control, and maybe you'll see him again soon.

Kent stuck his head out the window. "Yeah, OK. Hey—a bunch of us are going to go to Six Flags sometime . . ."

Seeger soared, nodding excessively. I'm in! Knew it. It'll happen. Kent'll go for me—if I don't fuck things up.

"Tell Cordelia I'm still up for next Wednesday," LaTonia interrupted, crushing Kent into his seat as she leaned across him, "if y'all want to double and meet you-know-who." Seeger nodded, still looking at Kent. She nodded and returned to her seat, patting Kent's chest. She gunned the engine and they drove off.

Seeger floated in to his house, shamelessly happy. Kent definitely likes me. Yeah, yeah, maybe more than likes me. Plus no more fucking fascist school, parental units aren't home, and a check sits on the kitchen table, next to some bloody pro-life brochures. He stuck out his tongue at the wrangled fetuses. Way subtle, he thought.

The $100 graduation check was from his grandmother, which meant he could afford to get Marc's "Mother Fish" 12" and "Melancholy Rose" double-7" with the special Kurt Weill B-sides he'd seen at Record Gallery. Life was giddily perfect.

He saw a note to call Cordelia. Rhonda had drawn a cartoon valentine heart with a crooked eyebrow and threatening scowl and written, "Soon!" Seeger hesitated in the center of the kitchen. He pocketed the note. He stretched out on the couch, awaiting Kent's call.

Seeger Weighs Loyalties

First Baptist chimed noon. Aimless depression blanketed Seeger. The glare of summer vacation's emptiness filled his room. His stomach growled. He stared into the box fan on the floor. Its hum lulled him to sleep at night, but the fan couldn't cool enough. Even with nothing but a thin sheet covering him, his limbs stuck together. He wanted to switch to AC, but Abe never allowed it till May 15.

He flopped over. His eyes focused on Cordelia's picture atop his desk, in a white frame Seeger had painted with cigarette holders, fish, grinning bagels and electrified spermatozoa. In the picture, Cordelia held a wine bottle up high, sitting on her beat-up Datsun's hood. A borrowed Journalism Department camera had captured this toast last year, when they'd sworn not to stay in Execution a year past graduation. Unlike their parents, they would not spend their lives in a community that included Karla's Kuntry Krullers and the Beauty Barn.

Seeger recalled the day of that picture:

Cordelia had seduced Seeger away from selling ads for the school paper. They'd returned from Christmas break only a week ago and were not yet prepared to take school seriously.

Cordelia had tossed Seeger her takeout carton of Peapod Beef. She'd grabbed the steering wheel with both hands and torn off onto the farm road. The cornflower-blue Datsun had charged heroically, rattling over an uneven terrain choked with tall, dry grasses. Seeger had nibbled his baby corn ear.

"There's Riunite White under the seat," she'd said.

Seeger had hesitated, assessing risk. What if Abe found out? What if Cordelia made them late to fifth period? Cissie Chamblin was in Seeger's fifth and she was Abe's Teacher Aide in sixth period. Could they stop and get breath mints someplace no one would know them? Gingerly, he'd set his Seven Treasures of the Sea on the bucking floorboard. Cordelia had cranked the tinny cassette, and Marc's "The Boy Who Came Back" had pranced forth, jaunty guitars jangling in time with the Datsun's lurches. Optimistic pools of midday sunshine had filled the car, and a seductive sense of liberty had heightened the glow. Seeger had shoved aside his anxieties and succumbed to Cordelia's spontaneity.

He'd reached under his seat. Greasy springs had pressed against the veins on the back of his hand. He'd fingered sharp bottlecaps and a sheer fabric—scarf? leggings?—before finding the cool glass bottle. Seeger had unscrewed the lid, and the road had become smoother.

"So Sam the Goon wants me to write in the *Journal* about his stupid band."

"Bad Boyz?"

"Yes! We have to maintain some degree of independence if we're

43

going to keep going out." She'd held up the golden wine with one hand and swigged.

"Yeah, and anyway, that'd be such a *girlfriend* thing for you to do."

"Exactly! I knew *you* would understand." She'd grinned at him fiendishly. "One must attend to one's own celebrityhood."

"Exactly."

"You wouldn't've designed a flyer for Jésus' band, if he had one."

"Of course not."

The car had tilted as Cordelia swerved up the side of a dirt embankment.

"Whoa, nellie!" she'd shouted in a decidedly non-Texan accent. She'd righted the car and shot Seeger a friendly look of concern.

"Not to say Jésus was the boy and you were the girl."

"Of course not. But not that there'd be anything wrong with me being the girl." Seeger had flinched as tree branches whipped the windshield.

Cordelia had shaken her head. "God, you and I understand each other."

She'd jerked the Datsun to a halt in a small clearing surrounded by cottonwoods raining seedling snow, dead sunflowers, and piles of rich, orange dirt. "This is the Spot!" she'd announced.

"What is it?"

"Sam thinks it's where they're building that retirement condoplex. But it's always empty. We come here to have sex." She'd pursed her lips, assessing the surroundings.

Seeger had nodded. "Oh."

"You and I are not going to have sex," she'd informed him. "Here—today, anyway. No offense, but I've had plenty lately. You're really not missing anything at all with Sam. Jésus was probably a much better lover." She'd raised an eyebrow at Seeger. "You'll have to tell me all the details sometime." He'd laughed and sucked his breath back in, like a smoker's French inhale.

She'd reached into her floral tapestry bag between them, shaking her head. "I probably couldn't come here with Sam and *not* have sex. Anytime we're alone, he jumps me. It gets old. You want a pear?"

Seeger had shifted in his seat, back against the door. His eyes had followed her, a bemused smile on his lips. "Sure."

"They're terribly overripe," she'd cackled, handing him one, its skin loose and marred with tawny dents. She'd settled back against her door.

"Oh?" Seeger had studied it suspiciously. Rhonda would've thrown it out days ago.

She'd bitten into hers with reverence. "Mmm-mm," she'd slurped, nectar dribbling down past her maroon lipstick. "I just love them, all mooshy and gushy and the little granules of grit between your teeth." She'd wiped the juice away with the billowy, lace-trimmed sleeve of her blouse. "And the smell is all rich and musky."

Seeger had bit in, sweetness fuming up his sinuses like gasoline vapors. The taste had synergized with the cloying alcohol buzz and overall delight of truancy to create a new high. He'd studied Cordelia, zestfully slurping as she basked in the magnanimous luxury of a January heatwave. The air had smelled of cut grass and manure. A sensual current had passed through him. He'd shuddered. Goosebumps had risen across his flesh. He'd licked the sticky juice around his mouth and leaned back in the seat. He'd felt giddy and smug, as if he'd gained a tremendous secret on the rest of the world, even if unsure exactly what the secret was. He'd looked over at Cordelia, smiling with nothing to say. She'd smiled back around a mouthful of pear and rolled her eyes. She'd looked out the windshield, and Seeger's gaze had fallen to her breasts, rising against the white neck of her blouse. The lace edges had fluttered in the breeze. He'd sucked juice from his pear, but much had managed to spill down his chin. He'd thought of the juice spilling onto her, what it'd be like to lick its grainy sweetness off her breasts, what sex with a woman was like. He'd decided she'd hate him if he'd tried something like that then, there.

The music had lurched into a grinding whine and stopped. The cassette deck had spat out the calligraphic label of Cordelia's tape.

"Holy Jesus, this tape always gets eaten," she'd complained. The radio had come on. "But it's one of my favorites and I just—"

They both had stared at the radio, dumbfounded. The space shuttle had exploded during their truancy, spraying the first Teacher in Space all over a beach somewhere. Silently she and Seeger had listened to the sketchy details. Seeger had wondered how Abraham felt. If Abraham were still a newscaster, Seeger had thought, he'd be reporting this now. Seeger had remembered his father's proud retelling of how he'd been involved with the first moon landing broadcast.

Seeger and Cordelia had finished their wine with nervous sips, searching for reassurance in their throats' warm glow while gnats circled the inside of her car, oblivious.

Seeger rolled over in bed, away from the picture, and frowned. First Baptist chimed on the fifteen. He thought of a more recent memory, both less festive and less dramatic, simply pathetic:

Last week they'd gone to the Golden Memories dancehall deep in downtown Dallas. Its neon stars and treble clefs had caught their Ecstasied eyes while searching for Club Uz after prom. Once settled into a vinyl booth, however, Seeger had felt too self-conscious to attempt their hypothesized fox-trot in front of the older, experienced dancers. The crowd of furs, polyester, and wigs had collectively swelled and contracted to waltz rhythms like cells of a single organism. Seeger had envied the synchronized multiple pairs of hands and feet. What would he and his peers have to unify them when they turned old? TV theme-song sing-alongs? He and Cordelia had drank amid emerald mirror-ball reflections and silver bunting, fabricating histories for the dancing couples. Cordelia had ordered martinis so she could say, "Waiter, I will have a martini," like Anne Bancroft in *The Graduate*. Seeger had sipped vodka tonics, Abe's drink. Cordelia had announced she was no longer sure she would move to New York when Seeger left for college, but not to worry because she wasn't sure that she wasn't sure, and would probably change her mind again. In the meantime, they should just enjoy their time together. Seeger's first reaction had been anger; his second, excitement over what effect this could have on his potential relationship with Kent.

This morning, he felt bleak. How can we keep being Andy and Edie if she doesn't come to New York? he thought miserably. I don't think I can be Andy without her.

He clicked on Marc and the Mambas' cover of "If You Go Away." He got up and showered. He dried with the lilac towel. Joan had told him purple was a color of transformation. Into what, he didn't know, but transformation in general seemed like a good idea these days. As he was tying back his hair, the phone rang. Although yesterday a distraught message had reminded him that he hadn't called Cordelia for three days, his gut told him this wasn't her.

"Hey, asshole," Kent said.

Seeger's heart rose; the day had a plot. Water dripped down his lips into the mouthpiece holes. The soapy steam of the bathroom faded, turned dark.

Seeger smelled Kent's sweat in the blackness, up close, and mixed with fertile earth. He felt their bodies press together, but he didn't see a thing other than murky green-black. He groped in the inky dark for balance. He smelled dank breath, felt Kent's cheek up against his own, beard stubble scratching him—except Kent didn't have any beard, and it didn't really feel like whiskers, anyway, they were bigger, deeper—scratches grinding into his face like gravel or glass—

"Yo, hello there?"

Seeger shook his head clear.

Whoa. This new thing's intense. Better sex than wrecks, though. Maybe this one wasn't symbolic, maybe it's partially straightforward prophetic, yeah.

"Hey, yourself." His towel fell and he fingered a new hardon. He wouldn't call Cordelia today. He'd do anything and everything Kent suggested, and he'd feel guilty later.

Seeger Surrenders to Athletics

Cordelia would be appalled, Seeger thought.

He furtively searched the Wal-Mart parking lot for anyone they knew. He'd been able to duck most everyone inside who would've commented on his purchases. Such base activities as sports defied every tenet he and Cordelia had established as Neo-Aristocrats, Jazz Age Inheritors, and Superstars-in-the-Making. Sports encouraged a complete mob mentality, like church or the Hypermart. Plus fashionable athletic clothes simply did not exist, you endured constant perspiration, and mixed drinks could not be effectively integrated. He flushed with embarrassment and chucked into the backseat a white plastic bag containing his new shorts and Reeboks. Both, Cordelia would've pointed out, were made entirely of unnatural fibers.

Seeger Plays with Kent

Panting, Seeger studied the weight room. Some mouth-breather in a tank top cut above the navel glared back at him. Seeger squinted and realized it was Bo Douglas, a distant uncle-in-law of some sort who was only two years older than Seeger. Seeger turned away. He felt edgy and exposed under the icy shower of blue fluorescent light. The aluminum-mesh bench chewed a chain-mail pattern into his thighs.

What the hell am I doing here? Everyone knows I never come here. I stick out like a flamingo and played racquetball like one, too. But Kent didn't seem to notice.

Kent. The boy landed beside him, catching his breath. Seeger inhaled the acrid funk of Kent's sweat, a sharp and metallic taste on the back of his throat. He glanced at rivulets creeping down Kent's dense tricep arcs, veering at bent elbows resting on thighs, and ultimately soaking into red-and-blue nylon shorts, the crotch already drenched.

Seeger imagined throwing him across the bench, holding his face down, shoving the racquetball in his mouth. He'd taste bitter neoprene while Seeger swallowed his dick's every inch. His thick-necked gym friends would gather around, spraying their chests with burning jism. They'd swim together in the empty pool, arm in arm, not breaking their embrace (if that was possible). They'd kiss underwater, then surface to stare into each other's eyes, touching chlorinated droplets on lashes and eyebrows. Kent would smile with an aching tenderness and put his head under Seeger's arm, nuzzling his armpit. Seeger would hold him and know they'd grow old together.

Seeger's cock rustled; he hoped Kent wouldn't notice its thickening when they changed.

"C'mon, let's get showers." Kent took off for a far counter.

Shit. Seeger had forgotten about showers. School reserved showers for the athletic elite. He'd mastered hardon camouflage when quickly changing clothes, but bare-ass showers would be rough.

Kent indicated an unamused guy at the PE desk. "Scott here will provide us with towels, courtesy of the Execution YMCA, for our showering convenience." Scott shoved two across the counter. Seeger tried not to recall Scott dragging him across the gym floor by his underwear in fifth grade.

"Such a nice young man," Kent said, "and cute, too." Seeger's heart tremored. Kent winked and trotted inside the locker room. Scott glared; Seeger followed Kent.

Neither spoke as they stripped. They locked away clothes and crossed over into an empty room covered floor to ceiling with white and hospital-blue tiles. There were no private stalls. Rows of gleaming, antiseptic showerheads, faucets, and pink soap dispensers jutted from the walls. Several drains lined up in formation across the floor. Seeger remembered straight guys' protocol of sitting several seats apart in movie theaters, but nevertheless took the shower beside Kent.

Kent arched his back, water splashing over closed eyes and running down throat and chest. Steam rose off his chunky gut, trickling around the black hairs of his chest and below. Seeger eyed them surreptitiously. Jealousy of the younger boy's superior development flared up, but a desperate curiosity to discover how they felt against his tongue tempered the flame.

"Feels great," Kent growled.

I'd worship him, Seeger thought. I'd give him long massages, lavender and patchouli oils, not even sexual, just paying tribute to every piece of his physicality. Kent shook his head like a dog, spraying water. He blinked droplets from his eyelashes and smiled at Seeger, soaping his pit. Seeger felt blood rush to his crotch and switched his faucet to cold.

He's so thick and squat, like some veiny, grinning tree trunk. If he was any shorter, Seeger thought, he'd look like some kinda dwarf. The idea was oddly appealing. Seeger imagined Kent lounging in a claw-foot bathtub, leaning back while Seeger washed his hair. Wasn't that some Meryl Streep movie?

"Hey," Kent said, "you can get hot water if you turn it the other way." Kent's gaze descended a few feet. He looked back up at Seeger with a smirk.

He checked out my dick, Seeger thought. No mistaking it, he just now looked at my dick. Seeger turned full front, focusing on the tile.

"Or do you like it cold?" Kent murmured.

"Yeah. It's invigorating."

"Maybe I should, too," Kent replied in a steady meter, staring straight ahead. "I get real horned up after playing. But I don't feel clean with cold." Kent stooped to wash his feet, and Seeger checked.

It's big. I mean, that *was* big, though, wasn't it? I mean, "Big" compared to what? Me? Jésus? Abe? And all that hair—fuck! All curly and so much blacker than on his head. Weird. Seeger turned his back to Kent as his own cock leapt up.

"Did you see who was in aerobics?" Kent piped up.

"Un-uh." Stop thinking about it, Seeger told himself. Focus! He tried reciting *Canterbury Tales: Whan that Aprille* . . .

"Laura Hervey! Damn, what I'd give to butter her muffin."

Seeger's dick arched against the frigid spray. *And bathed every viene in swich liquor, of which . . . of . . . which—*

"Don't you think she's hot?" Kent said.

"Sh-she's OK," Seeger stuttered over his shoulder. *Engendered is the fleur.*

"I guess with the College Woman you don't give much for high school babes?"

Seeger scrubbed his ankles. How did *Beowulf* go?

"Cordelia's just gorgeous," Kent said. "You two are an excellent couple."

"Yeah." Seeger jerked his faucet around and killed the spray. He backed around, facing away from Kent, and fumbled toward his towel.

His head felt thick and drugged as he dressed, trying to finish before Kent joined him. Laces and zippers snagged, rubbery and hard to manage, like when he'd been on codeine after his wisdom teeth. He remembered how he'd tripped out listening to Soft Cell's *Art of Falling Apart* album for three hours. During "Where the Heart Is," Joan had called. He'd heard Abraham's side of the argument, weaving in and out of the opiate, like dialogue samples from some melodramatic movie mixed into a trippy dub mix of the song. The loopy song had poured over his father like syrup: "No, you can not talk to him now. [Spiraling bassline and the piano picking up the melody.] If it's so hellfire important, why can't you let me take a message? [In come the Fairlight strings.] Well, if you can't tell me, then he can just call you tomorrow! [A phone receiver slams down, somewhere, very far away—lots of reverb—and the drums hit an emphasized breakbeat.]"

Seeger shook his head once, forcefully, in a poor attempt at clarity. Hair loose and wet around his face, he mumbled as Kent approached, "Meet you outside."

Kent Asks a Favor of Seeger

Outside the YMCA, Seeger's mind raced. What the fuck was this racquetball shit? Like, some jockish test? Did Kent just want to see what'd happen when we're naked together? Am I totally wasting my time with all this?

He scowled at the traffic on San Jacinto Road. And fuck, what does this all mean about Cordelia? Am I cheating on her? I've got to call her soon; we've talked only once since the damn ballroom dancing fiasco.

"When do you and Cordelia leave for New York?" Kent asked after joining him. They hiked past Dairy Queen's umbrellas, red-and-white aluminum discs reflecting 3:30 P.M. heat.

"Cordelia hasn't decided for sure she's moving there."

Kent looked directly at Seeger. "Really?"

Seeger stared back. God, why don't I have the guts to just make a pass at him? It may have taken a couple of tries, but it ended up working with Jésus. It'd be worth getting beat up. That might even be kinda hot.

A car passed, blaring some heavy metal song. Kent banged his head, tossing hair and waving devil's horns at the car. Seeger waited for him to calm down.

"She's not sure she wants to follow me around." They paused next to a fiberglass wall pressed into a brick texture surrounding Alamo Family Apartments. Abraham and Seeger had lived there shortly after the divorce. Seeger felt self-conscious, exposed to the cars. The wall shielded them to the east, but westward across the expressway lanes stretched a wide, open field of brown grass, leaving them vulnerable. "But I leave September sixth."

"Shit, that's too bad. My family's doing this trip upstate in August to get Cecilia all settled in her precious little dorm. I thought maybe I could ditch them awhile and hook up with you. I'm supposed to meet some coaches at SUNY. I'm not sure that's where I want to go, though." Kent wiped sweat from his eyes. "I won't get there till eighty-nine, but you'll still be at NYU for two more years, right?"

Seeger fought blushing. He wiped sweat off his face and looked down the expressway toward Eva's Craft Cottage. "Uh, right."

"Cool," Kent said. He pointed across the field. "Can we go over to Circle K?"

"Huh? Why?"

Kent turned around, watching for a break in traffic. "They've got these three-for-five-ninety-nine jack-mags," he said and darted across the asphalt.

"Jack-mags?" Seeger frowned and zigzagged between cars. He jumped over the curb and caught up with Kent. Burnt grass crackled rhythmically underfoot as they ran. "Jack-mags?"

"Hey, us single guys gotta have something," Kent said. "I'll give you the cash. I got paid yesterday, and this'll be my date tonight."

Seeger stopped in the center of the ocher field. "I'm buying this?" Seeger shook his head, scowling at a blue monster-wheel pickup over in the parking lot. His anger embarrassed him. "Look, Kent—"

"C'mon, Moral Majority's got 'em pulled out of 7-Eleven; this is the only place left in town, but the manager bowls with my ma. You can even have one to take to Mexico when you won't have Cordelia."

"No thanks," Seeger retorted, glaring at him. Kent returned pleading copper eyes. "Kent, you're trash." Seeger marched toward the store. Kent followed a pace behind.

Seeger listened to the beat of their breathing, the crunching of dead grass. His furrowed brow channeled sweat into his eyes, stinging. *Jackmags?!* Pornography seemed so seventies, and not in a good way like LaTonia's parties. All those heavy-lidded, spread-eagled women recalled velour sofas with chocolate and tangerine color schemes, dark cork finishes on table lamps, and godawful *All in the Family* always on TV. He could almost hear the sound of pool splashes wafting through the sliding glass door at Alamo Family Apartments.

Seeger flashbacked on how he used to pour through his dad's *Playboy*s and *Penthouse*s fanned out on the coffeetable of Abe's new Single Guy pad. Seeger would keep an eye out to make sure Abraham was downstairs at the pool. The pool lay in a cement pit central to the apartments, surrounded by a rusty metal fence with flimsy bars. Some kids had broken gaps broad enough to fit through. Seeger had watched them hang from the cement wall and scrape their fingertips raw sliding into the pit. Seeger had been glad to move in with Abe, because there hadn't been a pool where he and Joan lived.

Abraham had opened the sliding glass door and turned his stereo out for the pool partners. Elton John had sashayed through the screen, leapt off the balcony, slipped through the bent metal bars, and rappelled down the cement wall with more grace than any kid. He'd danced through chlorinated spray to add his cocky soundtrack to frosted perms, tanned skin, shell necklaces, and water volleyball.

Sweat tickled down Seeger's smooth chest as he ran across the field with Kent. He wondered why he didn't have chest hair himself.

Seeger recalled how, when he'd see his dripping father mount the stairs to their apartment, he'd scamper back to his room.

"Hey, Seeg, what ya doing?" Abe had called out, entering the apartment.

"Playing," Seeger had called back.

"Why don't you come on down to the pool? Tommy's down there."

Seeger had paused. The pool's chaos had generally intimidated him, but Tommy had been his friend who would play Playboys: rubbing penises together in school bathroom stalls or sucking them in bedroom closets.

"I'm playing Tidal Wave instead," Seeger had explained. Seeger had tossed his inflatable canoe on top his bed and squeezed inside the clingy plastic.

"Whole pool out there, and the kid has to play pretend water," Abraham had muttered.

Seeger had paddled around atop his bed with its Little Prince sheets from Joan. He'd imagined Execution and even all of Dallas flooded to second-story windows by a giant tidal wave. The only visible feature had been the new silver watertower across the highway he'd watched grow last winter, rising massive above the oily quagmire like the giant albino paw of the drowning ape in *Son of Kong*.

Kent skidded to a stop and crammed ten dollars in Seeger's palm.

Seeger eyed him closely and tried to vibe a reading of his intentions. Could this be another weird tease? Yeah, right, that's wishful thinking. You act like he's premeditating things more than you. If he was, he'd've done you long ago.

"Thanks, man."

Seeger nodded and stalked into the store. Amazingly, no one close to his family was there. He loitered near the checkout, gathering nerve. He feigned interest in the *People* cover story about Donna Rice, the "brainy Florida beauty" that had ended Gary Hart's presidential campaign. His interest became real as he recalled Nostradamus's prediction that World War III and the third Antichrist would arise during the term of a big-spending Democrat. Despite his hatred for Reagan and the rest of the parsimonious Republicans, Seeger had been worried that Hart actually stood a chance of getting elected and maybe fulfilling that prophecy.

"You want something?" Seeger recognized the checkout guy from the crowd of freaks that hung out at the car wash, working sustenance jobs to provide crash pads and party supplies for their less-motivated jell friends. He'd graduated EHS in 1985 then moved into "adult" living at the Hildago Heights Apartments. Kenny? Kevin? made a loud sucking sound with the tobacco between his lips.

"Uh . . . give me one of those valu-paks." Seeger noticed an Elton John song on the market's Muzak. It's wasn't "I'm Still Standing" or "Nikita," but an old one from back before he got married, "The Bitch Is Back," maybe, or—

"Jamaica jerk-off," he remembered Abe's stereo singing. Abraham had dripped all over the sofa, legs spread wide, drops curling down the hairs of his inner thighs from his Bud Man swim trunks. He'd sat on a towel spread across the fuzzy sofa, listening to Elton John and perusing one of his magazines from the coffeetable, *Oui*. Seeger had whispered the name of the magazine under his breath, "Oh-ooey." He'd crept up behind his dad, smelling sweaty, coconut-oil shoulders. He'd looked at the magazine.

The images had hit his retinas but didn't really register. Women with torrents of hair and mustachioed men, even the histrionic and clownish people in the cartoons, had all used a nonsensical body language, gestures and expressions he'd never seen real people use. They'd belonged to something complex and alien, of which he had not been a participant. Seeger had lacked the vocabulary to fathom these magazines. They hadn't been dirty, like *pee* or *dookey*. They hadn't been bad, like when he'd gone nigger-knocking on apartment doors with the pack of kids (or the word *nigger,* even). They hadn't been secret, like his father's special cigarettes. They hadn't been scary, like *child molesters* in the films they showed at school. Seeger had searched his experience for people or events that evoked parallel feelings. He'd uncovered seemingly unrelated phenomena: his father's "Mucho Macho" T-shirt and shark-tooth necklace, Trix are for Kids cereal, Dean Martin Celebrity Roasts, that *Jaws* movie he'd feared seeing, TGI Fridays (where Abraham had taken him and Rhonda for Happy Hour Buffet Dinner), and even racing around the complex at night with Tommy when the hot gold lights came on. They'd spat on the lights to make sizzling steam.

"Hey, you mind?" his dad had remarked.

"What?"

"It's really annoying to have someone peering over your shoulder." He hadn't closed the magazine.

"I'm not reading it, Abe." Seeger had pointed to the left-hand page, which was all words. He'd traced his fingertip down the text columns. "I'm just looking at the white spaces between words. If you just stare and don't read the words, the letters kind of run together, and I like to connect the white spaces to imagine shapes and pictures. With my imagination," he'd added for impact.

"Oh," his dad had said, digesting this. "Well, that's OK, but remember now: most people get ticked off if you go looking over their shoulder, whether you're reading or not." He'd returned to the magazine and flipped the page. He hadn't told his son to go away.

Seeger had stared at the words with exaggerated interest so Abe wouldn't think he'd been faking. The words had been about a movie called *The Sailor Who Fell With Grace From the Sea*. He'd tried to resist stealing glances at the man in the pictures named Kris Kristofferson. Waves of dark curly hair swarmed across his chest and between his legs in hypnotic, intoxicating whorls. Like Abraham's. He avoided looking closely at Abraham.

"There's nothing wrong with these magazines," Abraham had informed him. "Some people will say they're bad, but there's nothing wrong with the naked body or with admiring a beautiful woman." Abraham had smiled warmly and rubbed a wet palm through his hair. "And you'll appreciate them a lot more in about ten years."

Seeger had smiled back, glad his father was so nice.

"Come on," Abraham had said, standing up. "Let's get us both cleaned up. Rhonda's coming over for supper." Abraham had shaken his head like a dog, spraying Seeger with water. Seeger had giggled as Abraham grabbed him and threw him over his shoulder. "I got me a sack of dirty potatoes to wash! Dirty, stinking taters!"

Seeger saw Kent outside the Circle K, anxiously bobbing his boxy head. Seeger looked away, face red. Fucking pathetic. I'm so goddamn desperate that I'm following around this stupid straightboy like some puppy, like some nine-year-old girl with a crush on her older brother's best friend.

"Doesn't matter which one."

The store's frigid air dehydrated his brow, upper lip, and thighs, sweat crystallizing into grainy salt. Seeger looked back outside, down to the opposite end of the stripmall to make sure Eva hadn't stepped from her Craft Cottage for a smoke just in time to see Seeger, smut in hand. Kent blocked his view, leaning against the glass, peering inside.

Fuck that asshole! Seeger fumed. I don't need this. The checkout handed Seeger the paper bag with a smirk. Seeger flushed, grabbing his change and receipt.

Kent rushed over and grinned sweetly. Seeger chucked the brown paper sack at him and held out a fistful of change. "You know, I've got to hook up with Cordelia down, ah, at Whataburger and then we're going into Dallas. And . . . it's later than I thought, so I think I'm just gonna take off for there now." He eyed Kent to gauge the lie's transparence.

Kent was expressionless, squinting against the sun. He picked the bills and coins out of Seeger's sticky palm.

"Talk to you later," Seeger said. He slung his backpack over his shoulder, brusquely striding away.

"Maybe I'll head that way, too," Kent called.

Drenched in sweat from nerves as much as heat, Seeger continued dead ahead, ignoring his guts' shudders, not responding to Kent's call or footsteps. He rounded the stripmall corner behind Circle K. He stopped, waiting and listening.

Seeger peered around the corner. Kent had disappeared.

Bitterly satisfied, he watched traffic course along the expressway like blood cells in an artery. They moved slower and slower, creeping steadily enough so he could study each passing vehicle's occupants.

His parents' truck drifted inexorably into view, Abraham and Rhonda seated stiffly up front. The truck passed directly before him, and his parents silently exploded into pillars of flame. Putrid black smoke billowed from the windows, burning the inside of his nostrils. An electronic whine, like the Emergency Broadcast System, steadily clouded over traffic and all other sounds.

Sweat squeezed from Seeger's pores, hot bee stings across his face. His head swam light and swoony. The afternoon heat drew him into the conflagration, engulfing him. The world convulsed and imploded into darkness.

The electronic screech pulsed, jagged and grinding, volume increasing until replaced by a quiet breeze.

Seeger held out his hand, dizzy, and stepped backward. Spinning around into the alley, he clutched the brick corner for support. The rough bricks scraped his palm and fingertips. His sight sparkled with purple and red optic fireworks, and he slung his head down. Breathe deep, he told himself. He shuddered and watched acidic strands of yellow bile thread down from his lips onto the oily asphalt.

He crumpled against the wall, gasping, and wiped his mouth. *Don't hyperventilate,* a fiercely rational voice deep inside his head ordered. He stared heavenward and tried to calm his breathing. Slow, slow, slow . . .

Tiny cirrus wisps lay strewn haphazardly across the sky like angel-hair locks, lost from some paternal god's locket. They drifted, changed, and transformed with almost imperceptible subtlety. The sky's serenity reassured Seeger. His breathing steadied. He stared at the clouds, remembering a meditation exercise Joan had taught him—using mental energy to change the shape of clouds, sometimes even making them disappear. It was the only telekinesis he'd ever been successful at, but it reassured him that greater versions of the phenomena were possible. He searched the alley to see if anyone had seen him. Rising gingerly, he dusted off his butt and headed home.

Got to talk to Joan about this shit, he thought. Never heard of anything so . . . physical. Like, what if I can't control it? And what the fuck do these things mean?! Got to talk to Joan.

Seeger Gives His Mother a Psychic Reading

"Fuck, they thought y'all were at a Student Council slumber party?"

"Can you believe it? I'm just trying to keep them happy till summer's over and I escape." Seeger studied the M.C. Escher print above his bed: two heads unpeeling and joining together as a Möbius strip.

"Just can't believe they're still giving you curfews and all that crap," his mother said. "You need to stay out later, what with the drinking age gone up. Probably harder to find places that'll serve you."

"Yeah, it is."

"Anyhow, you've been an adult for years now. Your father should know better; his old man did the same thing to him, and he hated it."

Seeger sat up on the edge of his bed. "Hey, I've been having these weird—"

"Abraham probably fucking voted for Reagan again, didn't he? Fuck, that man is evil, but everyone loves him 'cause he's good ol' Granpappy! Iran-Contra's making me sick . . ."

Seeger slouched against the wall, disappointed. He crooked the phone under his ear and drummed his hands against his thighs, waiting for

Joan to finish. "Ollie North with those little puppydog eyes—" The line clicked.

"Joan, you hold a sec? It's the other line."

"Seeger?" said a quaky voice.

Seeger collapsed flat back onto the mattress. Cordelia, with a crisis. Fuck. He reached over and clicked off Marc's "I'm Sick of You Tasting of Somebody Else."

"Yeah, hey, what is it?" He tried to sound real concerned. Leaden guilt and resentment soaked him.

"Oh, I don't know, it's just everything!" she sobbed. "Unclefred is being a dick and Mom is siding with him, so she won't say whether or not she'll help pay for me to move to New York!"

Background shouting reverberated through the receiver. Seeger curled up on his mattress, knees to his head, phone and arms pulled to his chest. "God, is that her yelling at you?"

"No, I locked my door!" she said, sharp and furious. "I can't believe this, after she wouldn't even pay for my dorm this year, that bitch! Excuse me, but I am her daughter and I can't believe she won't help me— What?"

Seeger heard a muffled pounding. "Fuck you!" Cordelia yelled. Her mother shouted in Greek.

Seeger closed his eyes. "We can find a way to get you to New York," he said evenly, "if you still want to."

"Greek is not my native tongue!" Seeger winced and held the receiver away. "What?" Cordelia gasped. "Of course I want to go to New York! I was just feeling independent before; I didn't want to feel like a wife following you around. Don't you want me to? Oh, I don't know."

"Cordelia, shit—Look, I've got Joan on the other line. Can I call you right back?"

"What? I need you right now."

"It's just my mom—"

"Oh, fine, call back. Maybe I'll still be here. I have to work at stupid Student Affairs this afternoon."

"Try to talk to them in the meantime, OK?"

She hung up. Seeger clicked over and cursed his relief. "Joan?"

"Are Abe and her around right now? You have privacy?"

Seeger uncurled, stretching out with a frown. He stared at the ceiling. "Yeah. No, um, I've got a phone in my room now." He chewed his thumbnail. He knew what was coming.

"But can they hear you on an extension?"

"It clicks if anyone picks up." Seeger glanced through his miniblinds. Next door, JoJon Goodrich, an Execution High grad of two years before, rifled through the guts of his decade-old, primer-gray Camaro. Abraham marched by, unrolling a Popsicle-green garden hose.

"Oh. I need you to do a reading for me." Seeger moved his face away from the mouthpiece and sighed. "Are you relaxed enough," Joan asked, "or are you all stressed-out?"

"I don't know." Seeger fidgeted with a receiver-cord tangle. He was not in the mood for playing psychic therapist, especially if it might trigger more truck-wreck visions. But he'd feel guilty if he lied to Joan to avoid it.

"They breathing down your neck?"

Seeger scowled and looked at Cordelia's picture. Got off the line with the wrong woman, he thought. "No, it's just, I've been having these—"

"I really need your insight."

He closed his eyes. "Give me a minute," he said.

He breathed in deep, forcing Cordelia from his mind. He tried to relax. He visualized the Tower of Light protecting him. He cultivated energy pulses around his third-eye chakra and incrementally descended a nine-step staircase. The self-hypnosis still worked, despite feeling routine and perfunctory. Seeger rarely did readings for himself anymore; only Joan's requests kept him in practice. The last psychic thing he'd attempted for himself had been a spread from the American Indian tarot Joan had given him. Like his childhood Magic Eight Ball, the answers ignored Seeger's question: Kent's true sexual inclination failed to reveal itself. More important, it said, would be a secret message from a tall blond woman and a financial exchange among his coworkers. But Joan had always assured Seeger he was a strong clarasentient, able to sense people's emotions and motivations but not visualize specifics. He knew he felt hyperconscious of others' feelings: shadows of their emotions colored his own, as if their feelings were radiant light and he was some sort of photographic paper. Joan had urged him to become a shaman/-psychic-surgeon/therapist. If he'd learn past-life regression and basic counseling techniques, he could guide people into facing crisis situations, then take on their feelings himself and free them to untangle their growth-blocking traumas. He could be like a temporary, terrestrial version of Walk-Ins, extraterrestrials who take over the mortal lives of troubled souls like Abraham Lincoln.

The idea made Seeger queasy, like being dragged up a roller coaster's first hill. He preferred the more pragmatic ESP he had on his own: hunches and gut instincts about whether or not to bring an extra gym shirt or leave for school early. Trial and error had proved they were worth listening to. Trance-readings seemed too vague. Unwanted stimulation and information confusingly blended, cluttering up his consciousness like so much advertising. No consistent spirit guides had ever shown up to help him out, and after unscrambling the interference of his own feelings and desires, most often the information he got merely reinforced his common sense. Nothing in all his experiences with Joan's visionquesting, not even in Rhonda's Christian bliss or Abraham's rigid rationalism, had compared to the violence and clarity of the recent visions that had stormed his mindscreen like terroristic premonitions. Despite their force and clarity, he didn't trust them—perhaps because of their force and clarity.

Seeger smoothed his mind out like a bedsheet. "OK."

"All right," Joan guided him, "I'm thinking of a man, but I don't want to tell you who he is. I don't want to tell you anything, so it won't confuse you. Now, I'm thinking on him right now. Can you pick up on his personality from me? He's all I'm thinking about."

Seeger wriggled about on his back. Be still, he told himself. Focus! His face twitched, his lower lip stuck out, his brow furrowed as emotions registered. "Um . . . it feels . . . wadded tight. Clenched—it's a frowning feeling, not angry but superconcentrated like a scientist, or trying to figure out a math problem. Headaches."

"Mm. Mm-hm. Yeah, that could be. What all else?"

Seeger hoped this was helping. His upper lip sprouted sweat beads. "He's also sweet . . . really funny and frivolous at times . . . like he can turn things into a great caper and take everyone along with him—"

"That's him! You're so—Mother, shut up! I'll be there in a minute! I'm staying with Mother again."

I wonder if this guy's why she moved back to Port Arthur, Seeger thought. The man didn't feel like anyone he'd met over spring break in Amarillo.

"OK. Now, can you put me into the picture with him there and sense his attitude toward me?"

Seeger's abdomen clenched. Anxiety buzzed impatiently about his

mind like AM radio static. His sweaty fists curled in on themselves.
"Real deep compassion."

"Mother! Just a minute!"

"Sort of like aching." Is she thinking about another marriage?
Seeger's mouth tasted bitter and metallic. A tremendous anger, gouged
with strange chasms of sorrow, washed over him. The feelings had an
aged depth and dense texture he'd never experienced himself.

"It's not like an, um, infatuation or sw-swooning," he stuttered.
Going back to Austin would have so many more opportunities for her
than Port Arthur. His stomach cramped. He tossed his head violently,
trying to shake off the fury smothering him. He didn't want to cry.
"Real deep," he gasped, "this, like, piercing melancholy." If she gets involved with someone—

"What sort of future do you see us in?"

Seeger swallowed a clotty mouthful of spit, breathed in, breathed
out. Tension gushed from his body like a deflating water balloon. He felt
empty, grew cold, brittle—a piece of scrap metal.

"Whoa—oh, ugh. He's really a flake. It feels real, like, illness or
breakdowns. Impulsive, like, shattered—" The line clicked again.
Seeger shook his eyes open and leapt at the escape route. "Shit, I should
get that. Abe and Rhonda get real pissed if I don't," he lied. "Can you
hold on again?"

"Yeah. Mother!"

Seeger sat upright, wiped his face, and clicked the receiver.

"Hey, asshole."

Seeger held his breath. Kent. They hadn't talked since he'd left him
in the Circle K parking lot.

"Hey," he said tentatively.

"What crime against nature you up to?"

Seeger licked his lips. "I'm on the other line with Joan."

"Who's that?"

"My real—"

Kent snorted. "Oh, can't be better than talking to me, now, can it?"

Seeger looked down at his carpet. "Yeah, right."

"Besides, I called in sick to Oshman's and now I'm bored out of my
fucking ass. Can't you set a good example and come up with some entertaining and educational way of wasting my time?"

A loud smack against the window. Seeger jerked around. His dad had the hose on, washing down the gravel, and had struck the pane. Thick dribbles clouded Seeger's view; his neighbor's shoulders ran and swirled like a movie flashback.

"Hold on," he told Kent. He'd given Joan enough today.

Seeger Tests Kent

Seeger emptied his second box of candy. "That was wild," he said casually, "that they got to show two guys screwing like that, you know, in a movie."

Seeger had convinced Kent they should drive into Dallas to see a foreign film he'd already seen: *My Beautiful Laundrette*. It had again filled Seeger with heady romanticism. His heart felt X-like, ready to embrace and confess and pull the world up into heaven. Exiting the theater into the day's thick heat, facing another hour-long drive back to Execution without AC, however, Kent had turned sullen and sarcastic.

"Made me hard," Kent snapped.

Seeger tossed the empty Dots box at him, irritated now as well. "Yeah, right." He leaned forward, feeling his T-shirt already sweat-stuck to his back.

"No, those English dudes with spiky haircuts really pump my 'nads." Kent's voice was flat, betraying no emotion. "Really. Duran Duran dick. Gotta love it." He flashed Seeger a forced, insincere smile.

"Kent, look," Seeger said, "this little homo routine you pull—it's like some real stupid joke?"

Kent shaded his eyes against the low western sun, squinting at Seeger. "Sure," he said.

Seeger felt sick, his chest and gut hollowing, innards spilling out his asshole, pouring through holes in the floorboard, splattering across LBJ Freeway to be crushed by eighteen-wheelers and Harley-Davidsons. His heart would become roadkill to be nibbled by fire ants, scorpions, and armadillos.

He tossed Kent a look of reproach, quickly affecting the role of a pissed-yet-relieved big brother. "You know some people at school think it's true."

Kent stared straight ahead. "Maria and Vaniqua and them, they think it's all exotic. I just say shit like that to freak them out, then they end up hanging all over me even more." He rested his elbow on the window, burning it against hot chrome. "Fuck!" He pulled in his arm, rubbing. "You think that's why Laura Thompson ignores me? She's heard shit from the New Wave Babes?"

Seeger accelerated to change lanes. "This is a small town, Kent. Gossip's like part of the town charter."

"Fuck them. Fuck them. They're all so immature. I need to find someone like Cordelia," Kent said. "She wouldn't care what a guy did with his dick as long as she got some, I bet."

Seeger bristled. Was that flirtatious or insulting? "You'd like to find out," he growled.

"Yeah? What, would you two lock me up in a laundry's back office and spit champagne in my mouth, like in your little movie?" Kent faced Seeger, the hot wind blasting his bleached bangs around his face. He pushed them back, holding his bare arm in the air, wind whipping his tank top and wet underarm hair.

Seeger salivated. Stay in control, he told himself. Play Older & Wiser.

"You've only been in Texas a year, Kent. This isn't New York. Gay guys get shot here, even if they're just gay for shock value."

"I'm too cute to get shot at," Kent snapped. "Aren't I?" He stared hard at Seeger, eyes slits against the sun. "Besides, I don't act like a fag."

Seeger studied the road, face burning.

"In public," Kent added.

Seeger looked at him sharply. Kent levered his seat back into a low recline, propping his knee against the dash. He winced at the heat of the plastic but held his position. "You going to come along with all us over to Six Flags next weekend?" Kent asked, staring straight through the windshield at the road ahead.

Cordelia Learns About Kent

Uz had carded Seeger. He presumed they'd get carded as well if he tried bringing Cordelia to Dallas's gaybars. Those places intimidated him, anyway. He'd checked them out a few times on his own, only to leave after one drink, disgusted by the sweaters, cologne, and chattering fags.

As Cordelia meandered up and down Dallas streets, he searched for a dive they could explore. Nightclubs labeled El Foco Rojo and Super-Bailar loomed dead and silent. No people came in or out of either. A single red lightbulb hung in the breezeless humidity, desolate above the entrance to Copacabana. They drove on in quiet determination. They drank Mauna Laui Guava–Passion Fruit Juice with Gilby's gin and listened to Marc and the Mambas' chant, "Sleaze can be very tragic, but I only see the magic."

As Cordelia turned a corner, Seeger pointed to a marquee of rocking red letters. " 'Cabaret'!" he called out.

"Ooh, run over and open the door. I want to see inside." Cordelia slammed on the brakes in the middle of the empty sidestreet. Bolstered by music and drink, Seeger ran across the street, threw open the door, and surveyed Cabaret: a long, dark bar with two men. Pool table. Beer-piss fumes. A standard jukebox, only playing jaunty *conjunto* music with accordions rather than some guitar-rock power anthem. Seeger retreated to the Datsun.

Dejected, they drove over to the familiar territory of Greenville Ave. Seeger grew silent, watching the foreign neighborhood revert to 7-Eleven and boutiques. He'd always wondered if those Mexican clubs' drab exteriors housed grand secret fiestas, treasures awaiting anyone with courage to seek them out, Dorothy's farmhouse door opening into an other-cultured Oz of colored lights and festive syncopation. Portals, passageways between worlds and spirits, like power spots, lay lines, or folk shrines.

Seeger remembered Joan taking him to a South Texas folk shrine. He remembered inspecting shelves of spiritual aerosol spray: *St. Tomás: para protección*. Santo Ramon, a black saint, *El hermano bastardo del Christo, para causas perdidas.*

"I sensed this drought was coming," Joan had proclaimed to the stoic señora at the botanica's counter. "I had dreams and made my mother get a yardman so the lawn wouldn't burn and we can sell the house."

Seeger had crept away from Joan. He'd stood in the doorway between the gift shop and the shrine. Congregations of votives had illuminated a wiry migrant worker. He'd worn ragged jeans and a faded orange University of Texas T-shirt. A young girl had perched on his shoulders, jet-black hair clasped in fuchsia Care Bears barrettes. He'd bowed forward to give her a closer view of the painting of the folk saint and healer, Don Pedrito. As his arms had risen to steady her, Seeger had spied thick sweat beads in his sable armpit. Wonder if I'll ever have that much, he'd thought.

The man had ducked slightly to protect his daughter's head from the scores of cast-aside crutches hanging from the rafters. With a tiny finger, nail adorned in chipped but vibrant coral polish, she'd touched the painting, tracing Don Pedrito's wide-brimmed hat and pearly beard. Her father had pulled a tiny tin charm from his breast pocket and held it up to her. Together, they'd pinned it to the wall among hundreds of other minute tin legs, arms, eyes, and hearts.

"But dreams aren't satanic!" Joan had railed. "*¡No es diablo! Es como los sueños de los santos.* Everyone in the Bible had dreams." Lips pressed into a thin line, the matron had shoved the bundle of sage across the counter to Joan "*¡Es verdad!*" Joan had asserted.

Seeger had stolen away from the brewing confrontation, following the father and daughter out into the heat. They'd climbed into a primer-gray pickup and rattled down the dirt road, spawning a tiny dustdevil in their wake. Seeger had stood in the gravel lot, dustspecks sticking to the sweat on his temple. He'd dragged his hand across his face, smearing the salty mud. Seeger had squinted and seen astigmatic dustcircles drifting across the surface of his eye. He'd closed one eye, making half of the school of fuzzy circles disappear. He'd switched eyes, and the other half had disappeared. He'd only recently discovered that test, with which he'd proved to himself that the spheres he sometimes saw floating in the sky, despite what Joan had assured him, had not been water faeries.

Seeger looked out the window. They were deep into the Greenville Ave. cruise now. Cordelia drove past the Granada art-theater, past Record Gallery, Arcadia Theater, Assassins' Shoes, and all the other proper hangouts for Dallas's punks and 'wavers. They passed Zanzibar, a restaurant where Seeger used to sip iced tea for hours and tell people he was an orphan who went to private school in Highland Park. It had all been so exciting two years ago, when he'd first begun driving into Dallas. Now it seemed as routine as Execution. But tonight they had to find something to do, something to justify the hour-long drive.

Greenville was running out, turning into another zone of Mexican and Vietnamese neighborhoods. They'd gotten lost here before, searching for non-English-speaking liquor stores. Seeger couldn't think of anything to do, but they needed to find a place to X soon or they'd have to come home while still Xing. He'd once spent an ultra-cheery evening with Abe and Rhonda and Bill and Pam while Xing, and didn't want to repeat that creepiness.

"Bra-sil," sang out Cordelia and pointed down the block.

Club Brasil looked not only promising but safe. Brilliant banners draped across the windows; around their edges flashed nuclear shades of viridian, yellow, and violet. A white billboard sported a postmark stamp of BRASIL in vibrant teal. Teal was a safe, contemporary color, seen on last year's Vacation Bible School scrapbook that Rhonda had printed for her class, on the awnings of the new RV dealership down from Tony Hill's Cowboy Catfish, and Eva's new gift bags at the Craft Cottage. You could trust teal.

Brasil didn't card but welcomed Seeger and Cordelia, giving them lapel pins of the club's logo upon entrance. Cordelia led Seeger farther into the club, maneuvering around tables of smartly dressed dates and families enjoying the salsa-spiced disco.

"Hello, may I speak to Don Quixote, please?" a man asked over bleeping synth-samba. "N-n-n-no no no, señor," a woman answered.

"Disco *Man of La Mancha*?" Cordelia wondered aloud. She smiled over her shoulder at Seeger and pointed ahead. A spotlit café table, poised apart from the rest, graced a small stage at the edge of the dance-floor. They beelined for it. Once settled, Seeger removed from his pocket a tiny pair of purple grape clusters hanging from a silvery stem base. Dimestore plastic, they were intended as salt and pepper shakers. Seeger slid a black vase of gardenias out of the aqua-tinted pinspot and slid in the grapes.

Cordelia tapped the grapes once. "Where did you get these, anyway? They make lovely drug containers."

"Wish someone would get our drink orders so we could take them," Seeger fretted. "How late is it? Is there a clock anywhere?"

Cordelia grabbed his wrist and leaned forward across the table with a sense of dire urgency. "You have that iridescent paper? I'm going to perform origami."

"I think so." He frisked his jacket pockets.

A young woman appeared. "Thank you for waiting," she said, touching turquoise combs in her hair. "We're only open two weeks and there's little bit of craziness here. My name is Maria—"

"Hello, Maria!" Cordelia smiled radiantly, commandeering the situation. "My name's Cordelia, and this is Seeger." She touched Maria's hand, her own chest, Seeger's arm. Seeger looked up from searching his pants pockets and nodded, hands still under the table.

"Ah, hello. What can I get for you tonight?"

"We'll have two glasses of cranberry juice, please," Cordelia said. "It's full of vitamin C and so delicious!"

Maria looked askance at Seeger. "Are you doing drugs under the table?"

Seeger looked at Cordelia and yanked out the paper, sparkling with a thousand crystalline colors. "I was just getting this."

Cordelia grabbed the paper and held it to Maria's face. "Isn't it pretty? We found it at this shop called Off the Street that had a window display of mannequins in Max Headroom masks."

"Yes, it is very lovely." Maria tilted her head away from the cellulose. Cordelia stuffed it decisively into the flower vase, a gaudy, petroleum-based blossom dwarfing the authentic ones.

"Besides," Seeger said, "we'd never do drugs under the table. We do all our drugs on top of the table." They grinned up at Maria.

"Are you two married?" Maria asked. Seeger faltered, looked at Cordelia.

"*Blech,* NO!" she exclaimed, sitting up straight. "I don't even like this guy. He's been following me around for seven months. I may have you throw him out." She gave him a disdainful scowl. "I'm looking for a quarterback, a big hunkahunkahunka burnin' love. You know any?" She rested her hand in her palm thoughtfully, blinking up at Maria.

Maria headed for the bar. "I'll ask Jaime . . ." Seeger watched her leave, wondering which was Jaime.

Cordelia leaned forward across the table. "She's very friendly." Seeger nibbled his pinkie nail, nodding and staring over at the bar.

"God, I can't wait to see what this place will be like once the X kicks in." She picked up the grapes and shook them next to Seeger's ear. "Hey, you." He jumped, startled, and turned to her. She relaxed back into her seat, reclining confidently.

"You never told me about these." She waggled the grapes like a dinner bell.

Seeger blinked. "Oh. They're from Kent Lozone."

Cordelia set the grapes down on the table. "Who?"

"You know, he hangs with those band guys," he said offhandedly. "Just turned junior. Works at Oshman's."

Cordelia furrowed her brows, nudging the grapes with her finger. "I don't remember him. And I don't spend much time in Oshman's."

"He's on the wrestling team."

"A wrestler?" She rolled her eyes and looked at Seeger reproachfully.

"But he's not like that!" Seeger protested, too strongly. Get a grip! Nothing's happened that you have to hide. Make him sound appealing to her, too. "He's the guy that wrote those gravy letters to the *Journal.*"

"Those never would've passed my editorial standards." Cordelia eyed him suspiciously.

"He wears cute little red horn-rims," he offered.

She glanced away, appraising the couples on the dancefloor. "Why did a wrestler with cute little red horn-rims give you plastic grapes?"

Seeger's feet fidgeted under his stool's support bar. Somehow, he wanted them all three to be friends. He imagined some sphere of perfect companionship and sex with the two of them but hadn't figured out yet how to maneuver them into it.

"A bunch of us skipped one day and went to Blazer Bowl," he said. "He, uh, won them in that game where you pull out prizes with a crane."

She laughed with authority, blanketing the table with an insistent air of relief. "Oh, this is that sporty boy you've being playing racquetball with."

"How did you know about that?" Seeger uncrossed his legs, but the bar snagged his shoe and slipped it off. The table rocked, the grapes tipped precariously. He watched Cordelia for a reply, but she waited until he bent under the table to fix his shoe.

"Oh well," he heard her say, "you're not always home when I call, you know. It's very frustrating. But sometimes I have a little womanly chat with Rhonda. We talk about all sorts of things."

Act like you don't care. Keep him mysterious and she'll be intrigued, not threatened. Seeger noticed his sock smelled.

"You know," she continued as he rejoined her above the table, "she shares with me your handed-down family recipes for Frito Pie, heirloom bondage quilts"—she raised an eyebrow—"endless invitations to accompany you to church."

Seeger grimaced apologetically. He wondered if his hands now smelled.

"She really has no concept of my Catholicism," Cordelia sighed, shaking her head. "I don't know what you're going to tell them when you convert." Cordelia looked around the club. He sniffed his fingers. They were OK.

"I suppose this Kent boy is Protestant as well?" She shot Seeger an exasperated look of disappointment as she stretched her ankle across his. "Probably something really lax, right? Some horribly liberal denomination, like Methodists, that allows dancing and married priests and polygamous fornication?" She eyed Seeger closely, cocking her head and raising her ankle up his leg. "I don't know what I'm going to do with you Texans. It'll be very healthy for you to move to a Catholic time zone."

Seeger's legs felt frozen. "I don't know," he blurted out. "I mean, he might be Catholic, too. He's Italian. He's from Chicago." Keep Kent mysterious, he reassured himself. And keep her happy, be charming so eventually she'll want to charm him. Just don't mention you're going with him to Six Flags tomorrow. She'd want to come. Smiling at Cordelia, he visualized a general panorama of the amusement park and blanketed it with obscuring static.

"*¿Para señorita?*" Seeger jumped and pulled his legs away. Maria had reappeared.

"Say, Maria," Cordelia queried, "would you have sex with a wrestler who wore red horn-rimmed glasses?"

Seeger squirmed in his seat. Cordelia gave him a merry look. He smiled back tentatively, as if testing new muscles.

Maria screwed up her face. "Over his face mask?"

"He doesn't wear a mask," Seeger protested.

"Ah. Well, he would have to take the glasses off," she said. "But even then, I think, no. He would be very smelly and oily always. He would make very fat babies that would be hurtful to me." She set down two tumblers brimming precariously with juice.

Seeger flashed on Kent's armpit hair and swallowed excess saliva. We need to take the drugs soon. I can control myself. I won't say too much about Kent, what I'm planning to do to him tomorrow.

"I should think so." Cordelia shot him a significant look and handed Maria a five. He stared at the garnet-red juice and lush jade wedges of lime; red like two cauterized wounds, green like Cordelia's eyes on a clear day. Seeger reached for their drugs. Cordelia reached for the bowl of tortilla chips.

"Ugh!" she grimaced, chewing. "You could make a Frito Pie with these chips."

Seeger jumped at the chance to change the subject from Kent to something trivial. *"Ew,"* he said, trying to loosen the grapes from the stem. "You know, I used to know a guy named Frito."

"Really?"

"Yeah," he said, unscrewing the grapes, "one of Joan's friends in Texas City. He and his son lived across the street. I remember it had really dusty windows, 'cause I'd have to wipe them to see out to Joan's place across the street. He baby-sat me sometimes because his son and I were friends."

Cordelia watched his hands, his thin fingertips gently press open the grapes.

"I remember watching Joan drive off in her Bug through their window—did I ever tell you she had a VW Bug once? Complete with this ONWARD THRU THE FOG bumper sticker by that guy that did KEEP ON TRUCKIN'.

Cordelia laughed. "And Jimi Hendrix in the eight-track?"

Seeger frowned, fingering out a green-flecked tablet from the hollow plastic grapes. "Frito's son was named Ocean, and he was a year or two older than me but couldn't read. I used to read him his comic books. We hung out 'cause he was kinda fucked up and lonely. His mom had OD'ed on smack."

"Smack is heroin, right?"

"Yeah," Seeger said, passing Cordelia the X tablet under the table. "I think so."

Her fist closed around his fingers. He pulled free and returned to the tabletop to fish out the second pill.

"I remember her a little. She had dark circles under her eyes and liked that Rita Coolidge 'We're All Alone' song. Frito just smoked a lot of pot and listened to Cheech and Chong. I remember him playing the records for me and Ocean. Frito would be totally cracking up and I wouldn't get what was so funny at all. Ocean didn't either, but he pretended to, just to make Frito happy."

He slipped the pill between his lips and grabbed his juice.

Cordelia faked a yawn, popping her pill as she covered her mouth. She sipped her juice, tilted her head back, swallowed. She shook her head. "Our parents had such bad taste in drugs." Seeger nodded and swallowed, relieved she had stopped asking about Kent.

LaTonia Reveals Kent's History

"I heard a story about your boy," LaTonia announced. She and Seeger blinked against the sunlight beating down on the asphalt, squinting into the expressway's traffic.

Seeger sipped his coke and turned, raising his eyebrows at LaTonia. "He likes me? Check one: yes? No? Maybe? He wants to kiss behind the bike racks after school?"

"Dream on," she laughed. "Hey—now!"

They jumped out into the river of fumes, tar, and exhaust. Seeger quickened his pace as a car in the opposite lane approached; LaTonia walked steadily.

They regrouped on the grassy knoll before the school. The EHS marquee loomed above them, CONGRATULATIONS EXECUTION EAGER WORKERS 4-H HOG SHOW AND AUCTION. He wondered if the kids in summer school cared.

"He went to school in Dallas before here," she said, eyeing a couple of students sprawled on the cracked cement steps. "At North Dallas. His family moved there first after Chicago, then Execution. This guy in Typing went to the same school."

"Yeah?" They walked along the curb, cars whooshing past them, heading south toward the mall.

"Anyway, he was different there. He was real shy and quiet; he didn't have none of this smartass 'tude going on. He was all artsy, like you. He joined their art club there first thing, and no one told him that's a total fag alert. He got a load of crap, got beaten up. You know how sometimes the whole school decides someone is going to be everyone's punching bag that year?"

Smiling, Seeger pointed to his cheeks with both index fingers. "West Execution Middle School spittoon, eighty-two–eighty-three!"

She nodded grimly. "Yeah, well, he got that, too, looks like. Maybe worse. His folks moved out of the city before he'd even finished his first semester."

Seeger kicked the dirt. "So you think he's really gay?"

LaTonia rolled her eyes. "That's not the point! If every dude called *fag* around here was one, you'd be in hog heaven. That's not it." She thwacked him on the side of his forehead. "The point is, be careful. Not only are you fucking around—"

Behind them, the tardy bell rang deep at the school. Weird that it doesn't matter anymore, Seeger thought. I still flinch.

LaTonia stopped to get Seeger's attention. "Not only are you fucking around with you and Cordelia," she said, "you could be fucking around with Kent, too. You don't know what all he's been through, what all's gone down in his head. He's been through some shit. Keep that in mind, huh? He *is* younger than you."

Seeger resumed walking. "C'mon, we'll be late for the movie."

Seeger Dreams the Night Before Going to Six Flags

Behind Abraham and over his shoulder, a bilious President Nixon became an illustration of a space capsule and grinning skull.

"Look there's Da—Abraham! Abraham and the dead cosmonauts," Joan said. She peered at the baby boy in her arms. He seemed to frown back, as if disapproving of her waxy new flip hairdo. She sucked her upper lip.

"Look, here's your father again." She held Seeger's soft skull and aimed his face at the fluttering TV phosphorescence. He waggled his arms deliriously. Her thumbs pressed into the indentations on the sides of his temple.

"Yes, yes," Joan cooed, massaging her thumbs in circles. "That's Abraham. Can you say 'Abraham'? Aye-bruh-haym?"

"Ayeayemam."

"Yes, yes! That's very close!" She pressed in hard on the side of his skull. "Aye-bruh-haym."

"Nayprahm!" Seeger shouted. His eyes bulged.

"Yes, Abraham!" She dug her thumbnails into his soft baby-skin.

"Naypahm!" he cried, wrinkling up his face, waving his arms in the air as if to fly.

"Yeah, hon, you should be proud of your father." Joan lifted Seeger up by the sides of his head and held him to her face. She spoke directly to the child. "Just don't call him *Napalm.*"

She sat Seeger back on her knee. The TV replaced Abraham with a commercial for a local record store. Joan sang along with Carly Simon, "That's the way I always heard it should be . . ."

Seeger Touches Kent

Sweat seeped into his eyes as Seeger gulped back his coke. Orange tasted shitty, but running around Six Flags Over Texas all day had dehydrated him. A record 100 degrees had hit, and it wasn't even officially summer. Nevertheless, Kent and his friends had been determined to pilgrimage across the Metroplex to Arlington's history-themed amusement park.

"Warhol pictures!" Kent shouted, surprising the counter girl at the Republic of Texas's Nacogdoches Saloon with a close-up snap from Seeger's Polaroid.

Seeger smirked. "You know, Kent, you should remake *Blow Job.* It's this movie Warhol did that's a thirty-five-minute closeup of this guy's face while he gets sucked off."

"Oooh, that'd be special. Got the kit for it at the Craft Cottage?" He lifted up Seeger's shirt and took a closeup of his dripping chest.

Seeger saw a blinding white flash, even though Kent wasn't using one in the relentless sun.

He felt chapped lips chafing his nipples. He looked down at Kent pressed against his chest, and with a stomach-churning wave of vertigo, they fell down, rapidly sinking into a mulchy, brown-green sea of mud.

"Six Fags Over Texas!" one of Kent's less-appealing friends shouted, pointing as Kent lowered Seeger's shirt. Kent gave him the finger. Seeger stared dumbly as he tried to slow his breathing back down. He threw back the final drops of orange.

"So The Woman couldn't make it today?" Kent said, folding up the camera.

"She had to work," Seeger lied. He'd told Cordelia he was going to Six Flags as a Family Day with his parents.

"Too bad. If I could get pictures of her chest it'd be great: a matched pair."

"What?"

Kent snatched Seeger's cup and helped himself to a piece of ice. "A matched pair of chest portraits," he said, crunching. "His 'n' hers."

Seeger thought of an old portrait of Abraham and Joan and him, all squinting in front of the cactus gardens outside Execution's post office. He dimly remembered sitting in Joan's lap, Abraham burrowing behind his camera and tripod. Spiky yucca and century plants had sprawled uncomfortably close, insectoid thorns and antennae looming around mother and child. "This is so *Ozzie and Harriet,*" Joan had complained. Seeger had leaned in against Joan, turning to lace his arms around her. "It's just a holiday card. Joan, hold him—"

"I know! Jesus, stop clinging to me, you damn octopus."

"Hey! What d'y'all want to ride next?" called Isaac, Kent's lanky, sullen friend. He towered above the sweaty clump of sophomores and seemed to have been made leader by virtue of height. All day he'd co-ordinated bull sessions to determine the next ride (deferring to Seeger to map the shortest route from attraction to attraction). In contrast to the other sophomores' hyperenthusiasm, Isaac maintained an air of belea-guered heat fatigue. Seeger was growing fond of him.

"Decide for us," Kent yelled back. He and Seeger stood off to the side as the huddle shouted rides' names, continuing the day's boisterous spirit. Seeger found their alcohol-free ebullience startling. Their age difference from Seeger seemed much more than two years.

"I think he's trying to talk them out of skeet-ball," Kent noted.

"Hmpf. That's pretty boring," Seeger groused. "I don't play games much."

"Yes you do," Kent said, sucking on another piece of ice. Seeger glanced aside at him. Kent watched his friends, jaws grinding.

"Hey, y'all," Seeger called, "let's do La Salle's Haunted Fort. It's got AC. It's in France."

Isaac peered over the crowd at Seeger and nodded solemnly. They all sauntered downhill, shouting in agreement. As they rounded a bend in the path, Seeger spied the Haunted Fort at the base of the hill. "There's the mother!" Kent shouted. Seeger's heart fluttered. The fort offered not merely heat relief or jostling; it was opportunity. The slow spook ride had single-file canoes drifting in near-dark through the flooded ruins of Fort Saint Louis. This French outpost on Lavaca Bay had supposedly become haunted when its founder, Robert Cavelier sieur de La Salle, had been killed by his own men. They themselves then fell to disease and Indian attacks.

Seeger knew Kent would sit with him, as he had all day. Exaggerating centrifugal force to press against Kent on Texas's Spindletop and Mexico's Crazy Sombrero had been cheap and sweet, but unfortunately unacknowledged. Kent could've easily blamed the crowd when they'd pressed shoulder-to-shoulder at the Confederacy's Palmito Ranch Battle reenactment (one of Abraham's favorite attractions: "It's so goddamn *Texan,*" he'd say each time they visited, "celebrating a Civil War battle that took place after Lee had already surrendered at Appomattox").

In the Fort's dark, Seeger could make physical contact so obviously intentional, Kent would have to respond somehow, give Seeger some answer finally, some sort of yes or no.

Seeger considered LaTonia's warning as they waited in line. Kent, roughhousing with the other guys, certainly didn't look . . . fragile.

The group quieted inside the ride, drifting through mechanized scenes of scalpings and pox-riddled French ghosts. Four sat single-file in a polypropylene canoe. Seeger took the rear and Kent, as anticipated, sat in front of him. After the smothering heat outside, the AC tightened Seeger's skin. Everything seemed acutely tactile as they drifted beneath fluttering, spun-fiberglass moss.

Holding his breath, Seeger let go of the canoe's sides. With excruciating delicacy, he rested his arms around Kent's hips and across his bare legs. Each hair on the inside of Kent's thighs pricked the underside of Seeger's arms, sharp curls like strands of steel wool. His thumbs edged up underneath the hem of Kent's sweat-wet "I Just Ran Into Tammy Faye at the Mall" T-shirt. His index finger brushed the trail of hairs dotting the center ridges of his abdomen.

Kent was silent. They entered an undersea menagerie of giant seahorses, pirate skeletons, and treasure chests spilling out pearls. Phosphorescent jellyfish spiraled around their canoe, and flickering wave-lights undulated across their faces.

"Phantasmagoric," Isaac murmured from the front of the canoe.

A heavy purple mist enveloped them. Seeger laid his forehead at the base of Kent's neck, stroking his thighs and calves. Kent didn't move. No one said a word. The mist dissipated, and they emerged into the sun. Kent said nothing.

Leaping from the canoe, they all huddled, yelling about what should be the next ride. Kent scampered away. "Isaac!"

Seeger froze. He imagined Kent telling Isaac, the group, and everyone turning on him, eyes and eyes of disgust, his running away, making up some story to get Cordelia to come pick him up, Kent never returning his Polaroid.

Kent laughed and Isaac shook the fake moss from his hair. Kent mugged for the gang and ran over to a park map. He seemed wholly oblivious to anything having transpired.

The afternoon wore on. Seeger sank into bitter depression, sitting out rides to rest or walk around the park. He thought about going off to one of the johns but felt too bummed even for masturbation. He wanted some reaction from Kent—terror, disgust, joy—anything passionate and intense. They were all the same thing. He only had to feel emotions writhing between the two of them, a lovepainintensitypower arcing from heart to heart, cock to cock, eyes to eyes.

Isaac tried to engage him with sarcasm regarding preteen girls in halter tops. Seeger shrugged and watched Kent whack mechanical moles with a padded mallet. He was relieved Kent hadn't freaked, but now he felt disgusted with himself, lecherous. He trudged through the rest of the day in resignation. A sparkling adventure of potential joy had become an unpleasant and vaguely tacky chore, like bleaching come stains from his underwear with a toothbrush before Rhonda did laundry.

He wondered miserably what Cordelia was doing. Certainly something less sophomoric. He wandered forward, approximately with the flock of boys. The Judge Roy Scream roller coaster sped past noisily, its cars turning the dusk sun into a flashing orange strobe.

The light flickered, stayed on, grew. The screeching metal of the coaster leapt in intensity, and Seeger smelled Rhonda's perfume. Blinded in the coppery light, he spun himself around, away from the sound of screams and sirens and twisting metal.

He blinked. He stood up, steadied himself.

Across the walkway, Kent and Isaac were absorbed in photographing two giggling freshmen at the Pink Thing stand.

june, 1987

Seeger Prepares to Leave

Seeger snaked under his sheet, hiding from the ringing phone. His gut knew it was Cordelia calling, and he dreaded a replay of the night before. She'd left three messages while he was out driving around alone. When he got in and called back, she'd cried for an hour. He'd spun scenarios of NYC adulthood and celebrity. She'd hung up apparently comforted.

The ringing stopped.

"Seeger!" Abraham yelled from the front of the house. "Get the damn phone! It's Cordelia."

He turned on the stereo to brace himself: Marc's "Tenderness Is a Weakness" (with instrumental overture). Bad omen.

"Good morning, camarónito," she said brightly. "How are you?"

"Mmf. All right."

"Mmm. Lauren Bacall."

"Yeah, morning voice. Sorry."

"That's all right; I'm feeling pretty lesbian today, babe."

Seeger touched himself beneath the sheet. Soft. First Baptist struck 10:00.

"Hear that, young man? You have a plane to catch today! The Mexican delegation for Sonny Bono's mayoral campaign awaits your leadership."

"Oh, my."

"So get outta bed!" Cordelia laughed. "What time's your flight?"

79

"Three-ten."

"Shall I come by a little before two?"

He couldn't remember if they'd said anything about her, rather than his parents, taking him to the airport. She would definitely be better. The visions had made him queasy about riding with Abe and Rhonda. "Uh . . . OK. Great. Um"—he thought of them running through the terminals at Love Field—"no—make it one-thirty, so we're not late, OK?"

"Great, OK. Oh, I can't talk now, Unclefred's insisting on the phone, the asshole. See you at two, I mean, one—one-thirty, right!"

He hung up. Her resuscitated exuberance relieved him, tentatively. Just stay happy till I get out of here, he willed. Maybe if we miss each other a lot while I'm gone, things'll be stronger when I get back. Kent's confused everything so much, and she won't leave me alone with her New York–or-not traumas. Can't wait to get away for a while, just clear my head of all them. That's real shitty of you. Fuck.

Saying Goodbye

Seeger noted the time on the terminal's flight monitor. "Well," he said, "I don't want to miss it." He spared her a quick, awkward hug around his suitcase.

"Write from Mexico," she said, voice edgy, yet controlled.

"I will." He jerked away, veering into the boarding line. A collegiate guy with a stud earring butted in front of him.

Seeger shuffled forward in line, Cordelia's eyes on his back. Anxiety gnawed at him. He hadn't heard from Kent all week, since Six Flags. He'd been afraid to call, and now he was leaving town for almost a month. What if Kent loses interest while I'm gone? What if he starts going out with some girl? Or some guy—maybe he'll meet some guy really hotter than me, some other wrestler or something, and it'll bring him completely out. That'd be even worse. It could happen. The way he likes me is . . . it could just be like an infatuation. He probably doesn't find me attractive at all. I mean, after Six Flags, obviously he doesn't. He just likes me as a friend, maybe wants advice, has some questions. But we aren't even much as friends. He's probably disgusted with that part of me but too nice to show it. We don't have really much of a history.

Cordelia and I were friends for a long time before we realized we were in love. And Kent and I don't depend on each other for anything; we don't owe each other anything. We're not connected like Cordelia and I are.

Seeger's bowels knotted. He wondered if Cordelia was still standing in the concourse behind him, watching. He felt guilty, as if thinking about Kent constituted cheating on her. Following in your father's footsteps, he thought.

He remembered trying to sleep in the living room of Abraham's apartment when he'd first moved in with him. He'd been able to hear Rhonda say something about still feeling like an Other Woman, that the same thing had destroyed her great-grandmother. Abraham had complained about still being legally married to Joan and that he wasn't making very much money as a substitute teacher. Seeger remembered having been surprised to hear Abraham and Rhonda fight. He'd thought only Abraham and Joan did that, and that's why they had gotten a divorce. Their voices had bounced loudly off the thin apartment walls. Seeger had burrowed into the couch's velour crevices, trying to disappear into the furnishings of his father's new home that was now his, too.

"Call me when you get there!" Cordelia's voice faltered expectantly.

He stood still. "Look," he blurted out, stumbling out of line back to her, "I'm really—I'm sorry things have been so, you know, weird lately. Really. I mean . . ."

She looked up at him curiously. He shoved his face past hers, hugging.

"I love you," he said, sounding almost defensive, as if offering an explanation or justification. She relaxed in his arms, pressing against his chest. He inhaled. She smelled like pillows.

She nodded her chin against his collarbone and squeezed his waist. "Sure," she said, voice cracking.

Seeger wanted to squeeze tighter, to force their bodies together till they burst open, their disparate chemicals and essences flooding into each other, a swirl of liquids blended in a single casing. He thought of the two of them as one. With Kent, maybe?

"The rest of the summer'll be fabulous," he murmured through her hair. "We'll all have a great time."

She broke the embrace with a quick jerk and hugged her arms

around her sides. He sighed and smiled at her warmly. She flickered a return. He looked back at the emptying boarding gate and offered her an *oh well* shrug. She nodded.

He got in line. From the corner of his eye, he saw her back away from the gate and lean against the hot glass of the terminal windows. Seeger handed over his boarding pass and gave her a final nod goodbye.

The line shuffled forward, stopped. Seeger looked through a porthole in the gate's crew exit and saw, through another window beyond that, Cordelia, leaning against her panel of the long wall of windows. She stepped forward, looked up and down the concourse. Her chest and shoulders fell. She noticed the bank of payphones to her right and lunged toward them. Seeger watched her dial, jealousy rising in his throat. Who was she calling?

She waited, then smiled, speaking with effusive gestures.

"Young man?" The flight attendant motioned for Seeger to come forward. He adjusted his bag's shoulder strap and stole another glance through the windows.

Cordelia hung up the phone. Her shoulders slumped again, cheery expression vanished. She peered down the concourse as if searching for something or someone.

"Come on now, son," grumbled the man behind him. Seeger boarded the plane.

Seeger Lies to His Mother

"I think this will do." Seeger grinned, pouring his half-carafe of house blush.

"Goddamn, yeah." His mother raised a large ceramic beer stein. "A restaurant not full of diesel fumes." She drank heartily. "And they take El MasterCardito, so my mother can pay for it."

A moderate crowd dotted Le Veau de Bonheur, dining under potted ficus and white Christmas lights. Swarthy waiters in ivory linen glided from table to table amid the steady tinkle of flatware and tongues. An elusive piano warbled "Someone to Watch Over Me."

Joan slammed down her stein, rattling the lid. Seeger flinched. "So y'all excited about finally getting out of Execution this fall?" she asked her son. "Why your dad's so scared of leaving that hellhole, I'll never understand."

"Oh. Yeah," he said. He thought about his visions but resisted broaching the subject. Joan might want him to do more readings for her or maybe try to actually summon up one of them. Those intrusive truck explosions, and those other images of Kent, all felt too tied to Execution. Too many contradictory, angry, guilty, feverish feelings he was determined not to deal with while on vacation. He felt vaguely embarrassed that he'd let his summer become clouded with childish infatuations and fantasies. He wanted to clear his head of it all here, in Mexico, on one of his escapes to his other life with Joan. If he could maintain a balance, a separation, things would be fine.

"Saw this thing on CNN," Joan said, "about these 'designer drugs' that're all big up in Dallas."

"Ecstasy," he said, nodding. "Yeah, it's everywhere. All the premeds at SMU make it, so there's tons around. They used to advertise it right in bars' windows in Dallas 'cause it was legal up till last month. But now they just sell Eve."

"What's that?"

"Basically same thing. They reworked the chemical structure to get around the Ecstasy law. They're both big euphorics."

"What a Dallas drug, all clean and synthetic and soulless." She laughed. "The hick kids in Execution even know it exists?"

Seeger straightened up in his chair. "Nah, not really. Those that've heard of it don't want to spend twenty, twenty-five dollars when, uh, grass and acid are so cheap."

"No one really knows anything about what all the hell it can do to you, though, right?"

"It's supposed to be a combo of methamphetamine and acid." He wondered what all to tell Joan. He remembered her getting him drunk and stoned for the first time: "This is so you won't freak when other kids offer you some." But the press hyped X as a trendy plaything of hedonist yuppies, and Seeger feared his mother already considered him too much of a dandy.

"I don't know," she said. "Sounds scary. Y'all tried any?" Joan eyed her son over the stein's lip.

"Uh, no." He glanced away. "I hear it makes you all open and trusting and you love everyone real intense and tell them anything. Supposed to be, shrinks made it to help open up their patients." He looked back at Joan. She pursed her lips, thinking. She tapped her stein's rim.

"Fuck," she sighed, "you know, I did coke at parties—your dad was too piss-shy to even try that—but I never did acid or any of that real artificial stuff." She shook her head and blew a wisp of perm-fried black hair from her eye.

"Yeah?"

"Even after Abraham and I split, it was just grass, hash—God, I'd kill for really good hash again. You ever get a line on some, bring it down on your next visit, and I'll pay you back."

"Abraham still grows pot in the vegetable garden," he mentioned.

"No shit?"

"Yeah," he said, "guess he thinks I don't know, don't care, or won't steal any." He snorted. "None of which are true."

"He still lock himself in the bathroom to smoke?"

"Yeah, with the ventilator on."

"Fuck, he started that soon as he graduated UT." They giggled.

"It's like this big family thing never to say anything about it. But it's like obviously there, and Rhonda goes on buying me 'Number One Drug-Free Son' sweatshirts at Christmas."

"Shee-it," Joan drawled, staring into Seeger's carafe, "he always wanted to marry his mama. He certainly did this time."

Seeger shook his foot under the table. "Uh, I don't know," he said judiciously, "I think Rhonda used to smoke, too."

"Christ, grass doesn't do a thing for me now."

Seeger tried to maneuver the conversation away from his parents. "D'you ever do mushrooms?"

Joan shook her head. "No," she replied, "but, you know, I've always wanted to try. I mean, it'd have to be with someone who knew the scene. Did peyote once and that sucked, but I wasn't really prepared for it."

"Yeah. Hallucinogens scare me 'cause they're so unpredictable."

"Oh, I don't think so." She leaned forward, excited. "It just depends on locking your head in the right mental sphere, you see? I'd just want to see what kind of visions I could tap into, 'cause they're such a major part of the magical tradition. Christ, especially here! I don't know about Mexico City, but Oaxaca—where we're going next—is known all over as a mushroom center. It's ground zero! The Incas consider them holy; they used them all the time. I'm sure either of us could handle it. We'd just have to have someone reliable around in case anything went wrong." She lifted her stein but was too tongue-tied in enthusiasm to sip.

"I know we could handle it," she insisted. "It'd be great for us."

Seeger smiled with slight embarrassment. He held up a finger to quiet her and addressed the waiting waiter.

"Alsace Especial, por favor."

"Oh—ah, enchiladas de pollo," Joan stammered.

Seeger watched the waiter bustle off. "I thought German food in a French restaurant in Mexico would be funny," he commented. He smiled, hoping to shift Joan's mood to a lighter, less vehement tone.

Joan stared across the restaurant, frowning. Seeger couldn't tell if she was pissed at his interruption, absorbed in thinking about mushrooms, remembering some worry about their trip, or merely relaxing. What with her constantly changing lovers, locales, and careers plus her premonitions of nuclear holocaust, economic ruin, and environmental catastrophe, a furrowed frown had become her face's default setting. It locked in a tense expression even if she was relaxed, like how the feet of women who wear high heels maintain a stair-step shape, even when barefoot.

Mother and Son Make Mistakes Sightseeing

Seeger and Joan entered Chapultepec Park. The white-noise din of yelling children and yelping pets soothed their frazzled nerves. They admired pinwheels, turquoise cotton candy, sparkler guns, kites, papaya ices, animal-shaped balloons, and other paraphernalia of family weekends. Seeger felt an old youthful desire to run, wave colors, and caterwaul, but they were not such a family. Without wheezing grandparents and loud toddler cousins, they were solely two adults, possibly brother and sister. Many on this trip had assumed they were married, or lovers. Few guessed mother and son.

"This park is so much more soothing than Central Park. The way it's laid out? The size doesn't overwhelm you."

"You're right, yeah. And it's nothing like Versailles, no feeling of rigid aristocracy. You can't even see the castle."

"Where is it, anyway?"

"Around that crowd, I think. See the end of that other line? That big stone wall must be the base of the hill it's on."

They passed a kiosk blaring Carly Simon's "Haven't Got Time for the Pain," where smiling women in gauzy uniforms handed out Medipren samples. They joined a boisterous line at the base of the wall.

"This should be real fascinating," Joan said. "They've restored Maximilian and Carlota's imperial chambers."

"Ha! Revolutionaries profiting off those they overthrew?"

"Name of the game."

A few people in the line stared oddly at Seeger and his mother, but the two six-foot-plus gringos with matching shoulder-length hair had grown used to that.

"Sure are a lot of kids."

"Guess they get off on the Rivera murals."

"Looks like it's free, too."

Seeger stooped through the doorway at the wall's base. The line continued ahead down a dingy cement tunnel to an exit 150 feet away. The children's crowing multiplied inside with echoes. Funhouse mirrors lined the entire tunnel.

Seeger grinned sheepishly over his shoulder as Joan stooped in behind him. "I don't think this is the castle," he confessed.

The line crushed forward. Smirking, they pushed through. They strode past the mirrors, glimpsing their mutants: obese, skeletal, undulating—scores of freakish offspring. The last mirror created horizontal waves of sloping height. They stood beside each other; the mirror wove their images together into one crossbanded form, an Oedipal candy cane.

Outside, Seeger looked for someone to take their picture before their mirthful irony dissipated. It would make a great memory, a great story to tell Kent and Cordelia. But Joan had taken the lead, mounting the trail up the hill toward the real castle. He hurried to catch up, feet slapping flat on the cement path.

Sightseeing Separately

Joan threw tour upon side trip upon restaurant expedition, cluttering their days like mismatched silverware dumped unceremoniously into a kitchen drawer. Finally, Seeger convinced her they should split up.

He left her at the Museo Nacional d'Anthropología and headed downtown as the morning grew stale and hot. Once alone and surrounded by strangers, he felt the happiest he'd been on this trip.

Wonder where those transvestite stripper bars are, like Marc sings about in *"L'Esqualita."* If only I knew how to ferret them out. Wish there was a map. He jostled his cock through his shorts' pocket, imagining a bosomy Mexican she-male toying with him in front of a cantina's leering patrons.

He followed the crowds instead, to be safe. He drifted down to the main plaza. Pastries, pinwheels, and Lotería kiosks lined the Zócalo. He counted out pesos and bought a ruddy sugar lump. Vendors waved wares at him, crying, *"¡Muy barrato!"* He shook his head and meandered to the plaza's far side, stepping over a mosaic of the city in Aztec times. Two twelve-year-olds offered him a squirrel on a string. He sidestepped them and joined a crowd around a magician. Magic won't require fluency, he thought.

The magician covered a woman in an ebony cloth and asked her questions, winking at the crowd. Seeger understood only isolated words of the story. She answered hesitantly. He made a stupendous exclamation and removed the cloth. The woman was unchanged. The crowd gasped, laughed, and applauded.

Seeger felt lost, like a boat broken free from its anchor.

Joan Makes a Psychic Connection

Traffic's screech and blare still ricocheted inside Seeger's head, along with smog, beggars, earthquake rubble, soldiers' machine guns, and other souvenirs of Mexico City. The capital city had possessed only one functional highway in and out of town. One. They'd spent two hours imprisoned in traffic returning from the Tula standing figures. That night at dinner, nauseating iguana had been substituted, without warning, for chicken in Seeger's enchiladas. Joan had nevertheless insisted that Seeger join her afterward for a midnight drive into the desert. She was certain that a cab driver would trek out to the rumored UFO-viewing spot only at another male's directive. Without trying to rape her.

They'd seen nothing; Seeger's diarrhea had splattered on moonlit desert sand. The next morning Joan had announced she was too stressed out by Mexico City, they had to leave for Oaxaca right away, skipping the Teotihuacán pyramids.

The day of hectic travel finally over, they attempted recuperation with a lazy supper on a café's open-air balcony. Emerald and amber citylights spilled down into the valley below. Oaxaca's colonial architecture, flagstones pastel green like minty milk, collected elegant pools of twilight. Spiderwebs of tension, however, still clung to Seeger and his mother.

Joan surveyed the cradle of mountains surrounding the city. "The ruins are incredible around here," she said. "Monte Albán and Mitla, and I think some other, older ones." She shoved her falafel pita away to rest beside remnants of avocado salad, fried potatoes à la carte, *papaya líquida,* and *enchiladas suizas.*

What's the big deal about finding a vegetarian café, Seeger thought irritably, if you impulse out and order half the menu? He polished off his combo plate tidily and opened *The Vanishing American.* He'd never had an interest in reading westerns, but Joan had told him it'd be worthwhile to check out a couple and not be such a snob. The English section at the Mexico City airport had been small, but he'd recognized Zane Grey from his grandfather's dusty volumes. The "heart-and-guts characters" and "hard-shooting action" frankly got on his nerves, but nevertheless Seeger found himself drawn into the story of Nophaie, an American Indian born on a reservation but schooled in the East, who struggled to reconcile his two worlds.

Seeger opened to his bookmarked page. Unwritten postcards to LaTonia, Cordelia, and Kent fell out. He missed them, and worried what they were up to, but hadn't been able to bring himself to write.

Joan uncrumpled a flyer she'd torn from the café's wall: a rough sketch of a bearded man's face, line drawing of stars and planets and pyramids, and the prominent word, *Metafísica.*

A tight-jawed bearded man in a short-sleeve beige dress shirt marched over to their table. He indicated Joan's unfinished dishes and asked how their meals were.

"Oh, God, we're coming back tomorrow!" Joan nodded vigorously. "I can't believe we found falafel in Mexico."

"Seek and ye shall find," he said, deadpan. He studied Seeger with a face unblemished by emotion. Seeger said, "It's good."

"What do you know about this organization?" Joan thrust the flyer at him. "It was posted outside your café. I can't really tell if it's just a meditation group or school or what. It says, 'Ciencia de Energia'—"

The man waved the flyer away. "The organization is all those things and more," he explained. "Are you interested in metaphysics?"

"I do psychic readings," Joan blurted out. "Not professionally, just for friends or barter. I also do astrocartography and I've studied iridology."

The man's face betrayed surprise.

Seeger dove back into Zane Grey. Being an aloof bookworm didn't embarrass him as much as listening to Joan spill her Aquarian guts to some stranger.

"I run the society," the man announced, pulling a chair up to their table. "It's mine. My name is Mycall Powers." He turned out to be from Dallas and had studied at UT—Austin, like Joan. His parents lived in Port Arthur, the hometown of both Joan and Janis Joplin. He'd driven through Execution, even. Them psychic sparks are flyin', Seeger thought.

"Oh, this is so goddamn typical," Joan gasped. "I knew we were supposed to come to Oaxaca. I mean the ruins are nice, but I knew there was a *reason,* didn't I?"

Seeger lifted his head. "Yeah, we changed our whole itinerary. Blew off the pyramids and everything to come down here early."

"And I knew I was destined to work the café myself today," Mycall countered. "My local usually runs things, so I can spend days on my journeys."

"Really?" Joan said. "Living in Port A, I've been finding it real hard to intersect with other Initiates on a Cosmic Path. There are lots of little groups into meditation, positive projecting, UFOs; but no one really thirsty for the adventure of true growth."

"Such an adventure it is," Mycall remarked, narrowing his eyes. "Not just growth but complete transformation of body, soul, and mind. This is a great spiritual center, Oaxaca, but it is an ancient religion—"

"The only real kind!"

"All energy comes from the Primal Source, the forces of destruction and renewal, the winged serpent of rebirth flows through all religions, but the ancient practices are least tainted."

Seeger picked at Joan's cold potatoes.

"So you use the Indian healing knowledge? I want to write a book about Tex-Mex traditional healers—"

"Yes, healing." Mycall shook his head impatiently. "The natives knew of the Great Mother's life sciences. But they didn't fully incorporate the Father, the yang, the fire, life-destruction, and expansion. Transformative journeys of mind and spirit."

Joan looked pointedly at Seeger. He swallowed a mouthful of guacamole.

"The shamans here," she said, gaping at Mycall, "use the local mushrooms, don't they?"

"Yes," he answered, "we do."

Joan beamed proudly. "Goddamn! Did you know on the way down here we were just talking—"

Mycall held up his hand. "I felt your coming. I am your teacher."

Mycall Teaches

Mycall's society convened in a shut-down commercial sector of Oaxaca, half-empty cinderblock strips of stores standing testament to unrequited economic optimism. They met in a sallow rectangular room lit with dingy bulbs. Seeger felt he was inside a giant manila envelope.

Mycall held court atop a platform at the far end. On mats before him sat nine followers. Instructing in a serene monotone, he shut his eyes and spread his legs. His dick fell out of his red nylon running shorts. He ordered each student to stand on their neck. Desperate-looking housewives, hairy young Marxists, and gringo artists in native clothing all inverted determinedly, faces flushed with B_{12}.

Joan trembled, fell. Mycall's goateed assistant rushed over, frowning, and reinstated her bare feet in midair. Others faltered, but Mycall droned on, airing his dick. Seeger was unimpressed.

They reclined on straw mats. Mycall droned the commands for a guided meditation. Seeger didn't understand all the Spanish, but the rhythm pulled him under, anyway. He assumed it was the usual: "Picture a beautiful/warm/safe space, the sun on your body, orange liquid flowing out of your arms/leg/head," etc., etc. Seeger knew what to do.

He thought of the desert, at night, when coolness and moisture descended on your shattered senses like a savior. Vast, wide horizons without interruption, where all was visible. Nothing could sneak up on you in the desert, and at night the whole universe sparkled above. Staring straight up, you could almost believe you were an astronaut: the wide field of stars, the vacuous wind-whistles.

Seeger smiled at the thought. And big Prowler travel trailers were like space capsules; his family and their neighbors most definitely like aliens. Seeger stretched out on his straw mat and drifted back in memory to a vacation with his other family, last Christmas:

"I can hear you being all awake, Kody," Abraham had bellowed at the Kings' trailer. "Get to sleep!"

Bill had shot some Cuervo and passed Seeger the bottle. They'd chortled. Bill and Pam's son had been sent to bed in the Kings' larger trailer. Rhonda and Pam had been gossiping in Bill and Pam's tiny fishing pullalong. The men had been drinking around the fire.

Kody had sat up in his bed atop the dining table, throwing the sheet off his face and shouting through the window, "Yeah, you're what's keeping me up!"

Abraham had shaken his fingers in mock fright. He'd grinned at Bill and Seeger, reaching for another Lone Star.

"Dad," Kody had whined.

"Kody, shut yourself up and get to sleep," Bill had barked.

Seeger had struggled for precision while filling the cup of skin between his thumb and forefinger with salt. He'd licked it off, taken a shot of tequila and chomped a lime wedge, unsure if that had been the correct order. He'd passed the bottle back to Bill, face flushing hot. Bill had passed it on to Seeger's dad.

"What a Christmas," Bill had murmured. "Merry fucking Christmas."

"No lie," Abraham had agreed, taking a shot.

"Me and my family and my neighbors, out here in the fucking beauty of the Lord's goddamn fucking bee-you-ti-ful creation!" Rocking in his vinyl lawn chair, Bill had thrown his head back and howled.

"For a whole beautiful week," Abraham had added.

Seeger had tilted his head skyward and pretended his alcoholic warmth radiated down from the galaxy's silver spray.

"And tonight's just the beginning," he'd said.

"Here's to one hell of a first night," Bill had cheered. They'd all clinked together the Cuervo and Lone Stars, necks crossing.

"Jesus," Abraham had said after swallowing. "I figured we'd all cut loose sometime on this trip, but I didn't expect it our first night." He'd passed the tequila to Bill, who passed it to Seeger.

"Huh? What?" Seeger had been fixated on the campfire's reflected flickers making shapes on Bill and Pam's ebony pickup.

"What my poor son must think," Abraham had gone on, "seeing his father in such a state!"

Musty vapors had fumed up Seeger's nose as he'd sputtered out a laugh.

"Not to mention," Bill had added, "the most upstanding faculty member of the Execution Independent School District!"

"Yeah, right," Seeger had said. He'd passed Bill the tequila.

Abraham had slapped Seeger's back. "This is his last Christmas at home!" He'd leered. "A Christmas to remember! What would your new girlfriend think if she saw you like this?"

Abraham had handed Seeger the tequila. Seeger stared. The golden liquid sloshed inside, a magic elixir of distilled love passed from father to son. Primo stuff, 100 percent proof primogeniture. *Hijo d'oro.* Golden boy and Daddyalus. Sonshine fell softly on my Icarus today. . . .

Abe had laughed proudly and Seeger had rolled the liquor around, swishing it over his teeth. He'd held the taste in his mouth and the word in his mind: *girlfriend.* His throat muscles pulled the liquor down, and he remembered swallowing Jésus' come. Abe had chuckled and Seeger had smiled back at him, holding his flush, drunken head high. Can't wait to find out what sex with Cordelia is like.

Kody had rustled about, rocking the trailer.

Seeger had remembered one of Joan's mobile homes rocking when she'd have boyfriends over. He'd squinted at the trailer's window but could no longer see Bill's son. The firelight had dimmed.

Once inside the trailer, after joining Kody in bed, Seeger had been able to see well. They'd both peered through the louvered windows at the adults outside in the starlight.

"Don't worry," Seeger had said, "it happens when you drink too much."

"Are you drunk?" Kody had asked with a nine-year-old's frankness.

"Yeah, but not that much."

Seeger and Kody had watched Abe circle the trailers, climb into Bill and Pam's pickup bed, and pace around as if restlessly caged in the vast expanse of desert.

"Born in the U.S.A. . . . ," he'd rasped. Seeger had tried to ignore his singing as it became sobs. Abraham's crying—he'd only witnessed it two other times in his life—had infuriated Seeger.

"Abraham, just come to bed," Rhonda had sighed, sitting on the tailgate. Seeger had seen her through the window, chin in palm, watching that her husband didn't stumble out and fall face down into the sand. Abraham had fumbled his way around to the front of the truckbed, sick. Hot bile had smacked the placid sand, a sound firm and staccato in contrast to the lugubrious gagging.

"He throwing up?" Kody had asked.

"Yeah, but it's good to throw up when you're like that."

Rhonda had walked around to where her husband was hanging over the truck's side panels, resting her hand on his back and sighing, "Oh, Abe . . ."

That should be me sick out there, Seeger had thought, with him consoling me. Just like I should've let him teach me to shave.

"You ever been drunk before?" Kody had asked.

"Yeah."

"You throw up?"

"Sometimes."

"You and your dad ever throw up together?"

He'd lain down beside him, smelling the sweaty kid's hair. "We've never gotten drunk together before tonight." They'd listened to his parents' hushed talk, tiny scratches against the vast night. Coyotes had distantly called to kin.

"Wish we weren't on vacation," Kody had whispered.

"The rest of it won't be like this," Seeger had said. "It's hard to understand when you're little but—I mean, I know tonight seems like forever—but it's really just one night, and this vacation is just one week in your whole life. It's just a little blip you're visiting, like a little planet in the middle of the whole galaxy. It's not connected to anything else, and you'll never be here again."

Kody had considered the older boy dubiously.

Seeger remembered feeling dishonest—and old—as the boy had eyed him.

Seeger tuned in to Mycall for a moment but couldn't tell what he was now instructing the class to do. Seeger directed his memory to the next morning: Abraham hungover during the breakfast pecan swirls.

He remembered sun filtered by the trailer's windows, bright yellow and pink bands streaming through like headlights, headlights bearing down through a windshield shattering and the shriek of brakes, the impact of glass on face—

"*Unht!*" Seeger gasped and bolted upright. The class all stared at him. Mycall barked a command to his assistant, who rushed over to Seeger. Seeger brushed off the assistant's hands and walked outside, shaking the noise and heat from his head. Joan still had her eyes closed, concentrating.

Joan Tells of Seeger's Birth

"Sorry about disturbing class," Seeger said outside.

"Much stranger things have happened in that room," Mycall said blackly, not looking up. He drew a map while they waited for a cab.

"Seeger falls kinda deep into trance sometimes; all sorts of things contact him," Joan explained.

Mycall nodded. "Yes, I'm sure." He handed them the map. "Now, don't eat a thing tonight. You'll travel further on an empty stomach. And don't tell anyone where you'll be going."

"Great!" Joan grinned broadly.

"We're, uh, going a lot further than we planned," Seeger remarked. Joan laughed.

"You don't say very much," Mycall said, appraising Seeger. "Are you in agreement with Joan about all this?"

Seeger took this as a challenge. "Sure," he said stiffly.

"How did you two become acquainted?"

Seeger didn't bat an eye. "She gave birth to me seventeen years ago."

"Born on the very last second of the sixties," Joan detailed. "Last Child of the Sixties, that's what I used to call him. Born eleven-fifty-nine and fifty-nine seconds on December thirty-first, nineteen sixty-nine. That's not what his birth certificate says, but that's because the doctors fucked with the records so it looked like they worked more. Those doctors, they forced me under when I wanted a natural childbirth. The doctor asked me to do something I didn't understand, and I just said, 'What?' and he said, 'Oh, she's not going to cooperate, just go ahead and put her under.' So they knocked me out and I didn't get to see my son born. They yanked him out with forceps, and he's got these indentations on the side of his head from it. Abraham, his father, just waited in the waiting room; that's all he could do."

Seeger held his face locked, expressionless. He'd heard this story many times and knew what came next.

"When I went under, I had a vision of that Czechoslovakian student setting himself on fire. People were screaming, and grains of ash were soaring past. Mary Jo Kopechne and Sharon Tate reached out of the sky and welcomed him into this circle of dancing celestial spirits. But then everything became enveloped in this fiery light, and I woke up in the recovery room. It was the first vision I ever had, and I knew it meant Seeger would be a Seer, a special gifted soul." Joan laughed. "His whole life's been a trip!"

"Life is a trip that never ends," Mycall corrected.

Metaphysical pissing contest, Seeger thought. He offered Mycall a polite smile. Mycall narrowed his eyes at the boy. Traffic murmurs crept through the trees and lizards scurried across branches as Joan chuckled.

Seeger glanced away from Mycall. He touched his temples, feeling the undulations of bones. Didn't all skulls look like that? Was mine really abnormal? Maybe my visions are as unreliable as Joan's memory.

Headlights blazed around the corner. The cab's brakes screeched and Seeger flinched, anticipating another truck-wreck vision. He closed his eyes, bracing himself, but no images came. Mycall was staring at him when he opened his eyes. Mycall's face twitched.

"And when we see you in the morning," Joan said, bending into the taxi, "we'll really begin our journey!"

Mycall nodded beside Seeger, breathing heavily through his nose.

"What hotel should I tell the driver you're at?"

"Plaza—" Joan began.

"I'll tell him," Seeger interrupted, slamming the door. He didn't roll down the window. Mycall didn't wave, but he stood there, watching the cab as they rode off.

Seeger frowned, wishing he had a concrete reason for not trusting Mycall, for recommending to Joan that they blow him off, but all Seeger had was a gut feeling, an instinct, which should be enough. Should, but wasn't, given Joan's enthusiasm. What if there were an accident? What if Seeger got hurt, slipped and broke his leg or something, and the rest of the summer was ruined? No chances for sex with Cordelia and/or Kent as he whiled away his summer with a cast propped up in front of late-night music videos. He could tell that Joan really wanted this. He didn't want her to think he was too scared to go through with it.

A Postcard from Cordelia Back at the Hotel

Seéger Warholista—
Help! I am trapped in Vikki's psycho circle of restaurant employees!
I have been addressed as "Babe." I have drunk shots named after the
bodily functions of poultry and sex acts illegal in Texas. Last night I
sniffed coke from a meat cleaver. White billowing curtains are sure to
follow. Will be forced to track down racquetball-boy myself if you do
not return immediately. Love, Cordelia-Descending-a-Staircase-and-
Turning-Into–Demi Moore.

Seeger slid the card into his Zane Grey paperback, missing Cordelia and wishing tomorrow's mushroom trip would be with her and Kent instead of with Mycall and his mother.

Taking Mycall's Mushrooms

Seeger guided them via Mycall's map to Orozco Park. They marched to the *refrescos* stand in the far southeastern corner, where further instructions would lead them to the mushrooms.

A young Mexican girl sat there, reading a *foto-novella.*

Joan asked, *"¿Está Mycall Powers aquí?"*

The girl smiled at Seeger. She tucked hair behind her ear and, reaching from beneath the counter, handed them a map showing the way from the park to Mycall's house. "Bring OJ!" it read at the bottom. Seeger thought of his and Cordelia's vitamin C X-tender.

"Should we get some here?" Joan asked.

"He has some at the house," the girl assured them, shaking her head to dismiss Mycall's instructions. Who is she? Seeger wondered. What does she know about us? The girl buried herself back in her book, hair falling from her forehead.

96

They hiked past the jungle gym and monkey bars teeming with children, down into residential streets.

"God, this'll be such a treat," Joan said rapturously. "I hope I can grok some really good states."

"Mm-hm. Yeah." Seeger sighed. Although curious to try the experience, this morning he still felt wary of spending the day with Mycall. He didn't like or trust him in regular reality, let alone an addled one. Mycall was so anal, all masculine calculation. He'd shown them the algebraic equation for telepathy but was proud he didn't even know his astrological sign. He reminded Seeger to a degree of Abraham.

"After you left us at the café," Joan explained, "he invited us to join a visionquest group up in the mountains next week. We could change our return reservations tomorrow morning." She tossed her son a slack-jawed look of giddy amazement. "God, if only we could be here in August for the Harmonic Convergence."

Seeger bit his lip, guts squirming. No, he thought, I have to keep this from going too far, without being a downer. He rubbed his tongue across his teeth. If I play my cards right all day, I can probably get Joan to change her mind.

"This is it," she announced in front of a red-brick ranch house surrounded by a high iron fence. The driveway gate was unlocked. They followed a garden path down the right side of the house, banana trees and elephant ears towering around them. A plastic dollhouse propped open a side door. A pair of California Raisins kids' pajamas lay rumpled on the floor of the dark hallway.

Got to remember to keep a close eye on things, Seeger thought, especially Mycall.

They wandered down the hall, trying locked doors, poking their heads in closets stacked high with filing cabinets and metal fireboxes. A door opened into a small study with books stacked up from the floor. Loose file folders spilled papers across every horizontal surface. Mycall didn't look up from his desk, covered with maps and what looked like plane tickets, identification cards, passports.

"Good morning," Joan said, sounding casual. Seeger smiled warily.

"Oh. Hello." He closed his book. "Come in. I was just finishing." He rose, pushed past them into the hall. He directed them farther down the hall and locked the door behind them. Joan grinned over her shoulder at Seeger. He gave her a terse, jerky shrug. They entered a low-ceilinged kitchen with heavy, dark stone walls.

"You know," Joan said, "we almost didn't make it here. We slept through our alarm this morning, we were so relaxed from your class."

Cut the flattery. "It's the altitude, too," Seeger added. "We've been sleeping real deep ever since we left Texas. Lots of naps and stuff."

Mycall turned to them from behind the counter. "I wake up on my own every morning at five for meditation and study," he said. "I sleep only four hours a night; I need it less as I evolve."

"Really," Seeger muttered.

"Oh, yeah!" Joan agreed. "I've gone through times when I fasted or hardly slept because my body was telling me it didn't need it. One summer I didn't eat hardly anything besides milk and watermelons, just milk and watermelons, and I felt great. You really have to know to trust your body's signals."

Mycall withdrew a plastic Baggie from the stainless-steel refrigerator and extracted several imposing fungi. They weren't the soft gray puffs Seeger had anticipated. Dank moisture clung to their spindly, inky stalks. Their minute, drooping heads looked like veiled mourners at a rainy funeral.

"Here," he said, handing Joan a fistful, "*limpia* these while I make the juice. I must have some around here somewhere."

She took the mushrooms over to the large double sink. Seeger thought how the Frugal Gourmet admonished not to wash mushrooms but to brush them gently till clean.

"I'm a day behind," Mycall remarked, stirring the Minute Maid with a pair of surgical forceps lying on the counter. "I do this regularly twice a week." He poured the juice into a blender, and Joan handed him the mushrooms. He tossed in eight of the thickest ones.

"This should give you both a moderate trip." He hit PURÉE. "I'll take mine later," Mycall said offhandedly, halving the brackish cocktail into tall aluminum tumblers. "I want to make sure you both go positive."

He led them to mats in the open-air central patio and retreated inside to "do some work." Seeger could discern his shape through the kitchen screen, watching them.

It began with laughing. Itchy faces and fingers. Heightened sensitivity. Seeger grew relaxed and trusting, happy and intimate. It was very X-y. He drifted back to his first X trip:

He and Cordelia had been oblivious to the hundreds of ravenlike teenagers surrounding them, screaming for Depeche Mode's dour synth whining. Seeger and Cordelia had held hands tightly, staring into each other's immense pupils. "I never would've taken X with anyone else!" he'd said. "No one else could've gotten me to try something like this! You . . . you . . . you bring out so much more of a different person in me."

"I've done X with lots of other people, and it's never like this. It's never been like this with anyone else."

"It's us!"

"It's like you were there all along," she'd gushed, "but I never realized what a part of me you were!"

"I feel exactly like we're the same species," he remembered saying, "like those kids in *Escape to Witch Mountain,* different from everyone else!"

"I can't believe I wasted so much time with Sam!"

"I know but it was something you needed to learn."

"And you helped me through it so much! You were the only person I ever could've told when I really thought I was pregnant and that Sam wanted to marry me! Only you would've forbidden me from becoming Cordelia Sheppard—"

"You were the only person I could've told about that time when I thought I'd caught AIDS! I didn't even tell Jésus about those marks on my feet—"

"I knew I loved you when you told me that! And then, when you figured out it was just stains from your new shoes!"

"But it scared me so much!"

"Me too!"

"And now we have so much to learn about each other!"

They'd kissed passionately, gulping for air in an electric-indigo fog pierced with white diamond-shaped tunnels. It had been their first kiss, and Seeger's first with a girl since junior-high party games. He'd felt an explosion of new identity that night. Whereas Jésus had filled up some emptiness inside him, made him feel more completely himself, Cordelia had made him feel conjoined into something wholly new. She'd been taking him someplace altogether unknown, changing him into something new and powerful.

"It's so Lewis Carroll," Joan exclaimed. "I feel so tall!"

Seeger heard the wind turn each individual leaf of the eucalyptus above them. He saw vast depth between tiny ridges in the concrete. Joan haltingly voiced descriptions of a rose temple she could perceive, how it was the Zapotec poets' ideal architecture. Seeger's fist clenched, his mind gripped with a fear that if he relaxed too much, something sexual would happen with Joan. He didn't trust her, but he was losing a grip on his sense of control.

Joan sat lotus, swaying around, brushing too close to her son. Seeger felt wary of Joan, and nauseous from chugging the foul earthen smoothie. Seeger noticed the tree's bark formed faces, radiated tangerine and chartreuse coronas. He dove into them, fleeing Joan's presence. Zones of neon thatchwork vibrated around him. He wondered if they would weave into his skin.

Splat. Hot grapefruit rot scent. He heard Joan throwing up in the kitchen. He fought a gag.

"Fuck, I was starting to get some really good visions," he dimly heard Joan gasp. "Now he's out there having a great time. He'll probably contact ETs or something wonderful."

Seeger's flesh melted. He laced his fingers together, watching them separate at the root and knot into a worm orgy. Orange weasels pressed in, fluorescent cartoon whores leered and bounced through huge tubes in the air. Doorways opened to unsavory caricatured cantinas, blocked by loitering Salvador Dalí she-male prostitutes.

"Mom!" Seeger shouted. Mycall knelt before him, demanding that he describe everything. Seeger clutched Joan's wrist. She threw a blanket on him.

"What?" she muttered. "What? You want me to hold you or you want me to get you a drink or just what? You want some of this maternal action?" She groaned and sat down, grabbing him roughly.

Seeger craved the concrete, the stable.

"You're not communicating anything!" Mycall whined. "Don't resist communion, you have to experience Dark Night of the Soul before true growth can occur." Seeger peered though electric fog into Mycall's oyster-gray eyes. He thought hard, trying to telepath. Mycall didn't respond. Seeger opened his mouth and vomited on Mycall's knee.

"OK, time to leave!" Joan announced, walking to the patio door. "Mycall, you have to drive us back to our hotel. I can't deal with a cab."

Seeger felt vaguely guilty, as if they were disappointing their host.

They tumbled into his Pacer. Mycall muttered, "By my timing, he hasn't even peaked yet."

Joan collapsed against the shower tiles, overcome with laughter. "We—don't even have any—towels!" she gasped, doubled over.

Seeger leaned on the bathroom doorjamb. He jerked, blinking and squinting at the door. He touched it. He frowned at Joan. "Fall through," he said gravely. He spun around and careened into his adjoining room.

Joan shut off the shower and threw herself, dripping with giggles, onto the bed. She sat up and stumbled into Seeger's room. Crosslegged on the edge of his bed, he peered through blinds at an old servant woman mopping the hallway. "She's such a complete drone," Joan proclaimed from over his shoulder.

But no, his mother was at the funeral, behind him, in Mexico, right?

"Look at that primitive face. Fuck, that's the majority of people in the world right there: generations of mindless, numb workers."

Seeger turned around, eyes blazing wide. His mouth cracked a skewed, loopy grin. "Señora," he mouthed. The clanging hammers of the hotel's workmen echoed throughout the building. He cocked his ear as they looped inside his head in an endless reverberation. Finding a private rhythm in the cacophony, he rocked stiltedly.

"I'm so tired!" Joan yawned, drying her hair with the sheet. "All this goddamn noise! No towels, no room service. I'm so sick of dealing with all these hassles. I'm on vacation and I haven't even been able to relax! I can't even relax in this damn country."

Seeger lifted one foot in the air. "Oceans," he whispered, turning his ankle slowly. "Oceans and worlds."

"I don't even want to stay here any longer!" Joan announced, wrapped in the wet sheet. A tentative rapping drew her to the door. The desk manager handed her the mineral water and loaves she'd requested when they'd tripped through the lobby. *"Gracias, muchas gracias,"* she babbled. *"Mi . . . mi hijo es muy malo, muy enfermo."* Joan waved toward Seeger's room.

The manager peered in. *"¿Es tu hijo?"*

"Gracias gracias," she babbled, handing him a handful of pesos, and shut the door.

Seeger's head hung down off the bed's edge. "Christ, you're fucked up," she observed. He jumped up and squinted at her. She held out the bottle of Theuacan mineral water. He gasped and grabbed. He gazed at her with huge, vacuous pupils. He drank and panted.

She sat on the edge of his bed. "You didn't puke till a long time after me, did you? Huh. We should try to clean out your system." She tore off a hunk of bread and handed it to him. She watched his belabored mastication. "What a joke," she cackled. "You fixing to brag to all your friends back in Hicksville about your mama's latest stunt?" She swigged the mineral water and handed it back to him. "Your old man would love this one."

The bottle slipped through Seeger's fingers and spilled down his chest. "Jesus, you're still really fucked up. Here—" She put one arm on his shoulder to steady him.

Seeger thought, This scene, this tableau, this action's all a meaning. Some great universal truth of all human nature. He fell back on the bed, trying to untangle it.

"Oh, so now you're gonna go off on one of your privacy trips," Joan said, slamming down the water on the floor. "Have a nice time." She stalked into her room.

Seeger wondered if the feverish-pink ceiling plaster would drip down and mummify him, like being surrounded by a velvety pink casket lining. Only if he willed it to. But was he really in this room, or autistically looped in some Mexican memory? Or dead with his parents?

He dove with rollercoaster velocity fathoms down into blanket folds. Vermilion and malachite sparks spiraled through floorboards, drifted past his face, and ignited burning holes in the bedcovers. A winged white rat flew in close, brandishing albino feathers with muscular abandon, like a gymnastic angel. Its incarnadine, veiny ears ballooned out, transforming into a translucent graduate's cap. It didn't slip off his head the way Seeger's had.

"Classtime!" the angelrat roared, rapping a pointer twig on Seeger's shoulder. His feathers molted off, leaving slick, black bat wings, which unfurled into an Oxford gown. The blanket's folds swelled up, meeting and melding to form a vast amphitheater, with Seeger in the front row. The angelrat tapped his twig against a slateboard covered with equations and obscene graffiti.

"What are the differences between sex drive, sexual pleasure, and the reproductive instinct?" demanded the rat. "First, there is the reproductive instinct: the 'biological clock,' the ego drive to see yourself as object; the immortality thirst. These are not sexual yearnings but a disparate drive that outweighs the crisis of overpopulation and the specter of family genetics.

"Second, there is the sex drive. You experience sexual attraction as virgins, before your first masturbatory orgasm, even. You're drawn to have sex *before* you know how good it feels. It's certainly not because of media conditioning—you don't see media imagery proportionate to the homosexual population. Furthermore, after a negative sexual experience, one does not lose the drive. Also, numerous people claim to experience no pleasure in sex. The sensory pleasures are not a carrot on a stick motivating the sexual drive. Sexual impulse is independent of reproduction, with a purpose I shall soon address."

The angelrat delicately smoothed his sooty pencil-thin mustache. Seeger's upper lip quivered. He tried to move his head around to search the amphitheater for Joan or Mycall—no, they were in the hotel now, not Mycall's, unless Seeger was time-traveling—but his field of vision remained fixed on the stage.

The rat whipped out a segmented, violet cock with spiky silver hairs and low-swinging indigo nuts. It waved and squirmed in Seeger's face. "A very base function of sexual pleasure is satisfying the human sense of the literal. You discover sex feels good and acquire a false understanding of why you crave it. Sexual pleasure provides an answer to why you want to have sex, a question that would ceaselessly vex you otherwise.

"Why a smokescreen? The true goal of your sex drive requires unintentional discovery. An obsessive search destroys any chance of discovering it. Measurement influences behavior you know, like those pesky quarks and leptons that just refuse to travel in a continuous linear progression the more you rudely stare at them. That is why you are provided with a readymade false answer to keep you satisfied and distracted."

The rat's bloodshot eyes bulged against Seeger's corneas. His musky breath entered his nostrils like thousands of tiny, hot pinpricks.

"The reason you are compelled to have sex is the survival of your species—not reproduction, *survival*. The drive is an impulse to put yourself in an utmost position of vulnerability with another person. You are naked with your softest spots the unprotected focus of attention: human males' greatest source of pain, human females' most direct entry to insides. These, and the tongue, itself necessary for communication and taste (once a survival sense), are placed between the other's greatest weapon: the jaw, one of the most powerful muscles in your body, and the teeth, your sharpest and hardest body parts, poised to shred and rend.

"You similarly expose yourselves in a state of psychological vulnerability. Behaviorally, the power of the sex drive is given priority override to most other functions. In its service, you perform the most irrational and embarrassing acts, often in your partner's full view. They see you powerless, defenseless under your sex drive's sway."

Seeger frantically reached to touch the world around him. His hypersensitive fingertips felt every coarse thread of the blanket, the ridges of paint chips on the bed's footboard. These were the touches of the hotel room, but were they real? All he could see was the vibrant angelrat.

"Vulnerability is the condition of potential overpowerment. States of vulnerability foreground submission, dominance, power, control. Your own little goddamn power struggle with your sex drive becomes projected on, compared against, and psychologically entwined with, every other significant power relationship you experience. That parent/child Freudian miasma is an obvious result," he added nonchalantly.

"Once you consummate an active sexlife, it becomes irrevocably framed in terms of power and control, evidenced by rape, SM/BD, gender politics, and the preponderance of authoritarian scenarios in pornography. This makes exposure of vulnerability all the more acute.

"In short, during sex you are at your most vulnerable and in a situation that is explicitly about power and control.

"Thus, the survival of your species. Your own urges force you to make yourselves utterly vulnerable with another of your species in a situation about negotiating power and control. Through repetition of the sex act, you are forced to learn truths about yourselves and your species, truths applicable to all interrelationships, from law to politics. You are forced to learn about strength, weakness, irrationality, mystery, complexity. You are supposed to learn to see beyond that false answer."

The stentorian lecture hypnotized Seeger. Bewitched by the undulating priapus's cobra-dance, he imagined himself fellating it, taking the twitchy purple tube deep into his gullet, bat wings clasping his back, his own cock ripping into the furry white mousehole. Seeger struggled to refocus on the content of the lecture, to escape from the vision-within-the-vision or whatever it really was, whatever was really real. Where was the damn hotel? Joan—or Mycall . . . What's my dick really doing wherever, what would happen if I came?

"You're getting to the point, now, where you have to learn this lesson because it is necessary for preserving your species. The only way you will prevent nuclear holocaust, economic ruin, and environmental catastrophe is by learning, as a species, to accept difference within your global culture. It is your genetically instilled education, individual by individual, over the course of generations, to prepare you for crises you now face. Only through understanding this can you trust, only through trust can you ensure survival."

As a final note of emphasis, the rat lashed Seeger's face with his wet, rubbery dick. Seeger bolted upright. His groin felt scalding wet, but his pants were dry to the touch.

The amphitheater was gone. He spun around the room for something solid upon which to affix reality. Cordelia, Kent, he needed to write them right away, tell him he loved him, tell her he loved her. No, not a letter, just call, where was that card Abraham gave him to call home with? He fell into his suitcase, swimming among pens that slipped through his fingers, paper that flew up to the ceiling, a wallet that crawled away from him and Zane Grey.

Fiction! That whole world—*The Vanishing American*—could pull me out of this. Yeah, black and white, bolted on the page, real.

He opened the book to the page marked with Cordelia's postcard. The card fluttered to the floor, falling with tortuous slowness, landing image-side up: a lurid, oversaturated cookbook photo of a bloody prime rib. Seeger wrenched himself from staring at the meaty image and examined the book.

The words shuddered prismatic ghosts; he had to stare till type was discernible, serifs and descenders fusing into character. He stared till recognizing letters, till remembering the sounds they represented, till linking the sounds together. He pieced together language and reread words till he excavated meaning. He read that sentence at the top of the page over and over, till he understood how the words worked together as a syntactical sentence. He searched his memory for the plot of the novel thus far and, placing the sentence within narrative, tediously reconstructed his understanding of Nophaie's historical saga, till the whole elaborate structure gleamed brilliantly in his mind, perfect and regular like a stainless-steel bridge support.

Nophaie was at war with the intellectual forces that had robbed him of his religion.

He looked up from the book. The room stilled. Tinted flecks danced midair, and shadows had grown, but the walls did not bow. He knew what to believe. He let the paperback fall to the floor, page unmarked. The thud of the book hitting the floor grabbed Joan's attention. "You OK?" she asked.

"Yeah. I think I'm out of it."

"You had a bad trip, didn't you? Goddamn. I should've helped you come down. I used to make this linguistics professor I lived with diagram sentences when he'd go bad on acid."

"I'm OK now. I pulled myself out." He told her how.

"You're so literate," she scoffed. He turned on his light, knees unstable. "Hey," she exclaimed, leaping up, "we haven't eaten all day! Oh, we've got to balance out our body chemistry, man."

"Sure, let's go," he said listlessly, leaning on the doorjamb between their rooms. He thanked God it did not shudder.

Joan fumbled with blouse buttons. "If I have to eat another tortilla, I'm going to retch—again. I can't wait to change our reservations and get back to Texas!"

Seeger breathed deep, closing his eyes. He listened to his mother. "I want to get straight home and smell the salt air and eat fried shrimp at Snoopy's!" He tried to relax. He knew he was sober, but he still felt tense, wary, as if the journey was not really completed.

"Shit," she laughed, "what would Abraham and Rhonda think about this one?"

Seeger studied her. The light spilling in from his room carved out her dim chiaroscuro figure. He remembered vaguely that he still hadn't told her about those visions back in Execution. They seemed very long ago, very far away. All he'd had in Mexico was the brief burst in Mycall's class, plus psycho sex-education angelrat, and he didn't want to begin to try and tell her about that.

She sniggered in the dark like a naughty child.

No, he didn't want to tell her about anything.

Although nothing moved on the physical plane, he felt a sudden whiplash. He felt himself fall rapidly upward, a cobweb kidnapped in an updraft, stolen away into dry, thin atmospheres from which he could, for the first time, view her from above.

Seeger Writes

Hey Tonia—
Don't tell Cordelia/Kent you got this—haven't written them; they'll
be pissed. You know I love only you. Probably be back before you get
this. Mexico's a trip. Looooooong story. My mom's crazy, but I think
I'm OK. Will tell the tale when I get back. xoxox Seeg

Abraham Questions Seeger

Abraham drummed his fingers on the steering wheel.

Seeger lowered the passenger visor against the fiery evening sun.
"Joan doing OK?"

Seeger shifted uncomfortably. "Abe, come on, you know I don't like
to talk about it."

"I know, I know." Abraham straightened his change in the coin slots.

"Just makes me uncomfortable," Seeger offered.

Abraham accelerated and changed lanes. "I just hope you appreciate
someday," he said, "what a ton of trust I've put in her over the years.
I'm not trying to badmouth her or anything, I'm just saying it hasn't always been easy, just turning you over to her and never knowing what
goes on."

Seeger guiltily recalled his mother, incoherent at Mycall's, then collapsing with naked giggles at the hotel. He wondered if it was better or
worse than the scenes Abraham imagined that he experienced with her.

Abraham looked over with stern affection. "It ain't easy to turn off
being a father when you go off."

Seeger curled his toes inside the sweaty leather of his combat boots.
He felt his face flush. God, he just hated it when Abraham talked about
this shit. He hated himself more for getting visibly upset, not being
able to maintain his cool. "I know. Really, you don't have to worry,
OK?"

"Guess I better get used to it, though, huh?" Abraham smiled at his
son with a raised eyebrow. "You'll be hundreds of miles away in a couple of months."

Seeger stared at the blinking red light. Some new song about sex came on the radio, making Seeger more agitated. Stupid fucking song, he thought. Stupid fucking video: that faggy jerk writing, "Explore Monogamy," on some slutty model's leg. He mentally hummed Marc's "Two Sailors on the Beach" in auditory defense.

"No one but Cordelia looking after you." Abraham chuckled. "Now, there's something to get a father scared."

Seeger rolled his eyes out the window. "Cordelia's not going to New York," he announced. Seeger pressed his right foot down on an invisible brake as Abraham pulled up too close to the car in front of them.

"What?"

"I called her last night. She's going to leave North Texas and switch to religious studies at TCU 'cause they have a three-year degree program. She might come to New York for grad school." She had been exuberant, giddy about her new plans and Seeger's return. "So we can really make this the return of the 'Summer of Love,' " she'd said meaningfully.

"Cordelia? Religious studies?"

"She's real excited about it." Seeger grinned sheepishly. "More for the pageantry than theology, I think."

"Just what we need: another Jesus freak in the family." He glanced at Seeger with mock severity. "Don't tell your stepmother I said that."

Seeger laughed and nodded. He felt tense, trying to keep his anxiety in check: worrying about Kent and Cordelia in his absence, where they had gone, who they had met, what they were feeling.

They exited the expressway into the long corridor of brown grass fields, lots in development, and isolated office buildings. The squat corporate boxes lined the transition from Dallas County to Execution like glass sentries, mirrored facades relentlessly reflective like a highway patrolman's sunglasses. They drove silently until reaching the railroad crossing at Execution's border.

"So you'll be all by your lonesome up there with the Yankees?"

Seeger shrugged, embarrassed. "I'll be OK."

"Yeah, you probably will." Abraham opened his mouth to say more, but an Amtrak train hurtling past cut him off. The coppery sunlight strobed between the boxcars, flashing on them like a signal lantern's golden Morse code.

Seeger looked sideways at his father, in his tan corduroy sportscoat and Ray-Bans. He glowed, in the sunset, a rich, warm bronze, like a monument.

Seeger saw him fly forward and shatter the windshield. He strained against the chest harness, reaching out to save his father. Abraham's shredded bloody ankles slipped through his fingers and disappeared into the flame maelstrom before them. The thundering inferno lunged through the gaping mouth of the glass-toothed windshield, stripping flesh from his white knuckles and forcing its way into his mouth. The feverish French kiss blistered the inside of his mouth, cracking and splitting. The flame forced its way further down, a fire-cocked rapist plowing Seeger's throat with boiling, bubbling blister-pus, popping in his gullet like bacon grease, a white-hot load of come burning him from inside out.

He dug his fingers under his kneecap, concentrating on the pain of something he knew was real.

"Come on, already!" he heard his father say. The train reappeared. Seeger cautiously glanced to see if Abe had noticed anything. He unclenched his hand and pressed the sweat into his jeans. He shuddered and squinted against the sun. He turned the AC blower onto his face.

It's not real! he told himself. It's just a fantasy from all that psychic bullshit Joan's been feeding me all my life, and those damn mushrooms have made it worse. It's not real! he repeated till they pulled into their driveway.

july, 1987

Kent Meets Seeger's Family and Cordelia

Seeger watched his father. Abraham held court before his homemade BBQ/smoker/prep table. He placed PEPPER—WHITE, GROUND alphabetically between PEPPER—RED, FLAKES and ROSEMARY in the built-in spice rack above the mesquite chip soaker and utensil shelf. He looked up, beaming through smoke, and smeared crimson across his Father's Day apron. "God Bless the BBQ Chef" became "God less the BB Chef."

Rhonda bent over the aluminum patio table, slicing what appeared to be a pizza of hypersaturated, psychedelic hues. She looked sunny and fresh in an alabaster blouse, silver Christian ichthys earrings sparkling. Kent, broad and sturdy in his Spuds MacKenzie baseball jersey, sauntered toward Rhonda and Abraham, passing Bill and Pam in their "Ollie North for President" T-shirts. Kody was up on the roof, spying on them all with his new binoculars.

Kent reminded Seeger of Howard Hughes's *Spruce Goose,* monumentally boxy with ears jutting out like wings. Kent approached Abraham and Rhonda. Seeger's chest constricted. He told himself that there was nothing to worry about. What could Kent say to his folks—"I think your son's hot for me"? Still, having them around each other made Seeger nervous. Even worse, Kent had charmed his parents to death.

Cordelia appeared beside Seeger, dropping keys in her bag. "Who's he?"

"Oh, God, you're here," Seeger said stupidly.

"You didn't think I'd show up late to a Cleaver patio party? I told

Student Affairs I had to leave early so I could go have one. Speaking of which"—she shaded her eyes, already protected with faux oystershell and rhinestone cat's-eye sunglasses—"who's he—Garçon de Sportif?"

"That's Kent."

"That's Kent? The racquetball boy?" She removed her sunglasses.

"Yeah, my parents told me to invite him. He's totally pulling an Eddie Haskell on them."

"How fitting," she said, putting her sunglasses back on. She slipped her arm around Seeger's. He turned to her, smiling, and they kissed hello.

"He did mention, though, that Abraham's marijuana hidden inside the tomatoes needs watering."

Cordelia chuckled. "Not to mention, it's such lousy pot." They laced their fingers and watched the scene.

Seeger breathed in. The parched air had dried his nasal mucus, but he could detect hints of a lawn sprinkler's succulent mist. Some impatient gardener, probably a Yankee transplant, was watering too early. Under the day's remaining heat, each bead of fluorinated water, intended as life-giving sustenance, would act as a tiny magnifying glass, burning and scorching the emerald blades of grass into brown skeletal hairs. Wait till water rationing hits, then they're fucked.

"I've got Vikki's poppers in the car," Cordelia murmured.

"Funky."

They studied Kent as he pumped Abraham for grilling tips. Abraham aligned wieners parallel with the roasting ears and expounded on his technique. Kent, noting Cordelia's arrival, grimaced at them impishly.

"Oh, he definitely needs some corruption."

" 'Waitin' at the station for his train to ruination,' " Seeger sang, quoting Marc's "Road to Ruin," a song available only on the *If You Can't Please Yourself, You Can't Please Your Soul* compilation from Some Bizzare records. He and Cordelia had both been lucky enough to find probably the only two copies in the Metroplex.

Cordelia smiled.

"Yeah, he's pretty clean," Seeger said. He leaned against the splintery support post of the patio cover and shoved his hands deeper into the pockets of his white cutoffs. "God, he's just the type of son they'd prefer."

"What, you mean, all perky and polite and athletic and hopelessly heterosexual?"

114

Seeger pursed his lips. "Exactly."

Cordelia knelt to a hairy plant growing from a five-gallon paint bucket and plucked herself a deep-red cherry tomato. "Or it could all be a facade," she suggested, biting into the fruit. "Maybe he has a collection of medulla oblongatas hidden in his gym locker. You should be more careful and not go out with him alone anymore." She puckered her lips around the tomato's bite-hole, sucking out the plasm and pips.

"Yeah. You'll have to protect me."

Rhonda glided through the sunset toward them, holding aloft the Technicolor pizza. "Y'all want some Fruit Pizza?" she called out.

Cordelia looked at Rhonda quizzically.

"It's a roll of sugar-cookie dough for the crust; you just flatten it out," Rhonda explained, holding out the platter. Seeger and Cordelia both took slices. "Then you use strawberry pie filling instead of sauce, and fruit for toppings. Kent loves it."

"Much obliged," Kent munched, following beside her. Where'd a Yankee pick that up? Seeger wondered. No one says that outside of westerns.

"I was just telling your friend Kent here about Pat Robertson's presidential campaign," Rhonda said. "I was just yakking my jaw off about the good it would do this country to have some real Christian leadership"—she looked sideways at Kent—"and this little pill didn't even tell me he was just sixteen!"

"I'm a pill!" Kent shrugged helplessly.

She laughed, resting the platter against her waist. "He can't even vote with y'all next year."

Seeger flashed back on presidential history: Abraham calling him into their apartment living room to witness President Ford pardon Nixon. "Don't forget this," Abe had instructed him. "Don't ever believe that the president, a preacher, a teacher, or any other man in charge is someone special, someone better than you. They can be just as shitty as any other man."

Rhonda excused herself. "I'm sure y'all kids're really just dying to talk politics at a BBQ." She touched Kent's shoulder. "Need anything else? Want me to make you a sandwich?"

"Rhonda, we're OK," Seeger said, kicking the cement with his sneaker toe.

"Well, OK, then," she said knowingly, and left the kids in the jutting shadows. Kent watched her walk away. "God, your family's so cool," he said thoughtfully. "Totally nice people. And your stepmom's a babe. A Christian babe, but she's still hot."

"Holy Jesus, Boy Talk!" Cordelia turned away, covering her ears. Kent and Seeger grinned, eyes lingering.

"Well, aren't we just Boys," Kent said.

"Yes, you are!"

"You'll probably have to break down and spank us both silly." Kent offered her a saccharine smile.

"Don't think I won't," she threatened.

The phone rang inside. "Hey, Seeger," Abraham yelled, "get that, will you?" Seeger glanced from Kent to his girlfriend.

"C'mon, male," Cordelia commanded, taking Kent's hand, "I think we need to visit my car if we're gonna make it through this social event." She led Kent off across the driveway. Seeger went inside.

"You cannot go to New York," his mother announced over the line.

"What do you mean?" Seeger looked out the breakfast nook, watching Cordelia and Kent return to the picnic, all strawberry-faced smiles. He felt dizzily smug that both these fabulous people were enamored with him. His face flushed with pride, prickly hot skin like sunburn.

"Seeger!" she snapped. "Listen! I've been doing a lot of research into the Ruth Montgomery books, and she's positive the polar shift will happen by the end of the decade. New York's going to be entirely underwater in the nineties."

Seeger watched Kent and Cordelia whisper conspiratorially beside the garden. Cordelia was electrified with gold, the metallic thread in her tapestry pedal pushers and her battered favorite gold pumps caught the sunset. With a gilded toe, she nudged an okra plant.

Seeger blinked.

A black crowd of people filled the backyard, solemn mourners drifting about in ebony crepe.

He blinked again. Black disappeared; his neighbors, family, and loves reappeared in their bright summer garments, pleasantly eating and drinking. "Nostradamus totally supports her, and I'm sensing it's a high-probability reality outcome—"

God, I hate this shit! Seeger turned his back to the window. Probably some stupid fucking flashback from those mushrooms. Doesn't mean anything. He glanced around nervously for the angelrat.

"Seeger! You listening?"

"Joan," he said curtly, "I just can't change my plans this late. I'll, uh, probably be safe for at least my first two years and I could transfer after that to Chicago or something—"

"But Lake Michigan—"

"Do you have, like, a map or something of all this?"

"Yes, yes! I—"

"Well, um, great, can you just mail me that?" Seeger didn't have time for one of his mother's apocalypses right now. Besides, she was making him have those stupid visions. He yearned to get back outside and see what all Kent and Cordelia were talking about.

They smiled as he opened the sliding glass door, squinting and shading their eyes. The setting sun poured into their eyes like molten copper, piercing their retinas with blistering kisses. Artificially chilled air gushed out with Seeger through the door, gliding across evening shadows stretched long like claw marks. Sweat sprouted on his skin; it was getting darker but not cooler. The conditioned drafts mixed jarringly with the backyard's hot air, miniature fronts and convection pools swirling about Seeger's face. The antithetical temperatures made a disconcerting juxtaposition. When the same clash of temperatures occurred on a meteorological scale, the sky turned an ominous green, a sign of tornadoes that twisted Seeger's gut with anxiety. Even as a child, he'd known that when the sky turned green, things were serious.

Now the sky was gold and black; but swept up in eddies of hot and cold, Seeger felt an equivalent dread.

LaTonia Checks In

"Let me take off your panties—slowly."

"*Eeew,* Tonia!" Seeger grimaced. He sat on the bed, phone under ear, and inspected the polish on his shoes.

"This isn't LaTonia, this is Barry White, baby. I'm qualified to satisfy you. My family's gone, Ashton's out of town, and I got the love pad all to myself. Me, you, the Love Unlimited Orchestra and my marahoochie."

"What?"

"Mary Jane, baby. Dagga. Doobies. Maui Wowie. Mezz—"

"Tonia—"

"Splif. Viper's Weed. Zacatecas Purple—"

"Tonia—"

"Ganja, mon."

"I'm kinda laying off substances . . ."

"Oh." Seeger could hear LaTonia inhale over the phone lines. "Mexico still left you a little freaked, huh?"

"Yeah, and anyway, I'm getting ready to go out."

"You and Cordelia?"

"Yeah. And Kent."

Silence. Seeger eyed the corpse of a flying ant at the base of his windowpane.

LaTonia groaned. "Oh, I'm gonna have to get really fucked up tonight."

Cordelia and Seeger Take Kent on a Date

A man with a bushy handlebar mustache and parrot-green skullcap kissed Cordelia, pressing his card into her hand.

"Who was that?" Seeger asked, adjusting the pink tutu on his head. They'd decorated it with unpainted plastic baby-doll faces from Eva's.

"His name is Bob Eisenstein!" Cordelia announced. "He's a photographer and muralist. He and his wife painted *Whirlpool-Hair Woman* outside Assassins'!"

"Wow," said Seeger. "He sure seems to like you."

"He thinks I could make a wonderful mural," she said gleefully. "They're painting five inside this big cowboy saloon in Fort Worth, and he wants to do a test shoot with me!"

Seeger searched the crowd for Kent. "Does his wife know about this?"

"She was standing right next to us—that short woman with the glow-tape headband?" Cordelia glanced back toward the couple. "Her modeling days are over."

Kent stood on the other side of Record Gallery, smiling insincerely at some middle-aged guy in a rainbow Afro and Vulcan ears. A monitor mounted to the wall above them repeated patterns of computer-generated geometries; candles flickered on an altar with a rubber skull and half-full bottle of Chartreuse. Patchouli incense saturated the air. The Vulcan molded Kent's aluminum-foil turban into a phallus.

"Kent is so sweet," Cordelia announced. "He really does make a wonderful accessory."

"I can't believe we got him to wear his wrestling uniform," Seeger whispered. "It's making him very popular."

Kent caught their eyes and rolled his. He disengaged from the Vulcan and maneuvered through the crowd toward them, stepping high and wide in the ski boots he'd borrowed from work.

"I wonder if Bob would want to take pictures of all three of us," Cordelia mused.

"I think he's just interested in you," Seeger said pointedly.

"Who's all interested in you," Kent demanded. "Don't tell me I've got more competition."

Cordelia batted her lashes. "More than y'all can imagine," she informed him. "Last weekend I had twenty-seven gentleman callers."

"Great," Kent sighed. "It's enough work trying to get this guy out of the way"—he swung his foil phallus at Seeger—"now I'm never gonna get to be spanked by you."

"Oh, honey, Seeger and I spank as a team."

Kent didn't miss a beat. "Good, I've got a butt-cheek for each of you."

Cordelia slapped Kent's face more than playfully. Seeger glanced away nervously.

"You two were right," Kent said, rubbing his face, "this is a stupid party."

"It's *the* Stupid Party," Seeger clarified. "Record Gallery's annual, very exclusive; invitation-only fiesta."

"Wow," Kent said sarcastically, "just like the Starck Club!"

"Woo!" Cordelia called out, yanking off one of the daily vitamin packs stapled to her T-shirt. "Bust at the Starck Club!" She ripped open the packet and scattered the capsules across the hardwood floor. "Everybody drop your drugs."

"Cordelia's fixing to become an international modeling celebrity," Seeger told Kent.

"Just like Edie Sedgwick," she added. "Only I won't get a boob job and dance around in an empty swimming pool. Mr. Bob Eisenstein is shooting me for the cover of *International Celebutante.*"

"*Co-Ed Nymphettes,* more likely." Seeger turned serious. "Really, you don't know anything about this guy. You probably shouldn't go to his studio all alone."

"Oh, please." She rolled her eyes and gave Seeger a shove. "I can take care of myself, you man."

"Yeah," Kent joined in, "you man, you." He shoved Seeger. Cordelia shoved Seeger again, harder. Seeger took a step back from both of them.

Whooping cries rose from across the room as a couple in black cat-suits grabbed fistfuls of rainbow-iced three-tier wedding cake.

"Mmm," Cordelia said. "I could go for a piece of wedding cake; only that frosting kills my appetite."

"Y'all should've seen my parents' wedding cake," Seeger said. "When Abraham and Rhonda married? It had a man pissing on it."

"The Cleavers?!" Kent looked at him incredulously.

"The Cleavers have something of a Swingin' Seventies past," Cordelia informed him.

"Yeah, it was one of those 'adult novelty cakes' someone brought in addition to the regular wedding cake. They had a real small wedding in the apartment where we lived, little dump over by AmVets. Since Rhonda and Abe'd both been married before, they didn't want to do the big church thing, especially since it would've been the same church again.

"I didn't see it, but the other kid there, she saw it and told me. She cornered me in my bedroom, and I was kinda scared 'cause she used to like to get me to play all these Doctor games. I was afraid she was going to do that at the wedding. I was in like, fourth grade, but I guess she was fifth? Anyway, I remember the wedding was all late-seventies, like they had the Captain and Tennille's 'Do That to Me One More Time' play-ing, and we all ate fondue. The family and church people kinda stayed in one room, and all their young friends smoked dope and cut this adult cake in the kitchen. Tiffany kept trying to get me to play Wedding with her and kept telling me about the cake."

Kent studied Seeger, chewing his upper lip. He looked down at the floor, tapped his foot, looked over his shoulder. Cordelia smiled, watch-ing his edginess. Seeger fished in his white rayon dinner jacket for the pack of herbal cigarettes. He passed them around to Cordelia and Kent, smiling glumly.

"It creeped me out. We've got pictures of me being the ringholder, but I've got this freaked-out look on my face. I was probably on a major con-tact high, little fourth grader all paranoid."

"At least your folks were trying to be themselves around you," Kent said. "I mean, they treated you like an adult, not some stupid kid. They respected you."

Seeger lit Cordelia's cigarette. He held his flame out to Kent. "But I was a stupid kid," he said.

Kent inhaled, exhaled. He studied the two of them, shrouded in dank, spicy smoke. Cordelia removed her cigarette and kissed Kent's forehead. Kent clicked his tongue and rolled his eyes. "God," he said, shaking his head. He tapped Seeger on the chest. "You needed brothers and sisters," Kent told him. "Then you would've had allies. We should've merged our families: Seeger's parents and all us three as the kids."

Kent held his herbal cig in front of himself, grimacing as he licked the roof of his mouth. Cordelia squeezed Seeger's arm. Kent grinned and put the cig back between his lips.

" 'Scuse me!" sang out a tall man squeezing between them. His hairy back strained the straps of a Strawberry Shortcake flannel pajama top. Cordelia appraised him as he passed. "He can be an uncle in our family."

"And he won't marry his brother's wife," Kent added, eyeing Cordelia. She nodded.

"This one learns fast," she said to Seeger.

Joan Warns Seeger

"Joan already called once, to see if you got this," Abraham informed Seeger. "She wouldn't leave a message."

Seeger sighed and nodded. He took the envelope and walked down the hall to his room, turning up the AC as he passed the thermostat.

Dear Seeger—
Hope you're getting used to being back in Execution. You must be chomping at the bit to get out of there in a few months, but I need you to think about something else now. This is very important. I've felt very opened up since we had those visions in Mexico, and I've been channeling a lot in the evenings here. The air is real clear, and I'm getting strong signals.

Part of the message I'm receiving is that you are involved somehow, that there's some information I need that you are supposed to channel. I'm going to give you three words, and I want you to open up to whatever you get. Write it all down, or maybe talk into a tape recorder. Whatever you do, record every detail, no matter how little sense it might make. I'm not trying to be evasive, I just don't want to influence your reading. Call me with the results when Abraham and Rhonda aren't around.

I sense you might resist this, but somehow that is a part of the whole plan. Please, don't disregard your gifts. I can think of so many incidents when you were a child, and completely open, when you foretold events and had premonitions. Most of them were when you were so young, you probably don't remember them, or you remember telling me things but don't know their significance. Remember how you didn't like Jerry, that Scottish guy I dated in Galveston? Even though he took us to the Baroner's restaurant and we all had daiquiris and steamed mussels, had a wonderful decadent time? We all spoke fake French and mispronounced everything on the menu to the waiter?

Seeger remembered that evening: Joan had held court, sparkling amid stately china and the music of the live harpist. She'd slurped oysters (not mussels) with zest, tossing back her long black hair, jingling earrings of iridescent seashell triangles. She had always been able to enjoy "fancy things" in public without being stuffy. Abraham and Rhonda had never managed the balance, always embarrassed when a restaurant had forced a wine tasting upon them or Seeger had requested flaming desserts.

Jerry had watched Joan with smiling quietude. Seeger had recognized his stunned appreciation of Joan's upside. They'd joked, swearing and flirting, making fun of themselves for overstepping propriety in front of the child. Seeger remembered grinning at Jerry with that hint of mischief he knew put nonparent adults at ease. The kid's cool, they thought.

Remember how you instinctively knew something was wrong with Jerry?

Seeger had liked Jerry. Jerry had possessed the wildness of most of Joan's boyfriends, but also a European romanticism and elegance gave him added depth. He'd zoomed high in Seeger's favor when he engaged him in a very adult conversation about the *Columbia* space shuttle's maiden flight. Seeger had felt no jealousy, no need to be distant or assert his authority as son.

You told me to watch out for him and you were right; later he turned out to be a cokehead.

She never realized I was lying, Seeger thought.

That night, after dinner, they'd crashed back at Joan's new apartment, the top floor of a Victorian two-story in the Historical District. Galveston's nocturnal breathing had filled the rooms, humid salt breezes billowing white sheets hung over the balcony's French doors.

Seeger, Joan, and Jerry had made a threesome of spoons on a thick army blanket stretched across the hardwood floor. Summer winds had been coolest on the floor, and the occasional passing kitten had offered distraction from the TV news's rape tally. Seeger had felt surprisingly comfortable, his mother's body behind him and Jerry's body behind her. At eleven years old, with adolescence on the horizon, such casual physical affection had probably been something he should resist, but indulgence, trespass, and other contradictions to his Execution life had come with the territory of visiting Joan.

Joan and Jerry had softly gossiped about coworkers at the Food Co-Op, her managerial dirt mixing with his skinny on the other bakers. Tranquil, they'd sipped cheap brandy from small jelly jars. Seeger's had sat before him, still full despite Joan's urgings. Milk and sugar hadn't successfully masked the vapors too sharp for his green palate.

Bored with the movie on Home Box Office—Kris Kristofferson was helping Barbra Streisand become a star, which somehow involved lots of mushy love scenes—Seeger had absently reached for Joan's hand on his upper thigh. Securely enveloped in sultry breeze, body heat, and TV glow, he'd stroked her hand. Jerry had giggled, and Seeger had looked down. Jerry's hand. Seeger had bolted across the room, spitting out exaggerated sounds of disgust he knew he was still young enough to get away with. He noisily tried to camouflage his shock, the frightening, furious, green flame that sparked inside him. Next morning after Jerry left, Seeger had soberly informed Joan that he had a bad feeling about Jerry.

*I could've saved myself a winter of traumas if I'd listened to
my son then, so I want you to listen to yourself now. Here are the
words:* Explosion. Children. Submarine.

*Tell me every feeling and thought you get from them. You're
becoming an adult but don't become old. Don't lose your child-
like wisdom and intuition. Don't stop listening to yourself!*

Joan

Seeger hid the letter in his dresser. He really didn't want to think
about it. He could put off doing the reading for a few days. Maybe she'd
forget all about it by then, change her mind if he stalled long enough.
Worse came to worse, he could make something up and write it down.
He didn't want to plumb those depths so soon after Mexico.

He jingled car keys in his pocket. He'd borrowed Abraham's Impala
for when he and Cordelia and Kent went out, but decided that he'd ask
Cordelia to drive instead.

Seeger, Kent, and Cordelia's Second Date

Cordelia paused her Datsun at the railroad tracks on the outskirts of Execution. Silence descended around them; the flashing red light swung
overhead in the night. Dallas sparkled in the distance. A scorpion
crawled along the tracks.

"Damn," Cordelia sighed. "No train coming."

"So what do you want to do tonight?" Seeger asked Kent in the backseat. Kent bounced upright.

"What do you two usually do? Is there another Stupid Party?"

"No, I don't know of anything going on tonight. We usually just discover things."

"We find art and adventure in everyday life, just like Andy and Edie."

"Yeah, you know how, like, he painted soup cans and stuff? We've
had nights when we just went to the grocery store and had a fabulous
time, laughing at all the bizarre stuff we found."

"Clamato juice! Beefamato!"

"Stuff that is absolutely bizarre, but no one else seems to notice."
Seeger looked up at Kent's glittering eyes in the rearview.

"*Rocky Horror* is at the Granada," Kent offered tentatively. "I've never seen it, and it's not a midnight show, so we could get back to Execution before my curfew."

"It's awfully seventies," Cordelia said, thinking. "It's no *Vinyl.*"

"My real mom took me to see it on New Year's when I was, like, twelve," Seeger said. "So I'm kinda bored with it now," he added, apologetic.

"Something'll come up," Cordelia growled. She gunned the engine. They bumped over the tracks, jostling Kent. One hand on the wheel, she turned around and grabbed Kent's chin, squeezing his face. "Don't fret, little peachkins. An adventure will find us, one way or another." She patted his cheek, like a small slap.

Seeger stared out the window at streetlamps. Gray rows of steel temporary-storage buildings whizzed by, faceless pieces of business littering the zones between Execution and Dallas where no one made their home. *Rocky Horror* made him think of drag queens, and he'd read in a copy of *Dallas Gay News* at the library that there was a new drag bar in Dallas. He wondered if they could all three get in. Would Kent find it too faggy? Would Cordelia feel left out? Should he suggest it as the focus of their night? He didn't want to fuck up and do something not impressively fantastic with Kent. Cordelia and he could make anything, no matter how dismal, entertaining in some manner. He wasn't sure about Kent. He didn't want to disappoint him.

Seeger thought of the drag queens he'd seen in New Orleans one Thanksgiving. At first, he'd felt weird Joan didn't want to spend Thanksgiving with Meemaw, but the enticing odors that had invaded Seeger's nose, the airborne molecules of treacly molasses and turkey's soporific tryptophan, had reassured him.

Despite being on Bourbon Street, Seeger had felt ensconced in cultural symmetry. The whole country had been smelling those same aromas, from LaTonia visiting her grandparents in Detroit to Abraham and Rhonda in Execution. Seeger had felt himself confidently marching in Thanksgiving formation. Sort of. Joan's version.

"That turkey smells just luscious," Joan had said, "it's probably real decadent, with some pecan-mango chutney!" Joan had held her palm to her breast as if swooning. Seeger had nodded, speechless, as he'd looked through the plateglass window at a trio of costumed men marching past. An Indian maiden in hip-hugging buckskin had shimmied her fringe, headdress sparkling with multicolored sequins. A noble Puritan goodwife, severe wimple framing black lipstick and sweeping crimson makeup about the eyes, had waddled primly down the sidewalk, gait hampered by a studded-leather bodice binding her granny dress. A line of golden pom-poms had truncated the righteous Puritan reverend's silky black cassock midthigh. They'd bounced merrily with the assured march of his black patent thigh-boots.

"Oh, drag is *so* subversive in the nineteen eighties," Joan had scoffed. "I think we've all seen *Rocky Horror* by now."

Seeger had turned sharply from the window. "This place is so uh . . . *evocative.*" He'd sipped and held ice tea in his mouth, tannic acid a bitter astringent on his tongue and gums. He'd stolen a glance back outside but saw only a horse carriage draped in sable crepe trundling across the cobblestones.

"I just saw *Cat People* on cable, and it's in New Orleans, and this feels like that, like—a real otherworldly place, you know, where anything can happen."

"Yeah, I've always thought about living here."

Across the restaurant, a spumescent wave of glittering shards had sprayed over three rows of meticulous napkin pyramids as a window had shattered. Dripping rhinestones, the man who'd fallen through had grasped at waitpersons for support, smearing bloody palmprints across their punctilious linen.

Seeger's heart had leapt, his breath had stopped. What kind of lawless, magical place was this?

"Big fun in the Big Easy," Joan had quipped. "Probably some stupid drunk businessman."

Cordelia swerved out of the entrance lane and onto Central Expressway, jolting Seeger back to their present dilemma. "Blue films flicker," she sang along with Cindy Ecstasy on Soft Cell's *Seedy Films*, turning up the tape deck, "hands of a stranger—"

"Hey, we could do that for a theme night," Seeger suggested.

"Yeah, there's an idea." Cordelia smiled wryly into the rearview. "Wanna make a blue movie, hon?"

"I left my leather jockstrap at home," Kent replied. "What's a theme night?"

Seeger looked from Cordelia to Kent. "It's like a theme party, but it's a theme night. We could do this tape, 'Non-Stop Erotic Cabaret.'"

"Yes!" Cordelia blared the Datsun's horn into the empty darkness. "We'll all wear my black eyeliner."

"We can drink sleazy cheap drinks and go to adult bookstores."

"Pornorama!" Cordelia cheered. "Porndemonium! And this is the only tape we can listen to, all night. It's our soundtrack." The tape switched into "Sex Dwarf." She looked back at Kent. "And you're our little Sex Dwarf."

Seeger giggled. "Me, my little Sex Dwarf—" he sang.

Cordelia joined in: "And my Dumb Chauffeur—hey, I don't want to be the Dumb Chauffeur."

"You can be the Decadent Chauffeur!" Kent piped in.

Cordelia smiled at him, Seeger. "Oh, I like this boy," she said. Kent smiled proudly.

Seeger got mock-serious. "Now, most important detail: What should we drink?" He leaned back in his seat, humming thoughtfully. He clenched his jaw muscles and sucked in his cheeks slightly, trying to affect as sexy a profile as he could in the bursts of expressway light.

All Three at the Gay Cruise Park

Seeger, Cordelia, and Kent peered through the bars of the giant toy soldier's head, their faces shadowed in crimson.

"That's the red Pegasus god." Seeger pointed out a squat building's glowing outline of a flying horse peeking above the park's trees. "He looks over everyone at Sam Houston Park."

"From the kids during the day to all the queens here at night," Cordelia added over his shoulder. "Pass me that peach."

"Cheapy-cheapy-cheapy, cheapy Riunite," Seeger sang.

"How'd you two find this place?" Kent handed Cordelia the jug of Riunite peach wine.

Cordelia tossed back a swig. "These fag waiters from Vikki's work told her about it, and Seeger and I had to see for ourselves. It's very festive."

Kent considered this, appraising Seeger and Cordelia curiously. Whispered titters and clinking chains sounded below them. Seeger stuck his head between the bars.

"Oh, girl, there's some people already up there!" gasped one of the boys on the suspension bridge linking the soldier to the jungle gym.

"Orgy in the soldier's brain," Cordelia called out as they scampered away.

Kent laughed quietly, shaking his head. He swigged off the wine and gave it his verdict: "This is tasty."

"They had Royal Raspberry and Summer Apple," Seeger said, leaning back against the bars. "But those sound kind of gross, don't y'all think?"

"Mm-hm," Cordelia murmured, nestling up against Seeger's side. Only ten inches away, Kent pulled his knees to his chest, trying to get comfortable in their tiny metal bungalow.

"Non-Stop Erotic Cabaret Night has been a success, I'd say," Seeger said.

"Not that it wasn't a blast, guys," Kent said, rubbing his eyes, "but I really don't want to hear 'Tainted Love' ever again in my lifetime." He held his fingers in front of him, examining the smudges of eyeliner.

"When that song first came out," Cordelia said, "a bunch of my friends and I made a tape of nothing but that 12″: the full 'Tainted Love/Where Did Our Love Go?' medley, the original mix of 'Memorabilia,' and 'Tainted Dub,' over and over again. We filled up the whole ninety-minute tape. We'd take it to Manitowoc Park and play it on Vikki's portable Panasonic. That was when she was still just my cousin."

Kent wiped his fingers on his denim shorts and stretched out his legs. "Before my time," he said.

Seeger idly stroked Cordelia's hair. "We saw plenty of tainted love tonight," he said. *"Hot Milkin' Mamas* was my fave."

"Whale Fuckers!" cheered Cordelia.

"Oh, man, that one was harsh," said Kent. "And I can't believe the manager pitched us out."

"I know!" Cordelia said indignantly.

Kent slapped Seeger's thigh. "Well, your sketch of the Last Supper and Orgy on the viewing booth chalkboard didn't help any."

"Which did offend my Catholic heritage," Cordelia said. "And that was the only store with any male porn! Real men with penises, not that *Playgirl* crap. He threw us out before I could buy *Oversized Load,"* she pouted.

"Yeah," Seeger said. *"Kansas City Trucking Company* looked pretty good, too."

"*Ick,* that one guy looked like Village People!"

Kent studied them. He tilted back the bottle, frowned, and looked down in his lap. The crisp, sweet wine warmed his throat, and he felt very high. He looked back up. Seeger smiled tentatively, brows gathering in a muddle of fond confusion above his spooky, raccoony eyes. The three of them looked like delinquent Halloweeners. Kent didn't look away.

Seeger peered through the rusty shadows. Kent looks so sad, he thought. Protectively, he pulled Cordelia closer. She kissed his chin. Kent looked at Cordelia's conspiratorial smile. "Kent, you wouldn't date a Village People, would you?" she said, nudging his feet with hers. Kent shook his head. Seeger smiled.

A loud whirring and clicking below instigated a chorus of shrieks. They craned to look out the bars as the park's water sprinklers came on. Men scampered from picnic tables to parked cars, or up winding paths into the wooded hill. "Save the potato salad!" pleaded a man with peroxided hair as he frantically cleared off a picnic table.

"That guy looks like Andy Warhol's brother," Kent noted.

"His less-successful brother who does window display at Needless Markups," embellished Seeger.

Cordelia nodded soberly. "He's throwing a party picnic to overcome his grief from Andy's death, and it's getting ruined. But he doesn't have any aluminum foil to cover up the potato salad because Andy used it all to wallpaper the Factory."

"Good thing we're inside this soldier," Seeger said. They moved away from the bars. Kent swigged from the jug and hunkered down. He rested his head across their legs and propped his feet up high on the bars with a long, comfortable sigh, like a crumpled ball of paper unfolding.

"It is nice in here," Cordelia whispered. She leaned forward. She and Seeger fell into sweet peachy kisses. He closed his eyes, feeling brave and carefree, and tongued deeper. Kent's weight pressed heavily on his leg. Seeger broke from the kiss and smiled. He glanced down to see Cordelia stroking Kent's face while he looked up at them.

Cautiously, Seeger rested his hand on Kent's chest. He leaned forward to kiss Cordelia again, to reassure her. She tongued him straightaway, curling her tip along the roof of his mouth, scraping along the underside of his teeth like she was eating an artichoke leaf. She pulled back but kept her face close to his, breathing hotly around his lips, moving her head in minute circles, hypnotic. She pulled away more, arching her back and slipping a hand behind Seeger's head. Seeger's face slid down her cheek and neck, snagging the neck of her T-shirt and resting against her breasts. He closed his eyes and felt Kent's sweaty palm crawl up his back and join Cordelia's at the base of his neck.

Kent lifted up his hand and pushed himself upright. He sat beside Seeger, smudged eyes gravely serious. He glanced at Cordelia; she smiled and lowered her head. Kent leaned forward, haltingly, and his lips met Seeger's, sticky with wine-sugar. Seeger opened his mouth, inhaling sharply, but pulled back and broke the kiss. He glanced at Cordelia, whose Egyptian-looking eyes were fixed on Kent. She and Kent stretched across Seeger from either side and kissed over his chest. He leaned back to give them room. The wet metal bars pressed against his back. He put a hand on each of their legs. He craned his neck to see around Cordelia's curls: his watch read 11:00 in the red light of the flying horse.

He flashed on Joan's hair, black curls made reddish in the light of Abraham and Rhonda's front porch, on the last time all three of his parents had been together:

It had been years ago. Joan had dropped Seeger off a day early from his visit, unannounced. He'd been filled with terror at the prospect of her facing Abe and Rhonda. He'd tried to convince Joan not to ring the bell as they stood in front of his own front door. He'd tried to find out why they'd suddenly changed travel plans and arrived in Execution a day early. "I don't want to get a fucking hotel," she'd hissed, stabbing the doorbell. "Now you're home and can just go to bed and dream about your damn drawings."

The world hadn't exploded when Abraham and Rhonda had come to the door. His parents hadn't been mutually exclusive, cataclysmically combustible like some three-sided matter and antimatter. Joan had deposited him and stormed back to her car. Abe and Rhonda had taken him to his bedroom, carrying his suitcase across the threshold and through the living room where they had been married.

Kent's kiss yanked Seeger into the moment. God, haven't tasted that in a long time, Seeger thought. Not since Jésus. You wouldn't think a man's mouth tasted so different. I forgot how different it is. Cordelia nudged his shoulder, and he turned his attentions to her.

Rain spattered gently on the soldier's steel helmet above them. They kissed for an hour or so, rosy-red faces with black-ringed eyes, until they couldn't go anywhere else but home.

LaTonia's Advice

"I am so grossed out," LaTonia groaned.

"What? It's just like a corn dog only with jalapeño cheese inside—"

"Not that, fool. Give me some of that." She grabbed Seeger's wrist and took a bite. "Mmm," she said, chewing. "Glad you got over your little 'Just Say No' trip."

"Just to mushrooms." Seeger leaned back into the bench. The hum of the mall bathed them in soothing white noise. He surveyed the stores in stoned satisfaction. "I like Corn Dog on a Stick better than Fletcher's," he announced.

"That works," LaTonia nodded, chewing. "But they don't have cherry lemonade here. Mm . . . and I wanna get some waffle fries at Chik-Fil-et. Orange Julius!"

Seeger scraped the breading residue off the stick with his teeth. "So what's so gross?"

"This damn ménage thing you got going."

"It's not a ménage. We just kissed."

"You going to have sex?"

"I don't know."

"You and Cordelia talked about it?"

"Not really."

"You think she wants to?"

Seeger sighed, picking at the dirt in the rubber plant beside him. "I don't know! She seems to, like, like him, yeah."

"When was the last time you and her did it?"

Seeger stared at her directly. "You. Are. Really. Bringing. Me. *Down.*"

LaTonia brushed off her lap. "Buzzkill. Yeah, sorry. I get so nosy when I'm stoned." She stood up. "Come on. Waffle fries."

Seeger stuck his stick in the plant's soil and joined her.

"You know, though," she said. "You should make sure you got a happy home before you're inviting over guests."

"Downer!" Seeger clamped his hands over his ears. "Big downer! Improper topics for fucked-upedness!" She shook her head, laughing, and he stormed ahead of her down the mall.

Seeger and Cordelia Try to Have Sex

Seeger took his mouth off her nipple and drew a blank. Next? Getting the bra off had been awkward enough, scratching her shoulder in his own fumbling. Nothing was working tonight. His penis was sore from grinding against her hipbone to stay hard. They hadn't had sex in months, and tonight was supposed to fix that. Seeger thought maybe he should change the music again. Marc and the Mambas' "Your Love (Leaves a Lesion)" was not helping the mood any.

Cordelia twisted underneath him on the Eisensteins' overstuffed couch. She wrapped her legs around his waist, staring him in the eye. Neither spoke.

He looked away, down at her chest. Now go on, you know what's next, hands down to her skirt and those leggings. C'mon, why can't you do it? Do it for her. He fought a panicky urge to bolt from the house. His hands froze. Cordelia's writhing ceased. Seeger crumpled forward in stages, like a building demolition. He rested his head on her chest. He watched the Eisensteins' vine- and fern-draped studio rise and fall with her breathing. Self-consciousness fell over them lumpily like a splatter of cold grease.

"When do the Eisensteins get back?" he asked quietly.

Cordelia removed her fingers from his hair. "They're gone all night," she snapped. "That's why I'm housesitting, remember?"

Seeger's face burned. He softened. Fuck, why can't I do this? He sat up. "What time is it?" Cordelia said nothing, also sitting up.

"My folks want me home by midnight. Rhonda wants me to go to early service with her. I've hardly gone all summer." Cordelia stalked over and plucked her bra off an easel. "I think she wants to squeeze in a few more before I leave home," Seeger added.

"Well, we mustn't disappoint," she said in a clipped tone. "Good thing Kent is grounded all week or we'd be out till one again." She shut the bathroom door behind her.

Seeger tucked himself into his jeans. He checked for car keys in his pocket. He felt seasick, pitching and yawing between relief and guilt, unable to settle on one feeling or the other. They swirled around him, intertwining without mixing, like oil poured on rough waters. The two liquids could slosh and swirl, break and subdivide into hundreds of tiny particles, travel in close proximity, but stubbornly refused to blend.

Seeger, Cordelia, and Kent Plan to Stay Out All Night

Seeger viewed the truck wreck with perfect clarity, over and over like a film loop projected onto the real world. It had switched from sudden bursts to a steady, constant scene on his mindscreen, refusing to dissipate or fade, like the heat of an August day that continued relentlessly into night.

"But Seeger," Rhonda implored, "you haven't been out camping all summer. It'll be a beautiful night, and you and your father could go fishing tomorrow."

Seeger had to rub his eyes to see Abraham and Rhonda—the living ones—clearly.

"We were going to get supper somewhere fun on our way out; maybe Po' Folks."

"What's up with you?" Abraham interrupted. "You been getting stoned in your room? You might not realize, son, that I keep a close watch on you and your little friends, here and in class. I can tell if someone's stoned."

"Abraham, please, he's not—"

"My eyes just itch, OK?"

The truck's hood wrinkled like parachute material; Seeger tried to force the image from his mind, double exposures of the explosion danced around Abe's and Rhonda's angry faces.

"We just spend so little quality family time," Rhonda said.

Seeger's mind spun. This would happen, he knew. Tonight. This is stupid; you sound like Joan. You should warn them. They'll die.

"What's so all-fire important tonight, anyway?" Abraham barked. "You've gone out with those two damn near every night this summer."

Cordelia's parents are letting us stay over all night, that's what. And they're alive. Shut up! He thought of the fetid taste of Kent's mouth and felt wet and hot in his crotch. He called up the memory of Kent in the shower, but shattering glass and blood sprayed across the image like interference.

You want to get that crazy look in your eyes like Joan? That's it, admit it, it's not some magical fantasy world, it's just all crazy, and so is your mother. This whole truck-wreck thing is just your guilt about Cordelia; you're blaming your parents for your own situation. Some people make themselves have migraines, you're giving yourself visions.

"Just not this time," he said weakly. "I'm just not up for it, you know? I need the hours at work and I have to open this weekend. We've . . . we've still got all summer . . ."

No, they don't—yes, they do! Once you and Kent and Cordelia all have sex, you'll stop feeling guilty and this will all disappear.

Rhonda threw up her hands and looked to Abraham in deference to his authority.

"Fine," Abraham said darkly. "Have fun tonight. The keys to the Impala are on the table if your car gives you any trouble."

"Y'all're taking the truck!" Seeger said.

"Yeah? What's the matter, you want it?"

"No—"

"We always take the truck camping, Seeger." Rhonda furrowed her brows at him.

He felt his face flush, panic rising up in his throat. He felt crazy.

"OK," he said and bolted back into his room. He shut the door behind him and fell against the wall in the dark, catching his breath. He reached out and fumbled for the stereo switch. "Where was your heart when you needed it most?" Marc growled against the crunchy guitars of Soft Cell's apocalyptic third and final album, *This Last Night . . . in Sodom*. The music steadied his breathing. He braced himself, turned on the light, and pulled his T-shirt over his head.

Contemplating Theft

Seeger rewound and repeated over and over in his head the image he'd constructed of Abraham and Rhonda: arriving back from camping, trailer securely in tow behind them. They'd be sun-haggard, happy, and alive. He'd visualized the image all night, until it clung to his consciousness like the chorus of a maddeningly catchy song.

He sat on the picnic table beside Cordelia.

"You OK?" she asked.

Seeger nodded. "Yeah, why?" He wiped his mouth on the back of his hand.

"You seem kind of stressed."

"I told you, it's just Abe and Rhonda, they stressed me out with their third degree . . ." *burns.*

Cordelia nodded. Seeger swallowed. They both stared straight ahead. They watched as Kent led a tall Asian guy over to their table, talking animatedly.

"So, what's his name?" Cordelia asked, diplomatically changing the subject. She leaned over and curled her arm around Seeger's waist.

"Hm?" said Seeger. "Oh, him. Jung. Like Carl Jung."

"Hm," Cordelia said suspiciously, jutting her chin and chest forward.

"Hmm." Seeger grabbed her neon-green plastic sports bottle and sucked out a long draft of peach wine. He swallowed and scowled at the approaching outsider. Cordelia appraised the two boys narrowly through her sunglasses. She'd worn them all evening, even in the depths of the park's unlit areas.

"Kent says he met him here?" Cordelia asked. "When?"

"Kent's parents finally let him get his learner's permit," Seeger explained, "so he came here the first night he was off grounding. He wouldn't quit yammering about it when you were in Lone Star Market getting those vanilla cupcakes."

Cordelia nodded, sucking in her upper lip. Seeger couched and bit his thumbnail.

"Look what we got," Kent exclaimed, arriving at the table. He held out a maroon vinyl purse.

"There's eighty-two dollars in it," Jung said, blasé. He carried a boombox slackly in his left hand like a handbag. "C-c-c-can't you see," crooned a glassy-eyed voice, "back in your arms is where I wanna be."

"We could all buy some X!" Kent said. "I'm totally broke otherwise, since they made me miss work while I was groundified."

Cordelia blinked at the boys. Seeger stared hard at Kent, determined to flush away scenes of his parents.

"Whose is it?" Cordelia asked.

"Some friend of Jung's left it here."

"She's not my friend," Jung corrected, "she's a total bitch."

Seeger took another drink from the bottle and rubbed his eyes. "But, uh, where could we find any X now?" he protested.

Kent's face fell. "I thought—"

"Besides," Seeger interrupted, setting the bottle down and crossing his arms, "the bars, they all stopped. They don't sell even Eve or Eden anymore; you can't buy anything."

He clenched his teeth and pushed his willpower outward, a force of internal energy coming from the very center of his head, just below the nose. The fiery ball of mental energy pushed out in all directions, drawing on energy reserves of anger and hate, burning off the truck-wreck ghost images, radiating Jung with waves of hostility. The night flickered clear, a simple moment of the present.

Seeger released a steely sigh between his teeth, feeling powerfully in control. We can't have sex if there's four of us, he thought, scowling.

"Well, Vikki always knows where to get X," Cordelia said, uncurling her arm from Seeger's waist. She leaned forward on the edge of the table and lifted her metallic gold purse onto her knees. Seeger glared at her for not following his lead and dissuading the boys. "I've got her date's number somewhere in here," she said, pulling out a lipstick and compact and flashing the two boys a smile.

"Hey, there goes that guy," Kent gasped, pointing past them. "God, he's so cute." Seeger turned. Cordelia remained fixed straight ahead, applying lipstick precisely, never taking her eyes off the compact mirror.

"Oh, him," Jung sighed. "He tried to get me to go in his car once. 'I've got poppers,' he said, like that was some big thrill."

"But he's got himself plaid Bermudas!" Kent groaned rapturously.

Seeger turned back around, cocking his head indignantly. "Kent! No son of ours goes around with someone with such bad fashion sense. You should know better."

"We'll find you X, and some nice boy in a black turtleneck," Cordelia said. She clicked shut her compact and set it on the tabletop. She smiled at Jung. "Surely you have a black turtleneck at home somewhere, don't you, Jung?" He opened his mouth, closed it, nodded. "Good," she said and dumped her purse contents unceremoniously onto the picnic table. "Oh, look," she said, "here's my Outstanding Contribution to Execution High pen!" She waggled the pen disparagingly at Kent. "If you're a good boy, you'll get one of these, too, some day."

"Kent's already got one," Seeger said. "And Jung doesn't live in Execution," he added icily.

136

"I'm well aware of that. I meant—"

"So, are we gonna find some X?" Jung and Kent looked at them, shifting weight, hands on hips.

Seeger hesitated. Buying drugs with stolen money was certainly a new level of hedonism. He wondered what Joan would think. Taking something from someone, a bitch even, seemed to violate some ethical tenet so broad and universal that even the most wacked-out UFO-worshipping cult would probably frown on it. He wanted to X with Kent and Cordelia, maybe even just Kent, but definitely not with Jung along for the ride. Not if it was like some double date. X wouldn't trigger any visions, especially if it was just with Kent and Cordelia, people I love. If it was all love, it could wash away all of those visions like an exorcism. So Jung *can't* be there. His anger-energy welled up in his face, killing his moment of indecision. No way, fuck him, he thought firmly.

Kent looked right at Seeger. "Come on, I haven't even done it yet! You two get to all the time." Jung looked at Kent with narrowed eyes. "I'm sure I could find you some."

Seeger bristled and aimed his anger right between Jung's eyes. "We do have a responsibility toward our son," Cordelia pointed out. He looked at her, wiping lipstick off the sports bottle. She raised an eyebrow back at him. "And his little friend."

X would take care of all this, Seeger thought. That's all we need. No more pussyfooting. If we all three X'ed together, for sure we'd all have sex. It would be incredible, both at the same time, all perfect finally. And Abraham and Rhonda won't be home till Sunday (because they *will* come home Sunday, safe and sound), so I can stay out all night. We've just got to ditch Jung somewhere. We've got to get in a big crowd somewhere. This can all still work out.

"Didn't Vikki say they were going to Sassy's tonight?" Seeger said to the group.

"Yes!" Cordelia leapt off the table and slid her pile of belongings back into her purse like poker chips. "And she told me today she'd just found a card shop that still sells X: they have some loophole where you buy a thirty-dollar T-shirt, and there's a little plastic pack stapled to the collar with a pill in it, and a card that says, 'For novelty use only, not for human consumption.' "

Cordelia grabbed her bag and led all three boys toward her Datsun.

"She bought a bunch the other day for the rest of the summer; I'm sure she'll sell us some at cost. We'll check at Sassy's; if she's not there,

I'll bet she's back at home. I'm sure we can track down that girl one way or another. Or at least find out the name of the store."

Weaving through the trees, Seeger plastered a final bright poster of Abe and Rhonda's happy future across his mental viewscreen, exiling their automotive catastrophe from his consciousness. He crammed even the idea of any further images of burnt skin and flying glass far, far back, down deep into the furthest recesses of his mind. He filled in the crevices at the base of his skull with them like cheap plaster. They would harden there, acquiring tiny calcium crystals and barnacles, remain lost and forgotten like treasure chests, buried in his cerebral sea underneath memories of hate and horror.

Searching

Kent and Seeger stood beside the Datsun in the club's parking lot. Dykes on motorcycles and underage clubfags eyed them curiously. They watched Cordelia saunter authoritatively through four lanes of traffic, returning from the Mavrik Market's payphone.

"Your folks still camping?" Kent asked. "Maybe once we get it from Vikki, we can go to your house to X."

"No, they're fine," Seeger said brusquely.

"Huh?"

"I mean, yeah, they're camping all weekend; they're fine. But I don't want to be at my house. It—it'll bring me down."

"Vikki's at home," Cordelia announced, climbing atop an off-road pickup's bumper, jacked up four feet from the ground. "And I told Mother you're coming to sleep over." She perched on the truck's glistening, cherry-red hood.

"That's OK?" Kent asked incredulously.

Cordelia looked up from lighting a Honeyrose menthol herbal cigarette and nodded matter-of-factly.

"What about Jung?" Kent looked back at the club's door, where a woman with a salt-and-pepper crewcut was running her fingers through the hair of a fey boy with eyeliner. The fey boy gazed up at her in awe. She patted down his shiny black vest, dotted with strips of torn, multicolored ribbons, and he nervously looked over his shoulder, scanning the parking lot. He looked at Kent, Seeger, and Cordelia, then back at the bouncer.

"He left," Seeger lied. "He took off with that guy in the fringe leather jacket."

Kent's face fell. Seeger put his arms around him. "Come on," Seeger said, "it's time for you to meet the rest of the family, anyway." Kent pulled away from his arms and opened the door to the Datsun's backseat. He climbed in and slammed it behind him. Seeger looked over at Cordelia atop the truck. She slid down onto the gravel of the parking lot and walked over to the car, tossing aside her smoke.

Seeger circled to the passenger door, and she approached hers, leaning over the roof to catch his attention before he got in. "You might want to distract Kent when you get inside," she hissed flatly, "Jung's coming out of the club."

She got in, gunned the engine, and tore out of the lot.

Confrontations and Revelations at Cordelia's Home

Mrs. Herodotus stood silhouetted in Cordelia's bedroom door.

"And Mrs. Lozone called," she added. "She said Kent is to call home if he lands here tonight." She glared at Kent. "She said she called your church, and there is no lock-in tonight."

"Thanks for relaying the message, Mrs. Herodotus," Kent chirped.

"And Cordelia," she sighed, "when you told me you were bringing friends over, I assumed you meant girls."

"Seeger and Kent are kind of like girls," Cordelia quibbled and drained a tall glass of icewater.

"I don't want to hear about it!" her mother snapped, walking out the door. She stuck her head back in. "Don't drink vodka."

"Mother, this is not vodka; its just water! Mother—" Cordelia followed her. She stood in the doorway, watching her mother disappear down the hall. She tilted back her glass and munched an ice cube, watching. "Good evening Unclefred," she called out around crunches of ice. "Your daughter's outside." She jerked her head toward the front door and followed him with her eyes.

Seeger and Kent crouched near her corner bedroom window. In the front yard, Vikki laughed hysterically, clinging to the young weeping willow recently installed in their front yard. Her date swayed a few feet away, holding a cowboy boot in his right hand.

Cordelia turned off the hall light and crept back into her room. She crouched beside the boys. "That's Louis Garcia," she whispered. "He's like, thirty-two. They hate Louis Garcia but can't say anything because Unclefred is my dad's *older* brother. He's like twelve years older than my mom."

Light spilled onto the yard from the front porch. "Vikki!" Cordelia's mother demanded. "Come inside now. You woke your father up."

"This sure takes the heat off us," Cordelia whispered. "These are the times I truly adore Vikki."

"Louis Garcia!" she announced, taking Vikki's hand and leading her inside. "Your mother is coming to pick you up. You stay here in the yard and wait for her."

Cordelia stood up. "I'm gonna go hear what Vikki tells Mom and Unclefred. I'll be right back." She slipped out her door, leaving the boys alone in the dark.

Seeger rolled onto his side, appraising Kent. He stretched forward and kissed his cheek. Kent jumped up and sat himself on Cordelia's bed, bobbing his head with excess nervous energy. "I can't believe Jung left us at Sassy's," he complained, "and I'm sure Vikki doesn't have any X, either."

Seeger sat beside him.

"Let's go see if anyone's selling at Clearview," Kent said. "Before they close. Or maybe from people hanging outside the Starck. I read in the *Observer* that they sell it there."

Seeger touched Kent's shoulder. Kent shook off his hand. "Seeger, c'mon," he whined. "Look, I'm gonna go see what Cordelia wants to do, OK?"

Seeger followed Kent to the door, watched him slip down the hall. He threw himself back down onto Cordelia's bed, hanging his head off the side and staring up at the ceiling. A nagging guilt and urgency swelled in him, his face flushed. He tried to build a mental picture of Abraham and Rhonda, safely asleep in the tent, but all he saw were muffled clouds of red, orange, and pink, billowing and silently exploding against the dark ceiling of Cordelia's bedroom. He tried to turn the colors into something else, to direct and control his visions like you were supposed to be able to direct your dreams. He turned his imagination on the pink, the long, breathy explosions of pink, clouds splintering into hairs like mimosa blossoms. Yes, that's what they were.

Cordelia had been so tickled when she'd seen real mimosa trees in Texas, smelled their elusive perfume on late-night walks, Seeger having snuck out of his bedroom. Before moving to Texas, she'd known of mimosas only as champagne and orange juice. Seeger saw the delicate pink floral hairs with pale yellow roots, ethereal in the dry summer wind. He imagined climbing the mimosa tree in the backyard of the house Abraham and Joan had lived in. He pushed himself back into the past, away from the present, to memories of hanging upsidedown from tree branches, until he was a young boy again among the lush blossoms:

He'd reached for the nearest branch but reared back as his weight shook the fronds, the furry little creatures, the mimosa blossoms.

"Seeger get out of that tree!" Joan had shouted, her face pressed against the kitchen screendoor. "You'll bust open your stitches!"

Seeger had scampered down without hesitation. He'd stood dumbly at the trunk, blinking. He hadn't known the tree was off-limits. He'd gazed at the screen door—his mom had gone. Delicately, he'd pressed his scalp but found no scab beneath all his hair. He'd forgotten about his stitches, the hospital, his dive from sofa to console TV. All he'd been able to remember was his blood coursing down Mrs. Bowie's arm, how it had smeared on the yellow phone in her palm, and how he had worried that he'd get in trouble for the stains on his new stripey shirt.

Fritz had mewled from the garden. Injury forgotten, Seeger had trotted over and knelt in the moist loam. He'd reached out for the black kitten sprawled on her back. He'd giggled, glad to have been wearing play overalls so he could muck about.

"Hey, bud, you hungry, huh?" Seeger had tickled the thin fur stretched over tiny ribs. "You want a snack-time?" He'd bent aside the veiny fronds of the plants around him, searching for orange carrot tops. Fritz had liked carrots cleaned in the waterhose.

"I don't even have a damn beat!" his mother had shouted, voice spewing through the kitchen window above him. Seeger had bolted upright, staring at the window. The usual white noise of his parents' talking had focused sharply.

"I don't make money writing cotillion announcements and obituaries for that fucking rag—"

"Joan!"

"I just took the damn job to keep from going crazy sitting around the house all day! It can't support Seeger and me when you leave us—"

His father's voice had been thick and gristly. "What are you—"

Fritz had crawled under the porch floorboards, blinking sulfurous eyes out at Seeger and his grubby fistful of carrot babies.

"Did they fire her, too?"

Seeger had pounced onto the porch with a *thud*, dropping his carrots, and thrown open the screendoor. Looking downward, he'd marched right between them and held up his palms like a referee.

"All right, all right!" he said. "Who started it?"

Joan and Abraham had glared. Seeger had folded his arms and pursed his lips, inspecting them from the corner of his eye. He'd felt quite witty, like the Burger King kid on TV.

"Go to your room, Seeger. Joan and I are talking."

"He doesn't have to go to his room! He has the right—"

"Joan, that's exactly—"

Seeger had torn from the kitchen, his face burning, imploding. Eyes, cheeks, and lips all had collapsed into his brittle throat and chest. He'd gagged on sticky air and run past the spot where he'd gotten in trouble for coloring on the walls, past the aloe vera plant, past the seagull poster in the living room, past Kris Kristofferson and Rita Coolidge's *Full Moon* record jacket, which spun and sliced through the air in his wake. He'd rounded the corner into his room and leapt onto his bed. He'd coiled up and sat in the center, quivering, teeth and eyes clenched shut. He'd held himself, not crying or moving, a tight little ball, churning and burning violently like a new white star.

He'd waited for them to come after him. And waited.

He'd looked around the bed for a stuffed animal but Mousy, Kanga, and the rest were all in a pile across the floor beside the window, where Joan had set them to dry. Seeger had looked at the empty space where his aquarium had been. He'd recalled the dramatic splash of water, the shattering fluorescent rod, and the spray of saffron and teal pebbles flooding his room.

The aquarium's fragility had quite amazed him when it had broken the week before. He had stood speechless amid the devastated aquatic world, watching his fish on the wet hardwood floor flip, wriggle, and suffocate. Abraham had stormed into his room, demanding an explanation, but Seeger had honestly been so stunned that he couldn't remember exactly what had just then happened, or why.

Yellow-white exploded all around him, real light, not mental, and Seeger squinted his eyes shut. Kent had flicked on Cordelia's bedside lamp, a plaster-cast nude woman writhing around the base of a tree.

"We're going to your house," Kent announced above him. "After we buy our drugs." He looked down at Seeger hanging off the bedside. "What's your deal tonight?"

Seeger's head was thick; he struggled to right and anchor himself in the present. "Um, I should call first. Sometimes they change their mind and don't stay overnight."

Kent snatched the phone from Cordelia's dresser. "Here." Seeger dialed, fingers stabbing the buttons thickly through memory-fog. He rested his dizzy head against the receiver, slouching against the wall.

"There's a really long beep," Seeger said. "Shit, I bet they've been trying to call me." He punched in their code and listened as the machine clicked and beeped.

"Great, now you're in trouble, too," Kent said, watching Seeger listen to the message.

"No," Seeger said, expressionless. "It's the police."

august, 1987

After the Funeral

Seeger stared at the bed. The comforter rested smooth and flat. Russ's nimble hands had stacked the pillows neatly. Like a hotel. Seeger remembered kissing Jésus here. They'd had sex here. It had been their first time.

"Seeger, what you doing in here?" Russ entered Abe and Rhonda's bedroom. He rested hands on hips.

"Oh. Nothing." He swirled his ice tea. "Just checking on everyone. Making sure everything's OK."

His uncle surveyed the empty room. "Yeah." He put his hand on his nephew's shoulder. He guided him to the door. "You come back to the living room; everyone's all in there."

"Mm," he said. He felt Russ's warm hand through his graduation suit's shoulder pads. Did I get this drycleaned? He inspected the lapels.

"Come on, now, you look fine," Russ said. "Let's get you something to eat. Some of Rhonda's folks from Tyler brought homemade tamales."

"We have enough plates?" Seeger peered at him.

Russ stopped at the hall mirror. "Seeg, everything's fine. Don't you worry about nothing, OK?" He squeezed his shoulders. Seeger avoided his reflection. Russ smelled like his father, like Abe wearing different clothes and aftershave. Seeger tried not to think about it.

"We got more kinfolk here than I knew we had. Taking care this crap's about the only thing most them're any good for. So take it easy, OK?"

He led Seeger down the hall. At the living room door, Seeger looked through the slats, spying on the guests as he had on his parents before prom. Rhonda's whole clan from Tyler wandered about, stepcousins, -aunts and -uncles he recognized from reunions. Her parents sat stiffly on the sofa sipping punch, being tended to by a nurse and their children's families. Seeger hadn't seen them outside the rest home in years, but even wearing real clothes instead of robes and pajamas, they looked ephemeral, ghostly. Kody stood at the end of the sofa, blatantly staring at them until shooed away by Bill and Pam.

Meemaw, Joan's mother, had flown in all the way up from Port Arthur. When Seeger had asked if Joan had come with her, she'd simply smiled and shaken her head. Others had asked after Joan. He'd told them she couldn't make it. They'd glance over at Meemaw and give Seeger a similar nonverbal head-shake that spoke volumes: pity on Seeger, relief that they wouldn't have to deal with her.

Meemaw was out in the backyard playing with the kids. Herding them was more like it. She'd been Seeger's only real grandparent growing up. He felt a deep affection for her, having survived the stormclouds of her daughter's rebellion and her late husband's alcoholism. She sat on the lawn chair, calling out to kids. She directed their feverish games of running and screaming. She looked back in through the window and nodded at Seeger.

There were few relatives left on Abraham's side of the family. His parents had died in a house fire when he was a young man. He and Russ had been the only children. Over the course of Seeger's life, the remaining twice-removed nephews and grand-uncles-in-law had consolidated around their immediate families. They nodded at one another around town, but remained unclear as to exactly how they were related.

The crowd of friends and relatives formed a web of bloodlines and histories that normally wove throughout life in Execution with a vague but tolerable sense of claustrophobia. Now it gathered into a dense ball of yarn tightly spooled around Seeger. He resented their intrusion. He wanted to be alone. He needed an empty house. A clean slate. He needed to figure out what had happened. Where he was. Then get far away.

Cordelia and Kent stood in a corner, nibbling string cheese. Cordelia had been cordial. Quiet, though. Kent couldn't stay long. Had to be at work.

"Seeg?"

"Yeah. You're right. I know." Seeger blinked. "God—thanks for being here." He frowned. "Wish you hadn't lived so far away all these years."

Russ sighed. He folded his arms. "I'll be around hereabouts for a while. Get sick of me yet." He maneuvered Seeger into the living room. He deposited him with Cordelia and Kent. "Think your boyfriend here needs some tamales in him."

Cordelia smiled. "Well! Then let's get him some. Yes." Her eyelashes fluttered. She was not being flirtatious. Her hand slid around Seeger's arm. He did not lean into her. She held his arm, as if anchoring him to the ground.

"All right then." Russ nodded and backed away.

"I think your uncle's gay," Kent commented.

"Kent!" Cordelia said.

"What?" Seeger plucked at a carnation. He crumpled an ivory petal with his thumb and forefinger. He dropped it on the endtable. "Russ is a real cowboy. A rancher." He squinted. "We haven't really talked. If I were younger, he'd move me out there and be my dad. He wouldn't want Joan to take me. But I guess since I'm ready for college, I don't need a dad. Don't think he knows what to do with me in the meantime."

Kent crossed his arms. His lips pursed. "I still think he's gay. Butch bachelor rancher, like, really. He ever make a pass at you?"

Seeger looked at Kent blankly, trying to imagine the house later that night, after everyone had gone, just him and his uncle crashing out in front of the TV . . .

"Kent!" Cordelia snapped. "Rein it in."

He sighed at Cordelia. Cordelia put her other hand around Seeger's waist. "Let's visit the smorgasbord." She pressed her forehead against his. She kissed him. Seeger wrenched free.

"No, I can get it!" He dusted his fingers on his jacket. He stormed toward the kitchen. He faced a gauntlet of guests' outstretched palms and open mouths.

LaTonia was talking with Pastor Hank. The minister smiled. He raised chocolate-swirl Bundt cake. LaTonia shot Seeger a hang-in-there grimace.

"It's a terrible loss for this town," the pastor sighed. Seeger grunted.

"You did a really nice service, though," LaTonia said. "It was lovely."

"These are the hardest tests of faith," he said, looking at Seeger pointedly. "With sickness or old age, you see it coming and prepare yourself. But when the hand of God touches your life unexpectedly like this, it can make you wonder if there's any plan to things at all."

Seeger, nodding, shuffled to maneuver himself closer to the kitchen.

"I'll stop by and call on you," the pastor said. He reached out, but Seeger flinched his shoulder away. "And you can call on me anytime the spirit moves you," he added. "I've known your family a long time."

"Thanks," Seeger muttered. He bobbed his head and turned from them, only to find Eva standing there, hands clasped in front of her.

"Oh, my little darling, I can't believe this all has happened to you. Such a sweet child, all alone." She took Seeger's hands. "Your folks were such good people; this town isn't going to be the same without them."

"Thanks."

"Now, you just don't even worry about the store or your classes. I'll get my Earl in there to help. I was planning on bringing him in anyway, when you left for school. He'll pitch a fit, but he'll cover things fine. Don't you worry about a thing unless you feel like you want to come in and work a spell. Sometimes they say getting right back in the saddle is the best thing."

Seeger nodded, biting his lower lip. He squeezed her hands and put them back at her side. He wedged past her into the kitchen and nearly ran into his sixth grade teacher.

"Whoa! Seeger, easy there." Mr. Wilder smoothed drops of bourbon off his navy blazer. "How you doing there, son?"

Seeger shrugged.

"Terrible tragedy, terrible tragedy. The whole district's so sorry for you." He sipped his drink. He licked his lips thoughtfully. "You know, you might have a good legal case, son. Big explosion from a side-impact collision like that? Ain't right."

Seeger stiffened, anticipating a vision of the fiery wreck. There had been none since it happened. Since it *had* happened, it wouldn't really be a vision anymore. A flashback. A reminder. An indictment.

"Jap bastards don't know how to make a decent truck, putting the fuel tanks there like that, no protection." He poked Seeger's tie. "You oughta talk to a lawyer."

"I'll see what Russ thinks," Seeger offered feebly.

"Hmm, well." Mr. Wilder nodded and shrugged. He patted Seeger on the back and walked off.

No one seems to like Russ, Seeger thought.

John-Tyler, a cousin of Joan's who'd often taken Abe to the shooting range, stood up from behind the refrigerator door.

"Seeger, my man! Looking good!"

"Hey John-Tyler."

"Man, these things are a madhouse, huh? When Carrie's dad passed, we had these people living with us for days. Who all's camped out with you?"

"Just Russ."

John-Tyler nodded. "He's mellow. Well, no, he's a total tight-ass, but he's better than all these women breathing down your neck. Listen . . ." he leaned closer to Seeger, chewing rolled-up olive loaf lunchmeat with his mouth open. Seeger tried not to look. "You ever need to blow off some steam, come by and we'll go out to the shooting range, yeah?"

Seeger nodded.

John-Tyler elbowed him. He make a clicking sound out of the corner of his mouth. "Come by when Carrie's not around," he said in lower tones, "and we'll kick back with a little smoke, you know?" He jumped his eyebrows and smiled.

Seeger smiled. "Thanks."

He hid his angry flush, sidling past his cousin.

Everyone kept probing, reaching out, trying to touch him inside. He wanted to be alone. He couldn't act sociable. He walked till the sink stopped him. Seeger wanted a drink, but not to get drunk around these people. He couldn't remember where he'd set his tea. He looked for a clean glass. He grabbed a dirty one. He turned on water. He squirted clear dishwashing liquid. He held the glass under steaming water. He rubbed off lipstick. The glass's squeak pleased him. His fingers burned. He grabbed another.

He fell into steam and soap, the faucet's dull roar, not seeing or hearing anything else. Life felt dreamlike. Were dreams and visions the same? His parents were dead, as he'd envisioned, as he'd dreamed. Planned? Seeger had fantasized about being freed from his parents. He'd planned details years before the visions started. Had he set energies in motion? Had his daydreams taken on a force of their own, becoming spontaneous visions, then reality?

He remembered standing naked in the bathroom, planning his sleeping parents' death. Translucent streetlight drifting in had carved his hazy reflection in the mirror: a preteen charcoal-on-glass sketch posing for inspection. He'd run hot water until scalding and slicked his hair.

Rivulets had run down his face, neck, and back, tickling nipples and chest down, curling along ribs, lingering along five dark hairs beneath his navel.

I could kill my parents, he'd thought. Absolutely nothing stops me from getting the meat knife from the junk drawer and stabbing them. Wish Abraham had a gun. Or I could set the house on fire. The droplets had prickled his genitals. I could kill them and do the funeral. Handle all the details. I could make a tape of love duets to play in the background, married couples like James Taylor and Carly Simon, Kris and Rita, even that *Connie and Jerry Sing His Name!* album Rhonda's so in love with. I'd set up the Atari for the kids. Call a caterer, even though everyone'd bring food. You need too much food at funerals. Makes people secure. I'd invite Pastor Hank, and Patsy from Praisercize, who'd married and moved to Houston. Abraham's college roommate who'd moved to New York and come out. He'd be all built and we'd have sex in the garage. I'd invite Joan and her family plus Rhonda's family, Uncle Russ, all Abraham's obscure relatives. I'd set out snapshots of them. They'd feel flattered. Tell themselves it was grief. Everyone'd say, "We'd been out of touch so long, but I'm right glad I could be here."

They *had* been saying it, all day long, exactly as he'd imagined. Created.

A cool hand grabbed his. "Whoa, reality check." LaTonia took the fourth glass. She shut off the faucet. She leaned close. "Not that you need anymore reality, hon, but just what do you think you're doing?"

Seeger blinked. "Nothing."

LaTonia shook her head. "Un-uh. You're doing the dishes. Boy, you've got yourself relatives here up the butt. Make some of these weepy-ass church ladies do this, OK? Besides, you'll be getting this sharp suit all wet."

Seeger grit his teeth. "I needed something to do."

She steered him to a corner near the window. "Look," she said, "d'you see this here card from Tate and Jolene? Coach Wills brought it over with the flowers. Says they couldn't get a sitter but wanted you to know how much they loved your dad and you're in their prayers . . ."

Seeger stared through the lace curtain. Several mourners had joined Meemaw in watching the kids. Cheap sportscoats. Lace-collared dresses. White dress shirts rolled up at the sleeves. Only Eva, smoking beside the withering garden, had an all-black ensemble. She brushed ash off her pleated skirt. LaTonia waved the card before Seeger's eyes. "You listening?"

"Yeah. Tate 'n' Jolene. Nice."

"Yeah." LaTonia tapped the card against her chin. "They are pretty together for being stupid enough to get knocked up and married in high school. Least they got each other—for now." LaTonia cocked her head toward the living room. "How're your girlfriends doing?"

Seeger eyed Kent and Cordelia through the crowd. Seeger's great aunt Phenora from Gonzales pointed out antique photos on the wall to them. Abraham's ancestors posed stiffly amid horses, wooden split-rail fences, and adobe shacks. Rhonda had found them in the attic, packed away with first-marriage ephemera. She'd framed them in a black collage. She'd hung them beside Abraham and nine-year-old Seeger in cowboy gear: the State Fair Old West photo booth.

"Wasn't the funeral a circus?" Seeger said. "I guess. I don't know, it's all a blur. I hardly remember it. Feels like I wasn't even there. Russ said the *Daily Executioner* wanted to talk to me, but he wouldn't let them. The superintendent was there, I remember seeing him. Did they cancel summer school? Wouldn't it've been weird if this'd happened during school? We'd've had a big assembly."

LaTonia narrowed her eyes. She reached out. Seeger leaned past her. He filled his hand with Swiss cheese and saltines. He chewed thoughtfully.

"Russ said we shouldn't let anyone but family and you guys come here, though. Guess that makes sense. He's taken care of everything, just like my dad. Weird. I don't know what's going on with money or any of that shit yet." He laughed, "HA!" like a door slamming. He looked around the kitchen. His face clouded. "Everyone keeps watching me."

The phone rang. "I'll get it!" Seeger said. LaTonia slid her hand down. She lingered on the small of his back. He tucked the receiver under his ear. He turned away. She set her face. She headed over to Kent and Cordelia.

"Seeger, the fires are coming," his mother warned.

"What?"

"Don't play stupid, not now. The fire visions I've had for years, you know, where we're leading children out of Corpus Christi away from the firestorms? They're coming."

Seeger set down his cheese. Shit, I never told Joan about my visions. What if she says it was all my fault? "I thought those were mostly symbolic—"

"No, they're not symbolic, dammit! You can't indulge in wishful thinking now. I was meditating after Russ called about Abraham and I had a vision. Abraham was in it."

She knows! He told her how I ignored my visions—

"He came to me to tell me to get you out of there, your place is with me on the land—"

Seeger's shoulders fell in relief. He blushed over his panic. "Joan," he said, affecting Abe's schoolteacher-reprimand tone, "we just had the funeral. Everyone's here, and they all asked about you. Your mother and all the relatives."

"Oh, none of those hypocrites care whether I live or die! Now, snap out of this. You got to come back down here. There are times you can just be a content, small-town liberal and pat yourself on the back, but there are times when you have to accept what the universe asks of you and be a man."

Seeger gnawed his tongue-tip. What if she's right? I was right before. Maybe now she is. Maybe this happened with my parents so I'd learn and believe. So I'd help Joan. This could be real, serious. More than just two lives at stake.

Cordelia crept beside him. She held a note: Kent wants a ride to work. Do you need me to stay? She laid her palm against his chest.

"I need to get more ice," he informed his mother. "Can't we talk about this after everyone's gone?"

"Seeger. I asked Abraham for proof, and he told me to go to that silly red Unitarian church, the one where you did that psychometry about that woman's liver? I went there, and five other women were having apocalyptic visions. I'm sure the sub's here, that's what's going to start it all—"

You need anything? Cordelia mouthed. Seeger put his hand atop Cordelia's. He shook his head. She cocked her head, trying to discern the phone's squawks. Joan, Seeger mouthed. Cordelia frowned. She slid her hand behind Seeger. She hugged him around the phone. She stole a quick smell of his perspiration. He squeezed back, pulled away.

"What sub?"

"The nuke sub! I'm sure the government's hiding one here to use against Cuba or Central America. Voters didn't approve Houseport last year, so they're keeping them here secret. That's what'll trigger the firestorms, and I'll need your help."

Cordelia pointed to herself. She nodded. She pointed to Kent. Seeger nodded and waved across the room.

"Joan, Russ and I are going to have to do all this money and will stuff. He's executor till my birthday next New Year's. And I have to go to college." I really should believe her. My parents' dying had to have been a warning.

Cordelia smiled. Her brow clenched. Seeger noticed her eyes were bloodshot.

"You can't let me down, or the children! This is your calling, Seeger, you know it! You always felt destined for something worthwhile, more important than being some artsy stuffed shirt. But we got to act now, jump while the iron's hot. I know land for sale outside Uvalde with natural springs. We can set the refugee colony there, but I don't know how much time we got. You might not be able to use your inheritance yet, but you can get Abraham's credit cards or write checks. I can probably get the MasterCard back from Mother—"

Cordelia walked toward Kent. She tucked in her blouse. She raised her head. Seeger watched them leave. Wonder if we'll all go out later and fuck around.

"Seeger, goddammit! Listen—"

How can you think that now?

"This is it! When this sub explodes, the cover-up'll be huge."

Guess anything goes. I just killed my folks. I knew it was coming. I did nothing. Letting them die's same as killing. Fuck. Fuck. Why should I have to think about this shit? Why's it my responsibility? Why should I be some savior? No one's blaming me now. No one's going to blame me if hundreds of people die in Corpus while I'm kissing Kent and Cordelia.

"The government'll quarantine the whole Gulf Coast and exterminate witnesses. They'll never admit to a nuke accident; they can't afford it. This is the collapse of the world as we know it!"

Seeger studied his relations out of the corner of his eye. Living his own life, getting away from all this shit to college in New York was what he'd spent his entire fucking life working toward. He wasn't going to give it up. "Yeah, I know." He hung up.

Seeger watched the conveyor belt slide by. He hoped Russ liked orange buns. Nothing else sounded good for breakfast. Russ seemed only ever to have coffee.

"How's it going?"

Seeger looked up. Tate Kistwell from school smiled nervously from behind the register.

"Shit, Tate! I didn't even realize it was you."

"That's cool, that's OK." Tate dragged juice and pastries over the scanner. He punched up the total. "You doing OK?"

Seeger held out twenty dollars. "Yeah. My uncle's still here."

"Oh, that's good."

Seeger nodded. Tate stood there, change in his hand. Seeger recognized the woman behind him from Eva's and from church. She looked away, pretending not to notice them. Seeger held his hand out for the change.

"Well," Tate said, "if you . . . you know, if you . . . Jolene and I—"

"Yeah, sure," Seeger said. He moved his hand closer. He could see Mr. Dobie watching them from the Customer Service desk. One of Abe's junior-year students eyed them as he rolled a sleeve of grocery carts past.

Tate stuffed the money in Seeger's hand. "Take care, dude," he said. Seeger nodded and grabbed his bag. "Hey, Mrs. Carpenter!" Tate called out cheerily to the woman next in line. Seeger fought the urge to run to the car.

Fighting with Cordelia About the Future

Seeger and Cordelia drove through streetlamps' pulses. The LTV Tower's neon outline faded down a trail of expressway lights. It joined Reunion Tower's stippled orb on the horizon. An organic light show replaced downtown Dallas's klieg-lit buildings. Heat lightning cut the thick nightair. Wind screamed through the open windows of Abe's Impala. They sped through arid borderlands between Dallas and Execution. Seeger knew Russ wouldn't care when he got home but still felt obliged to approximate his old curfew.

"I don't like doing this," Cordelia burst out, "but sometimes I think I'm the most inhibited person I know!"

Seeger said nothing. He remembered teeth on ears. Hands in hair. One of them had kicked off the rearview mirror in her Datsun. Cordelia had chuckled and chucked it in the backseat. "Serves this damn car right," she'd said, "after all the bruises it's given me." Kisses. Fingertips. Nails hard down the back of the neck. She'd pushed his head off the seat's edge. He couldn't see. Blood had rushed to his head. The vinyl upholstery had clung to his neck. She hadn't touched him. She'd held her head close to his belly. He'd felt her breath.

"Maybe I expect too much. Maybe we're too young for a relationship. I think we have a wonderful friendship."

Silence. Seeger knew he should be consoling but felt incapacitated. Couldn't be the emotional rock.

They entered the causeway into Execution. Lake Ewing, a man-made square carved into the plain, reflected lightning. Jagged shards on choppy waves resembled scattered razors. Seeger could smell ozone and dried fish. Cordelia's powder. Fresh-scent laundry detergent. Gardenias. Sweat. God, he thought, wish there wasn't fighting or traumas or sex, only pale mornings. All naked against her back, semiconscious. Forever.

They pulled up to her house. He winced at the yang t'chin and cello intro to Marc Almond's "Broken Hearted and Beautiful" on the tape deck. The song was one of Seeger's favorites for belting out along with, clutching his heart and rolling his eyes. When he was alone at home. He clicked the tape off.

Cordelia uttered a choking sob. His neck stiffened. Seeger stared out the window. A few storm-glimmers remained.

"I just feel miserable!" she said. "And I don't believe everything will be perfect now that your parents are dead. I'm sorry! I don't mean that negatively, and I know this must be horrible for you, but it's been two weeks. Besides, it is the exact freedom you always said you wanted. They were what you always said was blocking you! I mean, we could spend every night together from now on! You know your uncle would let us."

Seeger looked at her, pained. What next? Perhaps:

"You're happy there, aren't you?" she would ask in several months. She'd be notably slimmer, with a portable phone tucked under her ear.

Silver sunglare would sparkle off her sunglasses. "I still miss you terribly, you know that; you're my dearest friend."

He'd be at a payphone in a sandy-carpeted hallway. Snow would dust a window beside him.

"We weren't the most frequent of lovers," she'd say pointedly.

"No," he'd reply in the warm familiarity of post-breakup confessional.

Cordelia would gaze down from a balcony overlooking a dizzying freeway spaghettibowl. "But I still feel like we had a more intense relationship than any of my other lovers," she'd say. "And now we're thousands of miles apart." She'd sigh.

Maybe. He couldn't see how their future would play out, but he was able to imagine scenarios. Maybe if he imagined hard enough, he would become able to see, able to make it come true . . .

"I just don't understand how you can be so uninterested in our future!" Cordelia looked away. She flinched at the silent lightning.

Seeger brushed away his bangs. The car was warm. The engine radiated through the dashboard. The upholstery's acrylic fuzz held his body heat. His back shirttail dampened. "Just give me more time. I don't leave for two months. NYU's letting me skip orientation."

"Maybe I won't be here that long," she said darkly.

"What?"

"Oh, nothing. Months, weeks; it's all time. I think we should either take complete advantage of all our remaining time together or not even see each other!"

Seeger's mouth moved silently. He put his hand over his mouth. He put his hand in his lap. "I'm still too . . . stunned by all this to figure anything out. I could blame them for everything before. Now, I'm not even sure what's wrong."

"Look," she said, "I'm sorry! OK?" She reached behind his skull, fingers combing his long hair. "I just really don't know what's going on these days anymore. I know, neither do you. I . . . I really can't imagine what you must be going through. And now I'm not going to New York, and I feel like I'm abandoning you. And I worry about your being all alone. But then I think, isn't being so alone really what you've always dreamed of?"

"I know."

She lunged over and kissed him. Seeger chewed her lip, ran his tongue underneath, over her teeth. He wanted to fall down her throat inside her.

She pulled back, eyebrows raised. "Oh, God, let's just forget the whole thing, OK? I don't want to go in mad. Let's get my Datsun and go ram some parked cars again or something. There's champagne in my closet . . ."

Seeger felt his heartbeat. He tasted her spit. "I need to sleep," was all he could say. "I'm sleeping a lot these days."

Cordelia set her shoulders. "It won't help for me to be there?"

Seeger looked hopeless. "Soon, I hope?" He glanced away. "I can't seem to be alone enough right now," he offered. He leaned back toward her. He kissed her lips, forehead. He slumped against her cheek. They sat breathing in what should have been silence, but the turbine-like drone of male cicadas possessed the night.

He left her standing beside spindly willows. The boa-like branches had lost many fronds in the storm. White plastic bows from the nursery clung limply to their trunks.

Russ's Parting Words

Amtrak was late. Seeger and his uncle killed time wandering around downtown Dallas. They could've caught the train at the Execution depot, but Russ had wanted to get some new boots at the Nocona outlet. He carried the ostrich skin beauties in a box under his arm. They wandered toward the Kennedy Memorial. The memorial was a huge cement cube, mounted slightly above the ground. It sat at the end of a sidewalk across from the School Book Depository.

Russ's old boots clacked softly on the cement as he and Seeger approached the massive cube.

"You know, I've never been here," Seeger said. "As nuts as Abe was on Kennedy, he never took us here. When me and my friends come downtown, it's to go to the museum, library, or over to Deep Ellum."

"They let you in those arty bars over there?"

"Yeah, sometimes."

"Well, you got the hair for it."

"It helps when Cordelia flirts with the doormen."

159

Russ chuckled. He punched his nephew's arm. "Li'l tit-flash! Womankind's secret weapon."

They moved closer to the cube. On the far side, a slit was cut into the concrete wide enough to walk through. They circled the cube. Russ sighed.

"So you never been down here?"

Seeger shook his head. "But I figured once I'm in New York, people'll ask me about it; I'll look like an idiot if I say I lived in Dallas all my life and never even saw the School Book Depository." Seeger looked across the street at the infamous brick building. "I'm not going to tell people I lived in Execution. I mean, it's too complicated to explain. I'll just say Dallas; everybody knows Dallas, especially after that stupid TV show."

Russ nodded. "Best thing about that show's that it made people forget about this. They think Dallas, they think Southfork, J.R. It's taken a long time to get out of the shadows of Oswald and Ruby."

They entered the cube. Seeger had expected an eternal flame, a monumental bronze like the Lincoln Memorial. There was nothing, not even a plaque. It was empty, hollow. It went without saying.

"Probably good you didn't get dragged down here as a kid. Most people my age are so freaked out by that day. You know that's what got your dad into TV news."

"Really?"

"Yeah, he didn't have his mind made up about shit in college. Little English, little journalism. Didn't really give a shit since he was on scholarship. But then after this happened"—Russ indicated the air around them with a nod—"he got all fired up about TV, about being able to show people what was happening, explain it for them. I guess it was kinda like teaching."

Seeger absorbed this. In the silence of the cube's interior, he asked, "You know why he got out of TV?"

Russ's lips pressed tight. "Don't know nothing about that. I's on the ranch then already."

"Oh."

"Let's get."

Russ strode out of the memorial, his mood brightening as they made their way over to Union Station. Reunion Tower loomed above them like a giant microphone.

"You're gonna be a man now!" Russ said brightly. "Feel like I should buy you a hooker or something." He laughed at himself. "Guess you got those bases covered. You sure you don't need me to stick around?"

Seeger shook his head. "Nah, I just want to get on with things."

"You clear on how to deal with the bank and your allowance and everything?"

Seeger nodded.

"Well, all right now. Just call out to the ranch if you need anything. And you got the accountant, and the lawyers' numbers. We'll get you all set up in New York. Meanwhile, there's plenty people in town who'll look after you. Never thought I'd see the day there'd only be one King in Execution. Soon there'll be none."

He appraised Seeger squarely. "But you've always known how to take care of yourself, I gather," he said. "Shit, with a ma like Joan, I guess you'd have to. No offense, now?"

"Yeah, I know."

"You heard anything more from her? Why she didn't come to the funeral?"

"She's kinda wrapped up in her own world. And I don't think she had the money to fly up here."

"Well, I suppose you're used to that. She was never a regular mother or wife. She was a goddamn pistol, though, when she was a kid. She used to run with us boys all over town, biggest tomboy in Execution. She'd even beat the shit out some of the sissyboys. She was a real hellion. Kinda reminds me of that girlfriend of yours."

"Cordelia?"

"Yeah, she's a firecracker. How you doing with her? She decided for good whether she's going up North with you or not?"

"It's still kind of up in the air. She changes her mind a lot."

"Joan again! Say, listen here, man to man, you got something on the side with that black girl?"

"LaTonia? She's got a boyfriend!"

"Well, so do you. A girlfriend, I mean. Y'all seem pretty pal-sy and, sure, Cordelia's a looker, but I'm a man who can appreciate a taste for a little brown sugar."

Seeger stared at him, aghast.

"And I'll give you a little piece of advice, college boy. Don't be turning up your nose at every gal who's not Vanna White. Lot of guys make that mistake and they miss out: the bigger the cushion, the sweeter the pushin'."

Seeger's mouth was dry. "I'll remember that."

Normalcy

Student Council dictators splashed drill team majorettes. Band captains cheered *Fat Guy Goes Nutsoid* on the VCR. Seeger kept his distance, avoiding their polite-but-anxious-to-get-away-from-him conversations. Difference rose from his skin like a stink. Execution had been comfortable with him as an eccentric, but now he was draped in an irrevocable cloak of death. No one could integrate the orphan comfortably into their daily lives.

A new song bounced through the backyard, a recent hit about not having to take your clothes off to have a good time. Seeger smirked. Probably only he got LaTonia's sarcasm. The song fit their Honor Society peers, whose end-of-summer party was her responsibility. In smiling passive aggression, she'd planned a party with absolutely nothing to "just say no" to, but added personal touches. There was only Tab, Canfield's Diet Chocolate Fudge, Carraway's Ginger Creme, and outdated Sesquicentennial Sasparilla to drink. If she could have only cokes, they'd be the worst possible. She'd scheduled the party on the night of the potentially apocalyptic planetary alignment astrologers were calling the Harmonic Convergence. If the world was going to end, universal peace break out, or some other major drama come down, she wanted to be throwing a party.

Seeger lingered under the slide. He didn't inflict himself on anyone. He looked at stars. Considering the Convergence, he felt nonplussed. Joan had dismissed it when he'd asked. It didn't fit her own apocalypse. While watching TV with Russ last week, he'd considered that maybe his visions, Joan's visions, and the fuss about the Harmonic Convergence were all different manifestations of the same event or energy. Mycall had said Quetzalcoatl's heart would burst out from some tree in central Mexico. Tonight Seeger felt only a vast blank, like Dallas's expressways, mirrored skyscrapers, desert plains. If the world was ending—tonight, by chance—he wasn't particularly concerned. He sighed. His shoulders dropped. I think I'm finally relaxing, he thought. It's kind of nice having Russ gone. He sipped his Tab.

The evening exuded seductive naïveté. Seeger was relieved that Cordelia, who normally required free-flowing gin, seemed charmed and content. She sat on the diving board, tossing glowsticks at the swimmers. She crooned, "There were glowsticks in the pool, but I never saw them glowing till there was you."

She wiggled her silver pumps above the waves. Isaac, Kent's friend from Six Flags, treaded below. Seeger hoped he would mention Kent's whereabouts.

"Wonder Twin Powers—activate!" Cordelia chucked a white glow-stick to Seeger. He made an exaggerated show of ducking. He shielded his face with his Tab rather than attempt a catch.

"Shape of—a wildebeest!" she prompted. She pointed a glowstick at him. He sipped his Tab.

"Come on," she said, "what form are you going to be of? An ice-unicycle? A water-schmoo?" She cocked her head at Seeger. She rocked back, gripping the board's edge. Seeger leaned close to the slide's ladder. He didn't want to join her spotlight, for once.

"Schmoo?" said Isaac. "I remember that show!"

Cordelia looked away from Seeger. She and Isaac sang, "The Incredible New Schmoo is going to please you . . ."

Seeger winced. His friends always bonded so fast over old cartoons. *Sesame Street. Zoom. The Electric Company.* "We're gonna turn you on," he muttered under his breath. He tried to recall a memory connecting *The Electric Company* and . . . tofu? Abraham and Joan fighting . . . Seeger pressing his fork into a frightening plate of white squish . . .

"Fuck the Wonder Twins!" LaTonia shouted, goosing Seeger. His coke went flying as he jumped. She cackled triumphantly. "Can't believe you were actually drinking that shit."

"Well you gave us such great choices," he muttered.

"Like this crowd deserves any better," she whispered. Seeger nodded. They watched Cordelia walk down and dismount the board.

"Well," Cordelia said with a smirk, "I guess now I'll have to go out with Aquaman!" She poked her glowstick at Isaac's dripping chest, standing beside her.

"Better get a white-knuckle on her." LaTonia nudged him. Cordelia led Isaac by the hand toward them.

"I know," he said, rubbing his chin.

"Yeah, I'm a model now," Cordelia said without apparent enthusiasm. She settled on the scratchy grass. Isaac, Seeger, and LaTonia sat beside her. "Bob Eisenstein's gonna make me some international personality." She dragged over her zebra-striped bag. She pulled out contact sheets and grew animated. "See? I got my proofsheets today. He wants to fly me out to L.A. with him next week and meet agents!"

LaTonia and Isaac leaned closer.

"Aren't they nice?" Seeger said. He sat up. "She could do a thing for Lots-O-Lash false eyelashes."

"I told Bob he should take pictures of me getting my hair cut on a fire escape."

"Like Edie outside the Factory with Ondine and Billy Name," Seeger explained for the group.

"Except no Dallas buildings are old enough to even have fire escapes."

"Another reason to leave," Seeger said.

LaTonia and Isaac squinted in the twilight at tiny black-and-white frames of Cordelia and her props. Cross sections of merriment. Silk and lace netting frozen around her. Her world of rhinestones, champagne flutes, false eyelashes, and ostrich feathers reduced to monochrome dioramas.

"Dig that breast action!" LaTonia fanned herself with her hand. She nodded approvingly.

"That's the last roll!" Cordelia squealed. "Several bottles of white wine later. Private collection only—those won't be my eight-by-tens."

Isaac glanced at Seeger.

"I think they're great," Seeger said. "They really capture you."

"Mom and Unclefred were livid. They thought because these didn't look like Olan Mills, Bob must be a pornographer or rapist."

"No," Seeger objected, "these are good. I mean, they're not, like, typical model stuff. Glamour photography. They're real different. You could get attention with these."

"He has shot for *Interview*."

"You're gonna be just like Mahogany!" LaTonia shook her head. "Wearing Versace gowns and getting in car wrecks with Norman Bates."

"Oh my," Isaac said.

"Film projects"—Cordelia shot her a knowing smile—"have been discussed."

Isaac and LaTonia went, "Oooh."

"Even though Seeger is now heir to the King family fortune, he will live the life of an impoverished painter at the Chelsea Hotel," Cordelia explained. "I'll jet-set from L.A. to New York for clandestine rendezvous with him, despite my marriage to an Asian foods–importing magnate, and the press will have a field day."

Seeger's smile faltered. Isaac shook his head. He looked back over to the house. LaTonia's brows knitted. She watched Cordelia leaf though her proofsheets. Cordelia should be famous, Seeger thought. Lots of other people looking after her. Not me.

"So, you're really going out to L.A.?" Isaac ventured.

"I'm visiting next week," Cordelia said. She stuffed the proofsheets in her bag. "We'll see if I return. Seeger doesn't escape Texas till next month."

Isaac frowned at Seeger. "Doesn't NYU start soon?"

"I've got to wrap up a lot of my parents' stuff first." Seeger sighed impatiently.

Isaac cringed. "Oh! Yes, of course."

"Least it didn't happen after you got to college and fuck your whole first year up," LaTonia pointed out.

Seeger opened his mouth to reply. Everyone waited in silence. He tried to think of something to say. He'd almost said, "I shouldn't have let it happen at all."

Feedback shredded the air. Everyone looked up the sloping lawn toward the house. Seeger appreciated the distraction. He felt a troubling haze descend. His confident clarity rotted, decayed. He felt stifled, hot, as if standing in midday sun. Sweat beaded on his upper lip. Everyone tonight had said they were sad he was leaving. They really felt relief. Next month Execution would be cleansed of him, the nagging reminder of his parents' death.

"Louie Lamore begged me to let his band play," LaTonia muttered.

Isaac nestled his damp head on Cordelia's lap; she leaned against La-Tonia's shoulder. Seeger couldn't watch. Hot violence swelled up in his chest. Fucking stupid band, he thought, trying to pawn off his anxiety. He searched the party. He glared at Dale Rogers from Yearbook. Sitting on the backyard porchswing toweling her hair, she moved to the music in a fringed overshirt. She caught Seeger's eye, and her smile faltered. Seeger pressed clenched fists into the grass. So fucking innocent. Totally stupid. Fucking backyard full of teenagers on a summer night and no one's making out. Fuck. Not even a cigarette or bottle in sight. Backyard Fucking Blanket Bingo. Not a soul with anything real to worry about.

We walked on the sand.
I held your hand.
I looked into your two eyes of blue.
Now I know, I've got too much love
but not enough for two.

"All the sad young men," murmured Cordelia. She smiled to the group but, looking at Seeger, rolled her eyes.

Kill them all, Seeger thought.

"Don't you make Fitzgerald allusions," Isaac chided. Cordelia narrowed her eyes at Isaac. She appraised him curiously. "Some of us still haven't found our Wonder Twin," he said. He stared at the stars. "Tonight hasn't worked at all."

"What, Isaac? Tell me." Cordelia smiled. She rolled her faux-pearl bracelet across his Adam's apple. Isaac scuffed up powdery dirt with his heel. Her smile grew.

"I came to this party specifically because Janine Cosgrove is in Honor Society with y'all." He nodded deferentially to Seeger and LaTonia. "Not that I didn't want to see y'all as well, but you've got to admit, this isn't a typical party, LaTonia."

"No shit; nobody's stoned."

As if on cue, the band launched into reggae-twang Dylan: "Everybody must get stoned."

Seeger flashed on his mother shouting, "Sex, Drugs, Rock and Roll!" from the window of her station wagon. She'd waved a bottle of Jack Daniels while passing friends on the sidewalk.

His resentment grew. He stared down at the earth.

"But Kent and I had planned that this summer we'd get Janine and Laura Thompson to fall in love with us," he heard Isaac sigh. "Now Kent spends all his time in Dallas, and the girls aren't here. I even wrote Janine a sonnet!"

Seeger closed his eyes. They were wet.

"I'd fall in love with anyone who wrote me a sonnet," Cordelia said. "Isaac, don't get morose. How could you love anyone with no appreciation of great literature?" She stroked his hair. Seeger remained absorbed in dirt but could see Cordelia steal a glance at him.

"Yeah," he said, swallowing. "At least it gives me something to write about. Kent and I were going to collaborate on an opera." Without looking up, Seeger made a contemptuous noise between a snort and a choke.

His lips pressed tight over clenched teeth. His breath came out his nostrils in short bursts. LaTonia eyed him.

Isaac sat up gingerly. "So where is Kent these days, anyway? I thought he'd show up again tonight with y'all." Seeger looked up. He glared at Isaac. His stomach twisted. Desire for Kent rushed back, swallowed him. He despised his own resolute weakness.

"No," he hissed. "I don't know where the hell he is."

"We've sort of lost track of that little peach," Cordelia said breezily, leaning into Isaac's shoulder, blocking Seeger.

"I'd say that peach was getting a little overripe," LaTonia observed.

Seeger tasted self-pity, bitter at the back of his throat like sticky aspirin. Where the hell was Kent? How come he never called? Fuck him, that's the last thing I need to be wasting my time with.

"Well, no matter," Cordelia said. She twisted around. She tapped her finger on Seeger's kneecap. "Now that Seeger's a wealthy orphan, he can afford a whole fruit stand." Her voice turned dry on the last words. She touched her lips.

Seeger met her eyes angrily. Her face was an impassive challenge. Her hand drifted over to Isaac's shoulder. Isaac rocked his head, watching the band.

Seeger looked away. The pool party, the band, the desperate flirtations, surrounded him. A trite, small town to which he no longer belonged. The familiar home scene radiated an unnatural aura. Mold had grown on the bread. Seeger saw all-important desires bottoming out into shallow pools of selfishness and spite. The others were blind to this, and happy to be so. He'd lost that gift. Their simplicity and sincerity made him deeply jealous. He'd always felt distinct from both Execution and Joan's world, to a degree, but adept enough to pass within both. Now he couldn't even fake it. He felt initiated into some new world but unable to find other inhabitants. Execution was sniffing him like dogs, recognizing an outsider. Soon they'd growl. Soon the pack would solidify. They'd circle their wagons.

He bolted up. "I've got to go."

Cordelia rose.

"No, I'm just gonna go to bed," he said.

Her face flickered embarrassment. Her eyes narrowed. She brushed dust from her skirt. She sat down, curling up beside Isaac.

"That's cool," LaTonia said, glancing up at Seeger standing above them. "You're probably pretty worn out these days." She smiled over at

Cordelia exclusively. "What's say you and me have a Girls' Night Out once this party crap's out of the way?"

Cordelia nodded sagely at LaTonia. "With real drinks."

"What about me?" said Isaac.

"Oh, Isaac," Cordelia snapped, shaking her hair out, "you're just gonna go home and brood, anyway, and you know it,"

"Yeah," he said with resignation. They all laughed. Seeger turned his back.

"Well then, Seeg—" Cordelia began, but Seeger was walking toward the back gate. He'd heard her but didn't stop.

He stalked down the alley. His father's, now his, Impala glowed in starlight, an eerie gray like underwater plutonium. In his fist, keys dug into his palm, drawing dark blood. He licked it. He thought of Kent.

Urgent Message from Joan

Seeger pushed the party from his head. He yanked the plastic vodka jug from the pantry. He slammed it on the countertop. He poked the blinking answering machine in the alcove beside the phone and coffeemaker. He opened the fridge.

"Seeger, it's Joan. You got to call me. Things're changing here, and fast. I need to know what the hell you're going to do. You can't still be going on to New York; I'm going to be needing you here. I'm making arrangements so we'll have money. You've got to stop worrying about everything; just trust your instincts. You can't control this; it's bigger than you. You know what happens when you don't pay attention to your psychic intuition—"

The machine beeped Joan off. Seeger turned it off before it could play the four other messages it signaled. He pressed ERASE. He debated pulling the plug. Not yet. Just in case. He'd deal finally with his mom and the end of the world tomorrow. If the world didn't end tonight.

The cranberry juice, a red so dark it was almost black, curled and billowed as he poured it into the liquor. They mixed like water turning into blood. He tossed it back. He checked the time. People would be showing up at the park soon.

Seeger Tracks Down Kent at the Park

Seeger pressed Kent against the soldier's leg. He raised his knee into Kent's crotch.

"Seeg, c'mon, I'm trying to find Jung. He doesn't know I got out tonight. I need a ride home." Kent rolled his eyes. His face looked cloudy and mottled beneath Sam Houston's trees. "Dad took my car away after I rear-ended Cecilia last week." He shoved Seeger's knee away and squinted past him.

"You found me," Seeger persisted.

"Finish up all that funeral liquor? I'm so sure they had drinks at La-Tonia's Honor Soc party." He cocked his head. He monitored Seeger with narrowed eyes. Seeger flushed, gritted his teeth.

Kent shook his head with a *tsk*. "If you see Jung," he said, wresting himself from Seeger's hands, "tell him I'm up on the Hill." He strode away, head thrown back, hands deep in his shorts' back pockets. He gave the park a brusque once-over. He disappeared up the tree-shrouded path.

Seeger reeled in his wake. His face burned. He stared up into the stars' pinpricks. Had the world ended yet? Scowling, he stormed off across the crunching gravel, in the opposite direction from Kent. He followed the driveway to the far parking lot, self-conscious in the cruising headlights. He passed the public restroom, dark and ominous. Someone called, "Hey, honey."

The lot came into view. A discofied air-raid siren blasted from someone's jambox. He squinted, making out two Hispanic drag queens clicking about on stilettos. He recognized Andy Warhol's Brother and Schwarzenegger-at-Large. And Jung. He treaded uneasily over to the shiny black Karmann Ghia.

"Hey, Jung."

Head twitching to the music, Jung glanced down from the car's hood at Seeger's ankles. "Wicked socks."

"Yeah. Thanks."

"Where's Cordelia?" Jung stared hard into a passing Jeep.

"Out with some people."

He shot Seeger a twisted smile. "What about the bi trade?"

Seeger frowned, confused.

"Kent," Jung sighed, face falling.

Seeger's face flared hot. "Uh, no. He's grounded all week."

Jung cocked his head to a different angle. He blinked and fluttered his hand behind him. "Vikki's here." Several cars behind, Vikki go-go danced in the truckbed of a gray El Camino. Black miniskirt hiked to the base of her oversized, dark wool blazer, she shook her hips in a wobbly shimmy, attempting to synch with the music. "Woo!" she hollered. "Woo!" On each *woo,* she opened a lapel, flashing alternate breasts.

"God, she's been doing that all night," Jung hissed. "Keeps scaring away all the cute guys." He licked his lips.

Vikki made Seeger queasy. Shit, she'll tell Cordelia if she sees me here. "Well. I'll see you around, then," he muttered. He backed away.

At the soldier's base, he glanced back. Vikki's shaky dance had mutated into a step-kick. Jung had disappeared. Seeger climbed into the soldier's head. He hoped to shut out the park's cacophony. He craved Cordelia's reassuring presence. He missed her reflection of the things in himself he felt good about. He couldn't remember if she and LaTonia had said where they were going. He kicked the pole in the center of the soldier's head.

Fuck. She's starting to realize what a shitty boyfriend I really am. Caring for her and treating her decent aren't enough. She really needs someone that can match her passion. Love her for real. Like I want to love Kent.

Seeger stretched out of the soldier's head. He hooked his feet around the side bars. He hung his head down the top of the tongue-slide. He stared down/up at his T-shirt falling toward his neck. He studied his exposed chest, skinny and gray. Blood rushed to his head.

Kent. Fuck. Now that was, like, a total dead end. Kent was turning into some stupid clubfag. Won't even kiss me. The whole mess swamped Seeger. Treacly black fury rose in his throat. Hot breezes blew over his skin. He got hard. His face and body flooded with itchy blood. He squeezed his dick through his shorts, hard, painful. He lifted his head up and slammed it back down against the metal slide. He yanked his feet from the bars and slid headfirst down the soldier's tongue.

He skinned his shins against the flagstones running up the hill. Panting at the summit, he steadied himself against a rust-stained cement fountain. He squinted. The circle looked empty, but it was hard to tell in the dark. He closed his eyes to listen but heard only his pulse whooshing inside his head. Dizziness hit him hard; he opened his eyes.

He stumbled along the flagstones until spying Kent, facing away, on a stone bench. He sat watching expressway lights through trees. Seeger crept beside Kent and flopped down on the bench.

"Hey, Kent?"

"Oh. Hey."

"Um. Like, I'm, you know . . . sorry, about—"

"It's OK," Kent sighed. "You're all drunk." He kicked gravel. "God, I get so sick of all these fags here, you know? Trying to drag me into their cars and shit. God, I just hate them!"

"Yeah." Seeger's heart raced. Take it easy; don't get all slurry like Peepaw.

"God, you know, can't I just, like, be gay or bi or whatever and just have buds, you know? Not have to hump everyone?" Kent threw his head back on the bench. He stared into the trees.

Seeger wrapped his arms around his chest, swaying. He sniffed, rubbed his eyes. "You should've come to . . . to the party tonight. Isaac, like, misses you."

Kent *tsk*ed. "Oh, yeah, right. Isaac just likes me 'cause I can get girls to talk to us. He hasn't even figured out I'm probably just some dumb faggot."

Seeger looked away. His mouth felt full of warm spit. His face burned. He swallowed thickly. He wanted to put his arms around Kent. He wanted to hold him and be held until they could think clearly.

Kent rolled his head. He looked sideways at Seeger. "Or you. Of course, that took me a while, too. At least you've got Cordelia. Your little ménage thing is kinda warped, but at least she cares about you. No one really likes me. No one knows me."

Seeger scowled. "Lots of people like you, Kent. Y'know, I mean . . . I do."

"Oh, that's fucked! Either I put on my, like, you know, Cutesy-Poo act and make people laugh or they're really just hot for me. That's the only reason you gave me the time of day."

Seeger swallowed desperately, not sure what he was hearing. He scrambled for a response. "No, I like you, Kent, really."

"You don't give preppie jocks like me the time of day! Like, *tsk*, God! You and all your snotty friends! Think you're all so *unique*. That's such a pile of crap. You and Cordelia, with your little special world. Andy 'n' Edie!" He shook his head. "What the fucking deal with *that?*"

Seeger's face weighed enormously heavy, thick, hot. His chest constricted. His eyes watered. He frowned darkly. The trees undulated. He reached for support. His hand landed on Kent's bare thigh.

"Fuck off." Kent shoved him with his shoulders.

"Kent, don't think I—" Seeger's voice cracked. He couldn't form words. Choking back a sob, he threw his arms around Kent.

"Stop it!" Kent wriggled. Seeger embraced him tighter.

"God, Kent, I just . . . ," Seeger hissed through clenched teeth. "Why won't you—"

Kent lurched aside. They fell to the ground. Limp, Seeger sobbed onto his chest.

Kent's body relaxed. "Asshole," he murmured. He locked his arm around the small of Seeger's back. His obliques flexed and he lurched to the side, tossing Seeger off. Kent sat up. He wiped dirt and leaves from his chest.

Seeger lunged blindly at Kent. He grabbed fistfuls of Kent's hair. He yanked back. He slammed his knee into Kent's ribs. Kent doubled over, a stunned look on his face. Curled up, he rolled onto his side. Seeger grabbed the hem of Kent's T-shirt where it rose high above his hips. He pulled it over Kent's face, yanking it back and gathering it in a knot. Kent scrambled upright, sitting on his knees, and Seeger crouched behind him. He pulled the shirt and the back of Kent's head tight against his chest. He breathed near Kent's covered ear.

Kent reached around behind his head. One hand tried to pry Seeger's fingers from the knot of his bunched-up shirt. The other flailed about wildly, seeking out Seeger's face. Seeger struggled to keep a grip on him while dodging the hand. Kent's palm smashed upside Seeger's nose. Blood dribbled down his face. Seeger let go of the shirt, and Kent spun around toward him. He reached up to pull the shirt off, and Seeger threw himself against Kent's chest. He knocked him back down on his back and planted his knee across his gut. His hands held Kent down by the neck, fingers spread across T-shirt and throat. Seeger's long legs and ankles locked around Kent's thighs, splaying them apart.

Kent froze again. Seeger ogled down, dumbfounded. Those pecs and abs heaved with Kent's gasps beneath Seeger's crotch. What was Kent thinking, what was he waiting for? Seeger knew Kent could pull out any number of wrestling moves and probably beat the shit out of him. Why was he just lying there?

Seeger took one hand off Kent's throat. He put a finger to Kent's dark nipple. "Don't leave," Seeger said.

Kent's wet exhales slowed, and he remained motionless. Cautiously, Seeger bent down. He closed his eyes, and his lips dusted Kent's chest, delicately—like someone kissing him goodnight. Kent's body unclenched. One-handed, Seeger pried apart Kent's shorts' Velcro fly. Kent still gave him no reaction. He released Kent's neck, watching him for a sign of attack or encouragement. With both hands, he gingerly scooped out his dick. Kent was hard and wore no underwear.

Seeger stroked the smooth skin stretched tight. The organ jumped, flexed. Seeger dove down, sucking Kent's dick with hurried gulps. He felt driven, as if making up for lost time. He listened for a reaction from Kent but couldn't hear over his own sucks, gags, and gasps. He paused midstroke, like someone being followed stopping midstride to listen for footsteps. He thought he heard Kent sniff, sob? Seeger's eyes watered.

Scattered honks and girly *yoo-hoos* floated around them like mist. Seeger sat up, catching his breath. He wiped blood away from his mouth. He rubbed his jaw, stretched sore. He forgot about that. He wanted a drink of water. He wanted to brush his teeth. He looked at Kent. He wanted to kiss him. He pulled Kent's T-shirt off his face.

Kent blinked warily. Seeger sighed. He lowered his eyes, turned away. Kent relaxed. They looked at each other, daring to hold the gaze. Their faces softened. Seeger smiled: a broken, limping thing.

Kent arched his back, raised his hip. His softened cock lolled to the side like a sleeping drunk. Seeger sat back on his butt, gathering his knees to his chest. He stared at Pegasus through the trees. Kent pulled up his shorts and sat beside Seeger in the dirt.

"You're still bleeding," he said.

"Yeah," Seeger muttered. "It got all over you. Sorry. I mean, it's not safe."

Kent stared at him. "It's OK."

"I don't think any got in your mouth or anything."

"It's OK, man."

Seeger wiped blood off his upper lip, cleaning his mouth on the back of his hand. He could feel the dried smears tighten across his cheek like scabs. The two boys faced each other in the dappled light, faces blackened from dirt and dried blood like camouflage.

Kent touched Seeger's face. "You look like some army freak."

Seeger popped out a soft laugh. Kent kissed him quickly.

"You look like shit." They kissed again.

"You are a shit."

Kent pulled back, dusted his shirt.

"I'll take you by my house on the way home," Seeger offered, "so you can get cleaned up."

"I don't want to go home," Kent said. He pushed his finger around in the wet blood on Seeger's neck.

Seeger Dreams While Asleep with Kent

Musk was attacking Execution. A fertile invasion of magnolia, bougainvillea, mimosa, and gardenia steamed off petals and branches, mingling, intertwining, joining forces. Floral vapors gained reinforcements from the narcotic fumes of freshly sheared turf, forming a multicolored mist that advanced down alleys, enlisting scents of garbage, feral cats' spray. The rich breaths pulsed and throbbed across dim patios and unwitting driveways, softly battering doors, saturating tar-paper roofs, steaming windows, but never penetrating the frigid domiciles.

Vinyl weatherstripping and rubber doorflaps kept red-brick entryways cool and dry, so that the prized air-conditioners could continue their protective, sterile roar.

Abraham set down the *Village Voice* his old roommate had sent him. "Fags are rioting in New York 'cause Judy Garland died," he told his wife. "Now there's a firm foundation for social change. Christ."

Joan looked out their window at the moon. "They must be getting close," she said.

"What?"

"The astronauts."

"Oh, God, don't remind me. That landing telecast is gonna kill me. I'm not going to be doing shit except local cut-ins, but I still have to be at the station all night looking my anchorly best. I tell you my director's making me interview that hick minister over at First Baptist? I have to ask him if he thinks man is playing God by reaching for the stars."

Mesmerized, Joan stared at the moon.

"Of course, getting seen at all during one of the biggest news events of the century is damn good." He stood beside her. "Wish I could stay home and watch it with you, though."

"Hard to imagine people are breathing that far away."

Abraham caressed her belly. "Any developments?"

"What? Oh, no." Her temple pressed against the glass.

"Too bad he couldn't've come along six months earlier and be here to see it with us," Abraham said. "This'll be the defining event of his life, his age. He's the first extraterran generation. He and his wife might honeymoon at the Sea of Tranquility."

"I wonder . . . what the moon-world . . ." Joan traced a fingertip along the cool, refrigerated pane. "I wonder what it smells like," she murmured, staring through all the mists outside.

Joan's Final Message

Seeger tried vainly to follow. His head throbbed. He couldn't concentrate. Joan's metallic reverberations from the receiver echoed through the house.

"So, I can't give you a forwarding address," she said. "But I'll be safe on the reservation. Miguel's promised to introduce me to their shaman. Maybe we can work together."

Nothing registered on his poisoned neurons.

"But I don't want Mother to be able to track me down. She thinks I've stolen all this money through her credit cards and is on the warpath—"

"Uh-huh." Seeger let the phone hang loose under his chin. He looked across the bloody sheets at Kent sleeping beside him. He'd kicked the sheet off and curled up fetal, brown blood and muddy smears on his T-shirt and shorts. Seeger had his clothes on, too.

"But I can't go to a hospital there because the computers will get both our names; I don't want to register the birth because they'll use it to track down the survivors after the blast. Luckily, the midwives on the reservation—"

Seeger watched Kent's face twitch. Seeger's lust was mercifully dead, but his aching romance, his dream of being a guiding, loving older brother of sorts hung around, lingering like a memory or a ghost.

"Oh, God, someone's coming. Listen for me telepathically—"

The line died. Seeger hung up. Kent stretched and uncurled sleepily. Seeger avoided his eyes. He looked out the window at their front yard rocks. All the grass yards on the block were matching the Kings' brown rocks now, burnt despite careful watering. Dry, beige leaves from the cottonwoods' summer molting littered the sidewalks and gutters.

Kent sat up beside him, yawned. "Shit, bled in the bed," he rasped in morning voice. "It's a mess."

"Don't worry. I'm not taking it to school. You can change into clothes of mine if you want."

"When do you leave?"

"Three weeks. Cordelia's still figuring out what she's doing, but she's going to visit L.A. next week."

"I start back next week." Kent leaned into Seeger's shoulders. "I'm glad."

Seeger looked at Kent's mussed two-tone hair, the trimmed patch running down the back of his neck. Seeger coughed. "You'll be careful this year, huh? Not go into Dallas all the time?"

Kent nodded. "Yeah, I'll watch out."

Afternoon sun blazed through the bone miniblinds of his parents' bedroom. It illuminated the walls with a scorching white glow like the inside of a microwave on high. A new day, Seeger thought. The world didn't end.

Seeger shifted to look Kent in the eyes. "I'm sorry, you know? I don't have any excuse, you know. I didn't know what I was doing."

Kent turned his back to Seeger and nodded. "Seeg," he whispered, "do you remember much of last night?"

"Not really."

"You know we didn't ever really have sex, and you didn't hurt me or anything. I don't want you feeling guilty for nothing."

"Oh."

Kent fell back roughly into Seeger's lap. He smiled up at him, dried blood cracking around the corners of his mouth. The soiled fabric of his shorts tented magnanimously.

"Want to now?"

Control

"I can't believe you're jealous!" Cordelia marveled, lounging back into the floral sofa. She sipped the grenadine-rich rum punch Seeger had concocted.

"Am not!" Seeger sipped and sat beside her.

"You'll have Kent to play with while I'm gone," she said, stretching her legs across his. "Or is he still all tied up with Jung?"

"I don't know." Seeger stared at her creamy ivory leggings, avoiding her eyes. "They all go back to school next week." He took a deep drink.

"Anyway," Cordelia said, "just because Bob Eisenstein is paying to fly me out to L.A., I am not going to sleep with him. Handlebar mustache, *ick!*" They laughed.

"He just wants to do sort of a screen test. Some shooting at the beach and my meeting some people."

"You really think he knows people? It sounds like such a bad movie." She nodded. "So, it'll be a screen test, like, The Factory, huh?"

"Don't worry, it can't be The Factory without you." She bent her knees alternately, calves flexing across his lap.

Seeger looked at her questioning and expectant face. He thought of Kent's subtle smile as he'd reached to touch Seeger's cock that morning. Just a wrinkle of cheek-muscle could say so much, like the tone of voice on a carefully chosen word: *forgiveness/invitation/initiation/closure/ hello/goodbye.* It sounded like a damn Beatles song.

Kent had wanted Seeger. Seeger hadn't forced it or manipulated him; Kent had wanted Seeger like Cordelia did now.

He set his drink on the carpet and stretched out alongside her.

She held her smile, but her eyes spoke *uncertainty/fear/hope.*

Seeger kissed her. He kissed her again and again, thrilled by his ability to initiate, to control. He kissed her neck, collarbone, eyelid, deep tongue. He flitted from location to location, almost flippantly, delighted with his array of options. He could do this or this or that. He wasn't making the moves he thought the script dictated or the costar demanded. He wasn't posing in the best angle for the composition of the whole canvas. He arched his back, pressing against her legs. He pulled back his face to gauge her reaction.

"Why, Mr. King!" she drawled in exaggerated Texana. Seeger flashed on a popular joke last year: Why are there no Texan virgins? Because it takes too long to say, "Kuh-wee-uh-it!"

"I've heard about these heah castin' couches."

He smiled but didn't affect a character to continue the joke. His hand reached under the waistband of her leggings. He was in control, Seeger King, and she liked it.

Cordelia Leaves

"I don't know why you insisted on coming; I'll be right back in a week." She kissed Seeger on the forehead. "It's just a brief business jaunt."

"I know, it's just I'm leaving next month and you start back up at North Texas soon. I feel like we have so little time left together." He handed her her carry-on bag.

"Oh, God!" she said, digging through the pockets, "where are the proofsheets? I know I put them in here—"

"We packed them in your big bag, wrapped them up in those scarves so they'd be safe—"

"But I wanted them on me in case my luggage gets lost! Why didn't—"

"You said they'd get crumpled in there."

"Oh, yes. Sorry. I'm so anxious." She eyed Security's X-ray doorway. "I guess I remembered everything. I've packed and unpacked so many times this week."

"That's all you've practically done."

Cordelia looked at Seeger askance. "This is important to me. I don't have a big college to go off to."

Before Seeger could register the edge to her tone, she hugged him. "Kent and LaTonia will look after you. You'll be fine. And I gave you Bob's number." She pulled back.

Seeger frowned. Kent hadn't returned his calls all week. He offered his lips to Cordelia, and she kissed his forehead again.

"I'll go to the gate myself. It's OK, really." She squeezed his hands and pulled away. "I'll bring you something shiny and shallow from L.A.," she said with adamant frivolousness. "Bye!" She grinned, waved and headed to Security.

Seeger stormed away from her, almost running through the concourse. He'd envisioned himself with the grand exit scene, the final goodbye as he left her behind in Texas for a new Yankee life. She'd one-upped him, cheated him out of the pleasure of that ending—because he knew she wasn't coming back.

He slapped his palm against the sluggish, motorized revolving doors.

He leapt out into taxis and piles of baggage. He threw himself into the Impala and gripped the steering wheel, hot rubber burning the inside of his tenacious grip. He sat there, pulling and pushing against the wheel, turning it slightly left and right. He nodded and reached for his keys.

Kent's Resolution

LaTonia settled into the Kings' sofa. "So you hunted the poor boy down?" Seeger handed her a glass of ice tea with a glare.

"I didn't 'hunt him down,' " he said testily. "He didn't return my calls all week, so I just stopped by Oshman's to see what was up." He sat himself in the easy chair.

"Was he freaked or something?"

"Well, no. Not about us. He was mad I hadn't told Cordelia about me and him, and he said he *had* tried to call me, that very night after we had, you know, that morning. No one answered and the machine was turned off because, ah, that was the night Cordelia stayed over." He swished tea around in his mouth.

"He said he tried Cordelia's house and Vikki answered and they talked, and she was drunk and wanted to go out, so they hooked up and went to Sam Houston. Jung was there and acted like an asshole—big surprise—so when he and Vikki went up on the Hill to get stoned, Kent stayed down in the parking lot and hung out." He looked at LaTonia. She smiled with eyebrows furrowed and swirled her lemon wedge around in her tea.

"Kent wasn't sure exactly what happened, but next thing he knew, he heard Vikki screaming his name. Jung had wandered off alone and some guy, ah, stabbed him. Vikki found him and freaked and got Kent to drive them to the emergency room. No one else would, and Vikki was too freaked."

"Shit."

"He's OK, he just got some stitches in his leg, but I guess there was a lot of blood. And Kent—the hospital was going to call all their parents. Jung didn't care evidently and Vikki gave them the fake name and number on her fake I.D., but Kent had his real driver's license on him and so he . . . he left them there. He skipped out when the nurse wasn't looking, before they could get his name and number. Kent was really freaked out. I mean, it could've happened to him—"

"No way, he's too smart; I'm sure that Jung guy was being stupid to begin with."

"Yeah, well, we're all stupid sometimes." Seeger sucked an ice cube into his mouth and spit it back into his glass. "Kent said he just needed to get his life back to normal, get ready for school starting back up. He told me not to call. He said, 'Good luck at school' and everything, but he told me not to call."

LaTonia whistled. "All that fucking and now they're both gone," she said. "You OK? How's your head?"

"Ah, fine. I'll keep busy. I've got to deal with this. . . ." He waved his arm about, indicating the living room. "Going through my folks' shit and packing and everything."

"Why didn't your uncle do that?"

"Russ did plenty. He would've had to stay a couple more weeks for that." Seeger stood up. "God, it's hot in here. I'm going to turn up the AC.

"What do you want to do?" he called from the hallway. "Gotta be something inside; it's over a hundred again today. It's so hot I don't want to eat or anything."

He stepped back into the living room. "You can just look out the window and see how hot it is. Even with the AC going, you still know it's hot out there."

september, 1987

Solo

Sleeping through another morning, Seeger dreamt of his father:

Seeger was choking, eyes bulbous. He was a toddler locked in his father's arms. Abe tightened his grip around Seeger's tiny belly but seemed to move in slow motion. Instead of the quick one-two! of the Heimlich they'd learned in Health, it seemed in dream-logic to be some sort of long, meditative adjustment.

"Seeger, I know this ain't nice . . . but you know sometimes you gotta have something bad . . . to stop something worse . . . later."

Seeger wheezed, an explosion in his chest unable to escape. He waggled his arms furiously, drooling.

Abraham's face crinkled and reddened. "OK, OK, OK!" he hissed, giving Seeger a rough shake. Seeger thrashed about like a baby merman in a net.

"Seeger, now you know what happens when you eat so much, gobble-gobble little turkey? Maybe someday something eat you up! A big, green dragon! He eats little boys . . . puppy-dog tails!"

Abe yipped like a dog, shaking Seeger by the waist. Seeger huffed and puffed, making noises like a clogged drain.

"Snap go the dragons!" Abraham barked back. "Snap! Snap!"

He tossed Seeger up in the air. Seeger floated, twisting and somersaulting like a skydiver, for what seemed like hours. His father caught him deftly in one palm, face down. He tapped Seeger's back with the other palm: Shave and a haircut . . .

Gag-gag!

Abe lifted his palm and flipped Seeger like a pancake. Seeger looked up curiously into Abe's face. "Wheeze-wheeze," he said delicately.

"Time for ancient family remedy," Abe said in a hokey Fu Manchu accent.

He stuck his large fingers into Seeger's mouth and pushed his jaw open. He bent over, still balancing Seeger in one palm, and covered his son's mouth with his own. Seeger felt an intense sucking, an implosion, as if his lungs were collapsing. Abe's gasp was loud like a roar as he pulled the air out of Seeger.

With a sudden *pop,* the cracker ripped out of Seeger's throat. Abe turned to the side and spit it out, *ptui.*

Seeger gurgled happily. Abe spit on his two fingers and rubbed the saliva over Seeger's raw lips and mouth.

Doorbell. Seeger bolted awake, squinting at harsh afternoon sun slitting through the blinds. He tried to catch the fading dream. What had that been all about? Joan had once said something about him choking as a baby, and Abe had something to do with it, but . . . had it really happened like that? The dream's colors had been garish and oversaturated, just like in the choking safety films they'd shown in sixth grade Science—

Doorbell, doorbell. "Fuck off," he muttered, closing the blinds. The bell continued. Maybe it was Kent, he thought. Maybe he's just getting out of school. Seeger hadn't called him, but he held out hope that Kent might reappear.

Seeger swaddled himself in a sheet and crawled from bed. "Hold on, hold on!" he shouted. He struggled with the crotchety doorlatch.

He flashed on struggling with his grandparents' doorlatch one night when he was young and Joan and Peepaw had been screaming at each other:

Joan had told Seeger to run to the car and wait for her, but he couldn't open the door. He'd heard her call Peepaw a drunk. He called her a bitch. Interspersed among his panic, he'd worried about whether or not Joan would remember their unfinished Kentucky Fried Chicken in its Bicentennial bucket. He'd finally given up on the door, slapping his hand against it. The futile protest left him feeling girlish and melodramatic as he'd contemplated his sticky palmprint over the swirls of dark woodgrain.

"What?" he barked as the door swung free.

Hot, dusty air swept into the house. A young girl, no more than eight, jerked up her head. Freckled brows knitted between blunt bangs and tight pigtails. She thrust out a white box.

"Wanna buy some candy?" she shouted.

"Uh, for who?" Seeger stammered, taken aback.

"For me!"

"No." They glared at each other. She grunted and spun around, pigtails flying. She marched down the sidewalk. Gleefully, she kicked the loose decorative rocks in the yard, battering black pumice against the cacti.

Seeger sighed and grabbed the mail: his last paycheck from Eva in a gingham-print envelope, more legal shit, junk for his parents, more letters from Rhonda's church, the *Dallas Gay Times* he'd subscribed to over the phone. He flipped it over. The door slammed behind him, sealing in the AC. Seeger threw the mess onto a nearby moving box. Still no word from Joan.

A familiar calligraphy caught his eye on a gray marbled envelope. He reached back into the mail. A letter from Cordelia. The first he'd heard from her since she'd gone to L.A. two weeks before. He set the letter down. He walked into the kitchen. He grabbed a ginger ale from the fridge. He walked back to the living room. He sat atop a box of Rhonda's shoes for the church's Ladies Auxiliary. He felt the need to brace himself.

He opened the envelope with trepidation, fearing that his gut feeling would be proven correct and he'd lose the comfort of doubt. He wasn't afraid of what she'd say but knew it would mark another stage in closing this phase of his life. The solitude he'd longed for after his parents' death was at last dawning, but the accompanying responsibility made him nervous.

Chalky sand, silver glitter, and a black plastic palm tree spilled from the envelope. The familiar handwriting cascaded across the pages with artfully wrought curls and flourishes. Tiny cartoons and asides filled the margins.

Dearest Seeger—

L.A. is quite chic, as I'd dreamed, but in a rather strange way. Most people and buildings are horrid, exactly the David Lee Roth Bikini-Poppin' Babe sort of thing you'd imagine. But the city's glamour isn't in its aesthetic so much as its energy (a new concept for me, I must say). Everyone is so driven and focused, working and doing things. It's a tremendous thrill and exactly what I need.

[Illustration: Wide-eyed portable phone with determined grin. Caption: Go! Go! Go! Go-go-a-go-go!]

All of our gallivanting adventures this past year have been an essential part of my life, which I know I will draw on for years, as I hope you will. Perhaps a ceiling mural of Sam Houston Park? A series of frescoes dedicated to the twelve Stations of our Torturing Sam?

Speaking of men who should be tortured, I've severed ties with Mr. Bob Eisenstein. Never trust anyone with a Russian filmmaker for a last name. I'll spare you the details until our first bicoastal rendezvous, but suffice to know for now I am making it on my own here. The only thing I'll give Bob credit for is, he really did know people out here. I met a few who I think are actually real people. We actually 'Did Lunch' when I first got here. I met an assistant casting something-or-other, and a modeling agent!

Bob turned out to be worse than a pornographer or rapist; he was just a boob. But I'm fine; I viewed him merely as a flimsy excuse to visit L.A., but I now I'm here to stay! North Texas State can kiss my fine ass; and thankfully I've gotten over that Religious Studies delusion. I may have to briefly return to the nightmare of restaurant hostessing, but the agent I met last week said it's standard for agents to support their clients on advances, so I don't need to worry about working a job for too long, just until I decide on an agent.

I hope the East Coast Sodom proves equally fabulous for you. I'm sure we will somehow manage a bicoastal Factory for our Andy and Edie; isn't that more fitting for the approaching nineties, anyway?

I still marvel at our enchanted existence, that these opportunities open up for both of us and that we didn't have to go through some awful boyfriend/girlfriend "breakup" thing. Ugh! I am so glad we have our exclusive brand of paradise-ical insanity at odds with the world's mundane insanity. I know, even though we're on opposite coasts (of course, making it now

mandatory that we jet-set), we shall maintain our bizarre bond.
I see us, years from now, meeting in Milan to shop for fish-shaped
wine bottles, and making our lovers insanely jealous!
I love you dearly and will keep you up-to-date on my fame.
Despite the endless health craze, everyone drinks like fishes here,
so I frequently quaff beverages blue in your honor. I hope you
find all that you want and need in your Life Nouveau in York
Nouveau. Please let me kneau.
                    Breathlessly, Cordelia

He folded the letter. It felt unreal to him, like a short story someone else wrote. He put it back in its envelope. He sat on the floor, listening to a grackle squawking out in the backyard. He sniffed the envelope: clean paper. He looked about for the nearest box labeled NEW YORK. He slid the envelope between the cardboard flaps.

His stomach growled. He looked in the kitchen and thought of nachos. That was fun for a big group but kind of pathetic on your own. He pictured Rhonda happily assembling the snacks for one of Abraham's football Sundays, when the other male teachers and coaches from school came over. He remembered Rhonda's smearing canned bean dip across individual nacho cheese–flavored tortilla chips, making motherly inquiries of Seeger:

"So Cordelia and Sam broke up?" she'd queried.

"Mm-hm," Seeger had replied, adding slices of co-jack cheese chip by chip behind her. "I think it's a good thing 'cause they were, like, always fighting."

"Mm-hm . . ." Rhonda had nodded. "So does she have a new boyfriend?"

"I don't think so."

Rhonda had set the bean dip can in the sink and rinsed off the knife. She'd handed Seeger a jar of sliced, pickled jalapeños to wrest the lid off. He'd frowned and twisted till it popped. Vinegar fumes had tickled his nose. Smiling, he'd handed it back to her.

"You want me to leave some plain for you?" she'd said. Seeger had wrinkled his nose and nodded. He'd eaten a slice of cheese thoughtfully, watching her top the nachos with the peppers. While being broiled, the jalapeño cross sections would burn pale white shadows into the melted cheese. Seeger always picked them off, but they left behind creamy ghosts, spicy memories, the stains retaining enough potent juice to hurt.

"So you thinking of asking Cordelia out?" she'd said plainly. She'd slid the tray under the broiler's flames.

"What?!" Seeger had hopped down off the counter. "Rhon-da!"

"Well, y'all spend so much time together—"

"That's just for school stuff or when we all go out in a group . . . ," he'd protested.

"Seeg, you're blushing!" Rhonda had smiled proudly and dried her hands on a dishtowel. "You two do like each other."

"Wha . . . uh, but . . . oh, good grief," Seeger had sighed and stuffed another slice of cheese into his mouth, concentrating on the soothing, curdled lactate.

No more. Rhonda was gone. Even though the summer's biggest news was now the oldest, the simple fact that they were gone still startled Seeger. He'd felt guilty throwing out Abraham's musk oil, Rhonda's feminine spray. Things he couldn't give away or use himself. He couldn't help fearing they'd show up, angry over their missing toiletries.

Seeger missed Rhonda. A simple, direct emotion twisted inside him. Her direct affection, her pure faith had always been reassuring somehow, regardless of how much Seeger had disagreed with it. Her trust in the Bible and its words were as unquestionable as her love for him. It was dependable and regular, a rare commodity in Seeger's life. He missed her. He wanted to call out to her from the other room, to pick up a phone, to write a letter or—

No, that's too ridiculous. That was one thing he'd never done, never even considered. Joan may have communicated with shrubbery and seen fauns and assessed whether people had been possessed by aliens; she'd studied the histories of the lost continents of Atlantis and Lumeria (where man and animals had fallen in love and mated to create centaurs and other new creatures); she'd searched for UFOs and dodged the Men in Black and geared up for the Earth's polar tilt; but the most common and traditional supernatural practice—communicating with the dead—she'd never attempted, as far as he knew. Maybe she considered it below her, sideshow sensationalism. She had talked a few times about being visited by spirits of dead relatives. And Janis Joplin.

Seeger had no idea how to go about it: none of that crystal ball and Victorian claptrap. It'd probably be just like doing any other reading—

"Jesus fucking Christ!" he sighed aloud and shook the thought from his head. Get real. He surveyed the room.

The emptiness grew around him like a solid thing: the packed moving boxes and plastic-wrapped furniture stacked on end. He slept on a sleeping bag unrolled between a dresser Isaac's younger brother was supposed to come pick up and some bookshelves for the church. His friends and school peers were disappearing to new jobs and colleges. Their calls, and those of family, coworkers, and churchgoers—all had tapered off. Enough time had passed. People felt reassured that Seeger could take care of himself, was beyond comfort, didn't need reminding. There'd probably be disapproving talk of Cordelia's leaving him, but talk of Cordelia had scarcely ever been anything but disapproving.

His physical and emotional landscape changed; now he only longed for the atmosphere to change as well: the thick muggy air, alternating with sterile air-conditioning. These were the inhales and exhales of Texas. Seeger longed for a cold, gray, dry environment to match how he felt inside. The anonymity of the city's crowd, like in Mexico. A school where nobody knew anything about him or his family.

Seeger slumped down off the box onto the carpet, kicking his feet up against half-packed boxes. He reached into one of his, not his parents', belongings labeled 82–83 and pulled out an oversized postcard from Joan. The front was a photo of a Mexican-American mural featuring a bold, iconic collage: the Virgin de Guadalupe, a lineup of proud Hispanic workers from many fields, a dollar bill, the United Farm Workers' bird symbol, an Aztec calendar, and a large, central image of a skeleton in full *vaquero* garb, sneaking along, bent over, rifle in hand. "MECHA mural, student artists directed by Sergio O'Cadiz," read the caption, "Santa Ana College, Rancho Santiago Community College District; Preston Mitchell, photographer." Joan's handwriting on the back: "Eddie finally died. July/Aug. better for your visit than June. We'll be living in Austin." No signature.

Speaking of family. Seeger sighed and shook his head. He didn't remember the card. He'd always filed them right after reading. He reached in for another: a letter on the back of a green YMCA summer camp flyer.

> *... it was a small but beautiful wedding in his uncle's garden. I just wish you could've been there. Ray-Daniel is real excited to meet you and take us all hunting at Christmas.*

Seeger wondered where that picture was now, the three of them awkwardly attempting a family portrait around a strung-up doe carcass. He'd endured the hunting expedition stoically, like his annual dental visit. Ray-Daniel was a pure-blooded redneck, and nearly everything he'd said or done had irritated Seeger. Seeger had enjoyed smug satisfaction when they'd divorced the following spring.

The phone jangled through the still house. Seeger knew it was Joan. He grabbed the receiver with mixed fear and relief. He hadn't heard from her in weeks, not since the message the night of LaTonia's party and of Kent. He hadn't had any visions, either. He'd tried to invoke them, but none came.

"Hey there, Seeger?" inquired a sharp, quavering voice.

"Hi, Meemaw," he said with surprise.

"How are you getting along?"

"I'm OK." Seeger leaned against the kitchen island and stretched the cord across his chest. "There's just still tons of packing and sorting to be done around here."

"You know I feel plumb wretched I couldn't stay up there with you, I—"

"I know, that's totally OK."

"—I fret about you all alone up there now."

"Oh, really, it's not that bad," he said. "Uncle Russ stayed here a long time. Rhonda's family brought tons of food; they only live about hour and a half away—"

"They're right good people, they are."

"My friends all check in on me." The words echoed in the empty house.

"Now, you heard anything from your mama?" she ventured carefully.

"Ah, no."

"Well, now. That ain't right."

"She called about the time of the funeral and said she was moving."

"Yeah, now, she was fixing to blow her top last time we talked, when I wouldn't give her no attorney power. She just took herself off and left."

Seeger sat at the kitchen table. "She didn't say anything to me about that. She said, she said that, um . . . you thought maybe she was trying to steal something—"

"Oh, Lordy, that girl. I never said no such thing." Seeger frowned.

190

"So you don't know nothing about where she's got to?" his grandmother asked. "Haven't heard nothing?"

Why am I protecting her? he thought indignantly. "She said"—he licked his lips, embarrassed. Jesus, this is my mother we're talking about—"I think she said something about an Indian reservation. I don't know. I was half asleep. I wasn't really paying attention."

"An Indian reservation?"

"Yeah. So maybe it's out West somewhere—"

"She did live a spell out in Santa Fe once. Seem to recall there's an Apache reservation out by way of Alamogordo."

Seeger felt a hunger pain. He craved Winchell's doughnuts, a dozen, apple fritters and long johns. "I may still have those old addresses," he said. "And she may've mentioned friends and neighbors in old letters. Actually, I was right in the middle of going through all those when you called—"

"Would you, now, hon, see what all you can find? I been digging through my mess of stuff but haven't found nothing hereabouts."

"I'll let you know whatever I find."

"Oh, hon, bless you. Well, now"—her voice took on a gracious tone—"I know you got lots to do—"

"I'll send you copies—"

"Yeah, I know you will, hon. Now, this is long distance so I'll—"

Seeger started, Joan's call flashed in his memory like a dream suddenly recalled with stark acuity during breakfast. "Oh! Meemaw! There's something else."

"What now?"

"I think she may be, uh, pregnant." Deep silence.

"This gets a might serious, then," she said. Her voice sank through him, the weight of generations scarred in its gentle undulations, like erosion floes across a boulder. Seeger realized that his grandmother was not . . . doddering.

"Yeah," he said weakly. "I'll let you know if I find anything."

"Seeger, hon, I don't know if I should be telling you about this. Hell, but I got me a feeling. Listen, hon: long time ago, when I first brought your mama home from the hospital as a baby, I was still mighty weak. Your mama was a hard birthing, and I'd done lost a good amount of blood. Your mama, she was fine, she slept happy and quiet-like, like her worrying was all over. I was plumb exhausted but I couldn't sleep. Your Peepaw had to work that night on the railroad, my first night back

191

home. I'd put your mama down in her crib and I was getting me some milk and corn mush to try and get myself sleepy. I was warming the milk when I heard this rustling and snuffling out near the kitchen door. We were renting this little cottage-house then, and the kitchen had a backdoor that opened out on to a field, on the other side was the tracks, and then other side of that there was Niggertown. I cracked the door and looked out. We weren't afraid of as much in those days, hell, the door was probably unlocked. I was just thinking some dog maybe got loose from Niggertown, but there was this javelina out there, this mama javelina. She looked up at me all scared when I opened the door, but she didn't run off. She just grunted and stood her ground, right there a couple feet from the backdoor. Her face was all bloody, and she looked like she'd been in a bad fight, maybe with some dog or something. You know how mean those wild pigs can be. Well, I looked down and there beside the door she'd been digging in the dirt at the side our house. She'd been digging in the dirt and there, next to it, was a dead baby javelina she'd drug up like she was going to bury it or hide it or something. Whatever fight she'd been in, she'd won, 'cause she was alive, but she'd lost most of all because she'd lost her baby, and that's everything to a mama.

"Here I was feeling like I'd just survived a battle with this awful birthing, but I had my baby with me, alive. And this other mama was coming to show me that you can lose battles, too. She was showing me you can lose your children. I just shut the door and soon I heard her grunting around back there. I never told no one about it. I don't know why I'm telling you now, I just—maybe you already know this, but I've always felt like there was something wild in your mama, and someday that wildness might decide to take her back. I always felt like someday she might not be around. I don't mean dead, I mean just gone. I'm not trying to scare you, hon; Lord knows, you been through enough. I think that's why I'm telling you this now. You can't afford not to know everything, the whole truth, even if part of that truth is made from an old lady's crazy superstitions."

Seeger breathed heavily. "No," he said. "I understand."

Seeger put up the phone. He felt haunted, as if Joan and her visions had died, disappeared from his life, only to have their ghost step in to fill the void, in the form of Joan's mother. Would there always be someone loading his scales with supernatural weight? He stood in the middle of the kitchen, hugging himself. He craved a chart, an outline, a grid from which to start a painting. Something clean and linear, like the Texan plains, horizon, sky. He made himself a drink and ate slices of bread. He pulled out address books and old boxes of letters. He unpacked. He copied down every different return address he found from his mother. Several additional locales he could only find in his memories. He added them to the list. He broke for a dinner of fishsticks with Mexi-Velveeta on top. He made another drink. He took the master list and transferred all the addresses to a new one, arranging them in chronological order. He transferred the final list onto a large sheet of drawing paper.

Seeger stabbed a thumbtack into the study wall. He left sticky fingerprints of milk, Kahlúa, and vodka on the floral wallpaper. He stepped back to survey his results, softly trampling envelopes. In skewed, black oil pastel, the list read:

> 2/75: 836 W. Mockingbird, Dallas, TX 75206
> 10/76: 905 Eldorado, Austin, TX 78703
> 1/77: Pecan Grove Trailer Park #43, 1518 Guadalupe Rd.,
> San Marcos, TX
> ?: (San Angelo, TX—adobe house near water tower)
> 3/77: 3231 Cibola Ln., New Braunfels, TX zip?
> 8/77: 1301 Mission St., Galveston, TX 77550
> 9/77: 3813 Karankawa, Abilene, TX zip?
> 10/77: 1630 Frontier Ridge, Houston, TX 77009
> 1/78: H.C.R. #43, Portland, TX 78374
> 5/78: c/o Luke Cardinal, P.O. Box 6220, Santa Fe, NM
> 87502
> ?: (that place in Pecos)
> 8/79: 624 Berman, Port Arthur, TX 77640 (Meemaw's
> house)
> 10/79: 513 Church, Agua Dulce, TX zip?
> ?: (Corpus Christi apt. across from dopehead house
> where we watched *Last Picture Show*)

He stopped, startled by the phone. He waited for the answering machine.

"Seeg, it's Tonia. Look, I know you're there, so pick up, OK? Seeg, man! OK, OK, cool. You're probably all busy packing. But I know you leave for New York soon, so don't pull some spook trip and disappear on me, OK? You might be all freaked right now, but you're gonna come out of this and then you'll want to blab. You don't want to get me all pissed 'cause you blanked out on me for months, now, right? Right. So here's my number at school *again,* 'cause you probably didn't write it down last two times: 617-555-1435. Call me."

Seeger had the number securely written down in pen inside the leather address book he'd gotten at graduation, sitting out in his pile of immediate-access stuff to put in his backpack when he left for New York. He wouldn't call her until after he got there. He wanted to wait until he'd escaped Execution and begun his new life, with new stories to tell. He looked back at the wall.

    1/80: 1028 N. Alamo, Rockport, TX 78382

    6/80: 624 Berman, Port Arthur, TX 77640 (back at
           Meemaw's)

  10/80: 509 Zephyr Pl., Austin, TX 78705

     ?: (Shared house in Galveston with female roommate
          and all those cats)

    9/81: 2201 Zapata, Austin, TX 78704

  12/81: 2529 S. Lamar, Del Valle, TX 78617

     ?: (Crystal City, TX, trailer park where you pass the
          house from *Giant* driving out there)

    8/82: 910 Spur St. #2, Corpus Christi, TX 78411

    2/83: 9320 S. Padre #1902, Corpus Christi, TX 78411

     ?: (Texas City apt. near drugstore with tipi out front)

    4/83: P.O. Box 242, Ingleside, TX 78362

  10/83: 624 Berman, Port Arthur, TX 77640 (Meemaw
          again)

  11/83: 305-C South Ranger St., Fulton, TX 78358

    6/84: P.O. Box 1891, Wimberly, TX 78676

    9/84: 7802 E. Longhorn Dr. N, Fort Worth, TX zip?

    9/84: Bluebonnet Park 22-202, 1501 35th Ave. W., Fort
          Worth, TX zip?

  10/84: #212-T, Vista Apts., 250 N. Bison St., Fort Worth,
          TX zip?

    2/85: 2034 Sentinel, Corpus Christi, TX 78418

    4/85: 624 Berman, Port Arthur, TX 77640 (Meemaw)

    9/85: #81 Rolling W.N.H. Ranch, 1600 W. Johnson,
          Kingsville, TX 78363

    1/86: 2420 S. Rustlers Way #606, Kingsville, TX 78363

9/86: 624 Berman, Port Arthur, TX 77640 (Meemaw)

2/87: 10507 Seminole, San Antonio, TX 78213

3/87: c/o Luke Cardinal (again) P.O. Box 4532,
Sweetwater, TX zip?

6/87: 624 Berman, Port Arthur, TX 77640 (Meemaw)

7/87: Indian Reservation? NM?

He'd type Meemaw a clean copy, with relevant possibilities high-lighted in yellow. He looked back up at the top of the list: 2/75: 836 W. Mockingbird, Dallas, TX 75206.

That had been Joan's first place after the divorce. She'd immediately left Execution. Seeger had gone with her. Seeger had helped her move in. They'd lived together a few months, until she'd decided it would be better for Abraham to have custody. Seeger had gone back to Execution, joining Abe at the Alamo Family Apartments.

Seeger sipped his drink and fell into an extended daydream about that time with Joan, when the list began:

Seeger had flown higher. Stiff peaks and valleys had loomed close, yearning to scratch his succulent cheeks, those unblemished hills of breathy pink. Shiny specks had glistened among the crags, elusively buried like mica, eye-catching and glittery like glass. The reflective flakes in the craggy ceiling stucco had looked like stars.

He'd landed on the couch cushions and crouched into a deep squat, hoping to increase his apogee with a more powerful takeoff. The crouching had offset his center of gravity, and he lost balance. Feet sliding out beneath him, he'd tumbled off the couch and into the surrounding ocean of cushions he'd made for exactly this inevitability. Carly Simon had skipped a verse on his mom's turntable. One cushion had absorbed his impact, others had slid across the slick hardwood floor until hitting moving boxes.

"Seeger?" Joan had called from her bedroom. "You OK?"

"I'm fine," he'd reassured her.

"OK," she'd said, distant and preoccupied. "Oh—if you're going to jump, set up some pillows so you don't hurt yourself."

Seeger had contemplated the cushions around him. "OK, Joan," he'd called back. "Good idea."

He'd picked at a cushion's upholstery like a scab. He'd dug his long thumbnail under the raised pea-green texture. It hadn't come off. The milky canvas with raised green puffs had reminded him of frozen peas with pearl onions. Wonder if Joan'll make me eat those now? he'd thought. Maybe she only made them for Abraham. Maybe she thinks they're yukky, too. That'd be fun.

He'd hopped up, surveying his scene. He'd stretched a socked foot to a cushion and pulled it toward him. I could stack them in a tower, he'd thought. But I might want to jump again. I could stack all the cushions on top the couch and jump off that—

A bell had rung. He'd turned his head and frowned. Again, a loose jangle. He'd tiptoed across the floor and poked his head around the corner. He'd peered into his mom's room. She'd balanced precariously on a woven cane chair, stretching out lithe and gangly like a stork. She'd been trying to hang a chain above the window. Three crooked pieces of metal linked together, with a chunky bell hanging from the bottom. It had been brackish green, like the dirty toilets at the city playgrounds here in Dallas.

"Where'd that come from?" he'd asked.

His mom had stepped down. "From my friend Tom," she'd replied. "Remember Tom from the college? He took us to see *Blazing Saddles?* With the farting cowboys?"

Seeger had nodded. Tom was younger than Abraham, probably younger than Joan, with little round glasses and big, curly cinnamon hair.

Joan had crossed her arms and frowned. "He made it," she'd explained.

"It's metal?"

"Yeah, it's bronze. I think, or something like that."

"How'd he make metal?"

"Well, he probably just bought the metal, got it real hot so it melted, then poured it into a mold, let it cool and then . . . I guess"—she'd reached out and grabbed the bell brusquely, inspecting it—"he painted it or used acid or something to give it this patina."

"Oh," Seeger had said, losing interest. He'd looked around the room: wire hangers and books, open boxes spilling out tangles of earrings, scarves, eight-track tapes, fortune-telling cards.

"I thought I'd set out a few fun things," she'd explained. She'd dug into a milk crate and removed a tiny china dish topped with a fat, grinning Buddha. "I'm too tired to put up any more stuff today." She'd fished around more and recovered a small tin of incense cones.

"It's so boring, anyway," she'd said, striking a match.

"Want me to make you a drink?" Seeger had offered.

"Oh, no," she'd said, waving out the match. She blew on the cone till it glowed.

"Didn't you like the one I made you before?"

She'd set the cone in the dish, sulfurous smoke circling her head. She'd smiled and shaken her head. "No," she'd said. "There's more to making a drink than just throwing a bunch of liquors together."

He'd nodded. Joan had climbed back up on the chair. He'd wandered into the living room. He'd crawled onto the couch and hung upsidedown off its edge. Joan had walked in. Vanilla smoke had crept in behind her, mixing with the crusty Frito smell of the floor.

"Can I listen to *Really Rosie?*" he'd asked her.

"Or you wanna go out and get a smoothie?"

"I don't know."

Fresh magnolia had breezed in through the window screens, the thick floral musk charging the room. Seeger had looked up, which felt like down. He'd watched dust particles spiral in the overripe light of late afternoon, maelstroms from his mom's passage through their space. A new generation had flown up and around as she'd sat beside him on the couch, oblivious as to how her movements had ripped apart their universe. She'd tapped his belly with her fingernail and sang, "Net-net nah, net-net nah." It was how she'd imitated the dancing mice in the old *Flip the Frog* cartoons, something they'd always laughed about. But it had been hard to laugh upsidedown.

Watching the floating dust, Seeger had thought of Dr. Seuss's *Horton Hears a Who!,* a story about an entire world that existed on a dustspeck and no one knew of it except Horton the Elephant. To prove he was crazy and shouldn't care about dust, his jungle friends had tried to drown the dustspeck in boiling oil.

"Boil that dustspeck! Boil that dustspeck," they'd chanted, giving Seeger quite a scare. He'd always wondered, if it were true, should he look for the dustworlds and take care of them? Or should he just go about his life and ignore them, like how the planets and stars went about their business in space, ignorant of their effects on our lives? Joan had taught Seeger about astrology; he knew his sun sign was Capricorn and he was a leader.

"Net-net nah, net-net nah," she'd sung. "We'll have such fun parties living together." She'd looked up at the sparkling ceiling of stars, motionless far above. Seeger had watched a tiny cinder from the incense drift down past his face. It had ignited the upholstery, creating a tiny burning circle. The circle had grown.

Seeger bolted from the kitchen table, realizing he wasn't the only one with files on Joan. His father had kept a file on the divorce. Seeger had glimpsed it when Abraham had pulled him a copy of his birth certificate for the trip to Mexico. Maybe that file held more addresses, new information on his mother. Seeger had no idea.

He stumbled into his parents' old bedroom, past the sheets still stained from his night with Kent, and into their closet. The black file cabinet, wedged around boxes of shoes and ties, was locked. Seeger had seen a keyring mixed in with rings and bolo ties in the dresser and packed it in JEWELRY. He fished it out and unlocked the drawers. Although he'd already sorted through and packed most of their effects, he still felt furtive, as if snooping through his father's *Playboys*.

Seeger shoved aside medical files, old report cards. Mortgages, repair receipts for the truck and car. Stuck unceremoniously midway through the bottom shelf he found DIVORCE. He opened the file: it held only several copies of the final divorce papers. Nothing else.

Seeger reached back behind the files and felt some solid objects. He yanked out the files—they'd have to get boxed up, anyway—and peered into the back of the drawer.

The tin stashbox held a treat for later; Seeger hadn't been very successful drying out what was left in the garden. The vibrator was a slim, featureless model—batteries still worked. Seeger was excited at first, having something to jack off with besides kitchen utensils, but he thought about where it had been and changed his mind. Too weird. It would've been sweet if Kent had fucked him that afternoon. No, save that for New York. For his new life.

He set the stash on the carpet beside him and left the vibrator inside the file cabinet. He leaned back against the closet doorjamb. His gaze drifted around the bedroom. He spied the family portrait on their dresser. He flushed angry, imagining how his father would've reacted if he'd known about Kent, X-ing, Cordelia—everything. The moral inconsistency frustrated Seeger worst of all. Despite Abe's sidestepping religion, he'd expected a highly responsible moral code from Seeger. He thought of Abraham's libertine sexuality during the year between divorcing Joan and marrying Rhonda: the porn lying around the apartment and, in later years, his allowing Seeger to watch British comedies and R-rated movies despite Rhonda's protestations. But at the same time, he'd chased Seeger into his bedroom, shouting at him, when Seeger had accidentally walked in on Abraham and Rhonda having sex. He'd sniffed Seeger for traces of the pot from their own backyard. If only he'd been regularly liberal and rational. Joan let Seeger do what he wanted, but he ended up parenting *her* half the time. If only she could be magical but not crazy. Rhonda had been the least open-minded of his three parents, yet strangely the most open-hearted. Seeger had always known that she would ultimately understand and forgive whatever truth came out.

You'd think between the three of them, I could've been myself with *someone*. Big fucking deal, another part of him said. They were fuckups like you.

He closed the file cabinet and stood up, stretching his stiff arms and legs.

He wanted to feel angry at his parents but couldn't. He wanted to rebel, but between the three of them, they covered all the bases. There was no direction for him to go in. He'd go North, become a Yankee, and see where that led him. The least he could do was get away from them, their land, their country.

He flicked the closet light off and shut the door. He loped into the kitchen for a new drink. The clock on the stove ticked loudly. 10:45. He wondered if he should eat more. He opened the pantry. Just about the only thing left on the liquor shelf was Irish Cream. What the fuck d'you drink with Irish cream? Must be for Irish coffees. Seeger eyed the Mr. Coffee. He loved the morning smell, but coffee tasted like tree bark. He shuddered, remembering an endless demitasse of espresso he'd ordered once to impress Cordelia. A hot drink sounded terrible—the night had not relinquished the day's muggy heat as it progressed. Seeger had the AC on but knew the heat was out there nevertheless. He was getting woozy, though. If he wanted to stay up, he'd have to go to the store for cokes, and there wasn't anything left to mix with that. But coffee, Irish Cream might go in coffee, maybe ice coffee, blended, even: a frothy Irish café au lait–shake kind of thing. Enough milk, sugar, and Irish Cream should make anything taste bearable, right? He dumped in the Hills Brothers and waited at the kitchen table as it brewed.

The liquor shelf was hollowing out, he worried. He'd have to try and buy some himself, with Cordelia gone. He balked at the stereotype: hanging out underneath the two-story neon cowboy at Big Tex liquors, flirting with grizzled old men to buy him a fifth.

He blinked and would've smoothed his tie if wearing one. Of course, he'd do exactly that, he thought. He'd do whatever was necessary to get what he needed. Pride and glamour were lovely but irrelevant. The burst of crystal-clear pragmatism, its irrefutable simplicity, reminded him of Abe. His father echoed inside him. In some perverse way—no, not even perverse, merely atypical—he felt Abraham would've been proud.

His mood darkened like a filter popped over a lens. He wouldn't see the pride in Abraham's eyes. Unless he tried to contact him.

Seeger rolled his eyes, shook his head. He paced around the kitchen, self-conscious of looking like a bad actor emoting "Struggling with a Decision." Mr. Coffee gurgled and uttered a final, satisfied *plink*.

Why not? No one would know. He felt uneasy, remembering the crash visions, the angelrat. No one was here to help if things got heavy. But then again, no one had ever helped him before with these things. His parents were already dead, so there shouldn't be any visions like that; and he wasn't taking any drugs, so he should be able to maintain reality. Maybe that's what the choking dream had been; maybe Abe was trying to contact him from the other side . . .

No, I *can't* . . .

The blender's scream stood out, glaringly incongruous in the September night silence. That mechanical whine was a summer sound, one of fresh margaritas and daiquiris. ("That's a virgin batch for the kids," Abraham had assured Rhonda, but they certainly hadn't tasted chaste.) The sound meant whirling junebugs underfoot, purple martins swooping through the air in mosquito-hunt. The incense of acrid lighter fluid, sweet melting fat, and roast corn blending in the BBQ's censer. These all comprised the milieu of a blender's whine. The house smelled of dust and Endust's lemony chemicals. The burble and chitter of backyard cookouts had become the thundering silence of an empty tract house, wood paneling reflecting silent moonlight, palmetto bugs tickling across the stainless-steel sink, and the air-conditioner's protective, sterile roar.

Seeger poured out his drink, stared at the creamy mix. The house was quiet and he was alone. OK.

He turned and opened the kitchen junk drawer, one of the things he was waiting till the very last minute to pack. He dug through rubber jar openers and chipped mushroom refrigerator magnets. He pulled out a box of six white emergency candles. He pulled out five, a power number he knew from Joan's numerology phase. He grabbed a frozen pizza's cardboard circle from the trash. A circle's powerful, he thought.

He yanked the black grease pencil off the string attached to the wipe-away shopping list magnetized to the fridge. He drew two perpendicular lines on the pizza circle, dividing it into equal quarters: the original, pre-Christian cross symbolizing the four elements. He lit a candle and dripped wax on three of the endpoints of the cross, near the very edge of the circle. In each pool of hot wax he secured a candle. He dripped two pools forty-five degrees to either side of the fourth terminating line and put candles there, so the five candles formed a pentagram, a five-sided star, Wiccan symbol, symbol of man's head, arms, and feet, like the five-sided sugar molecule found only in certain dates. He set the arrangement in the middle of the empty spot on the kitchen floor. He checked the clock. Damn, already missed midnight.

Seeger shivered despite the heat and went to put music on. He sipped his drink—not bad—beside the stereo and picked through the jumble of tapes. Debbie Harry? Pseudo Echo? No, none of that inane happy dance shit. That's not right for a seance. God, there's tons of it. Bananarama? Ugh, don't want to drive them away. Something relaxing, serious, but not too distracting. Tape after tape of Marc: *Soft Cell Volumes I–IV,* including the *Pink Culture* bootleg of rare outtakes and live performances, *Marc and the Mambas Volumes I–III, Miscellaneous Mambas* with the *Violent Silence* live EP from the Bataille festival and the *Kickabye* EP by Annie Hogan (his longtime keyboardist), plus tapes for each of his solo albums and their related singles, EPs, and B-sides—*Vermin in Ermine, Stories of Johnny, Mother Fist,* and, of course, an all-occasion *Miscellaneous Marc Faves* tape. Seeger traced his fingertip along the side of *Soft Cell Volume II,* with its pink and rust cover he'd drawn with map pencils in geography class, approximating the inner sleeve of the *The Art of Falling Apart* album from memory. He felt fond and protective of the Marc tapes, their chronological precision, their discographic thoroughness, the rarities lovingly washed and deionized to reduce static before being committed to high-bias Maxell tapes so he would rarely risk scratches to the actual vinyl. In New York he could get a new stereo with a compact disc player and begin replacing as many of them as possible (could you even get Marc on CD?) with those indestructible things. They said you could bury them in the backyard and not hurt them.

Seeger tapped his fingers on the cassette cases. He hadn't been able to bring himself to listen to Marc for weeks. There'd been enough real emotion in his life. He eyed his parents' tapes: James Taylor's *Dad Loves His Work,* Carly Simon's *Torch.* Maybe that would help him connect with them, plus they're real relaxing. He read over the song list: "Her Town, Too," "What Shall We Do with the Child?" No way, fuck it. Deal with the silence.

The creamy mixed drink ice-burned his throat. Grimacing, he shuddered as the throat burn synergized with his growing sugar/caffeine buzz. He poured himself a refill. He sat before the candles in the lotus position, with hands resting palms up on his knees, fingers and thumb circled in an energy-building loop.

He called on the four cardinal points and their elements. He imagined the Tower of Light protecting him. He called on any and all spirits and guides who would help him, to come to him. He prayed to God, and Jesus. He told all negative, hurtful, or disruptive spirits to stay away. He did circular breathing through his nose and mouth. He mentally repeated a positive affirmation of his innate ability to accomplish this. He visualized blackness slowly overcome by a growing white dot; whiteness slowly overcome by a growing black dot. He imagined the psychic energy coursing through his body, circling through each of the seven chakras, radiating out of his head in kundalini and stretching across the dimensions to his parents. He tried to keep his mind clear and receptive. He tried not to worry about the candles burning out or setting the cardboard on fire. He tried to feel his parents; he tried to summon them to him. He visualized them all together. He waited, relaxed, and called to them. He tried words, he tried images, he tried feelings; every language he could think of. Growing desperate, he tried to imagine the wreck, hoping a triggered vision might get him into a more altered state.

He swayed slightly, as if on a ship. A vast wave swelled up under him, washing over him, inundating his mind with a roaring black force, devoid of imagery or emotion, a huge black roar.

Seeger's head hurt. A dull, steady ache. He opened his eyes. He was on the kitchen floor, crumpled in the narrow space between boxes. He sat up. He rubbed his sore skull. Only hard, white wax remained from the candles, pooled off the cardboard. Long branches snaked across the kitchen floor like veins of Saint Augustine grass on sidewalks. Another white residue pooled in the corner: his drink had spilled and rolled away. All the ice chunks had long since melted, leaving only a sticky white film, almost like dried come.

It was pitch black. Crickets and cicadas droned. The clock on the stove read 4:34. He stood up, legs creaking. He poured himself the last of the thin, niveous liquid in the blender. He added ice. He turned back to the living room. He set his drink on the coffeetable and threw himself across the couch.

He remembered nothing, yet the air felt charged around him, thick and palpable. It wasn't the lingering emotional shadow of a dream he felt, but a much more concrete presence in the air, like steam. His skin felt prickly. He didn't feel as if he'd been asleep. All he could remember was doing his relaxation steps and waking up on the floor hours later. He had no idea if his seance had been a success or not.

He sighed with disgust. He wriggled his toes into the pile of yarn afghans at the foot of the couch. He rolled his head to the side. At eye level before him was "can wait" mail overflowing from an open packing box. Catalogs, condolence cards, bank statements, and *National Geographic* rested underneath his nose. He reached out, flipping through the envelopes. Concerned Women for America newsletter, Pat Robertson Presidential Campaign Fund—and the Baptist Missionary Service?

He hadn't caught that before. He sat up on the couch to inspect the thick legal envelope. Had they been thinking of becoming missionaries after he left home?

An ice cube numbed his upper lip as he drained the mixed-drink dregs. He ripped open the envelope, removed a stapled sheaf of papers, and set his empty glass down on the envelope. The cover letter read:

> Dear Mrs. King,
> Bless you for your recent inquiry and kind donation to our ministry. Your Pastor Wills (a devout soul I had the blessing to share fellowship with at our '85 conference) is correct in his recollection of our application processes. All applicants submit to a lengthy screening that includes, among other things, writing an autobiography.
> Enclosed are copies of our file for your husband's parents, including the autobiographies. I spoke with one of our elder deacons here who actually interviewed your in-laws. He recalled Pastor and Mrs. King as outstanding Christian brethren, full of the joy of the Spirit and spreading His Word. Deacon Hildago had been deeply saddened at the time of their death and knew that although the service had

lost two potentially great assets, the Kings had work of an even greater calling with the King of kings.

I hope you and your husband find these materials a true blessing. I must apologize on behalf of BMS that it has taken seventeen years for you to receive them! Since no requests were made following their departure, it was assumed the family already had copies of the originals.

As always, we trust in the Lord that He possesses a higher reason for waiting until now for you to get these materials. I'm sure you will find that they answer some prayer of yours, perhaps one of which you were not even aware.

God be with you,
Brother Wayne McMurtry

Seeger set down the papers. He feared reading them, making contact with the cipher of his grandparents. He tried to imagine them, real people with lives, but couldn't. He could only think of them as forces affecting others' lives.

He imagined Joan anxiously smoking a cigarette, waiting for Abraham to come home so she could tell him their Christmas had been ruined by his parents' death in a fire. Seeger would've been almost one, gurgling happily unaware, while she tried to mask her relief that the rigid preacher and his self-righteous wife were gone. The day would've been strained already; before Abraham had left for work, they'd gotten in an argument about whether or not to put out the Nativity and other specifically Christian decorations they'd never used before. Abraham wanted them for his parents' first Christmas with his new family. Maybe Seeger had even exacerbated the issue, gurgling something about Baby Jesus he'd picked up from TV or the baby-sitter. Maybe Joan had tried to balance things out, reading Seeger bedtime stories about Hanukkah and Winter Solstice. But the holiday was now a funeral, and Joan's main chore, instead of acting happy, would be to act sad.

Or maybe it was nothing like that. Seeger's grandparents had been barely mentioned by Abraham and only negatively referred to by Joan. And Joan, he reminded himself, could be wrong about many more things than previously thought.

Seeger ripped open the inner envelope and read. His caffeinated pupils jittered rapidly left to right across his grandfather's life: Small-town Texas. One-room schoolhouse. Dead parents. Wild, reckless days

as a ranch hand, getting a rancher's daughter pregnant and their marriage. Seeger had never heard of this:

> . . . the first great love of my life. I was obsessed with her,
> her wild, unpredictable nature, her spontaneous caprice, her
> tempestuous disregard for society around her. My mind con-
> stantly harbored sinful and violent thoughts.

Who was their child? What relation would he be to Seeger, a distant
uncle or aunt? There was no further mention.

> But then I met Evangeline, who brought me back to the
> Lord and changed my wild ways.

A phrase caught Seeger's eye. He stopped and read word by word:

> When Evangeline saw Jesus for the first time, he ap-
> peared to her when we were first courting. She was thinking
> of going out with some other fellow instead, and Jesus ap-
> peared to her, high in the sky at sunset. He told her my soul
> was her responsibility and that we would have a blessed and
> holy life together doing the Lord's work if she would com-
> mit to it. Next morning she invited me to her church social.
> She dedicated herself to reforming me, and the Lord's power
> flowed through her. Drinking and gambling and my wild
> ways simply lost their appeal compared with the spiritual
> richness I found with her. Six months later I told her I was
> entering the Baptist Seminary and I asked her to marry me.
> She said it was the happiest day of her life.

Seeger scanned the pages: an increasingly dull catalog of churches and
ministry positions.

> . . . tried to impress my sons with the glory of knowledge,
> the reward of passionate dedication . . .

Seeger thought of Abraham's long years working his way up in teaching, studying on weekends for his certification, dashing through the

apartment between his job at the deli and night classes. He thought of himself, studying in the A.M. for all those report cards.

> . . . in fit health for the job. Only serious hereditary conditions being the King flat feet . . .

Seeger peeked his grubby toes out from under the afghans. Guess I did all right in the genetic roulette, he thought. Beats Joan's craziness; at least I didn't get the full dose of that.

> . . . my call to God. It seemed the world blossomed around me like a rose. I became suddenly aware of so much outside my sinful self . . .

His grandmother's conversation with the Son of God was never mentioned again, nor were further miracles noted. Seeger tossed the stapled pack aside and tore into his grandmother's autobiography. Parents fighting brushfires and cattle deaths. Loss of the family farm. Uncle's conversion to Christ—damn, more preachers in her family, too. And schoolteachers: her mother had been a local teacher, too. Teenage girl watching shrimp boats on the horizon of the Gulf Coast and taking God into her heart.

> The sky was solid clouds that day, the sky and water were equally uninterrupted fields of gray. You couldn't even tell where one ended and the other began, the horizon seemed to have disappeared. I was a simple girl, fretting over which of the boys I was courting should receive my affections. My parents were sweet on one boy from a wealthy shipping family from down the coast in Fulton. He'd taken me to visit his family's mansion there once. There was another boy who I thought was most handsome. The man who would become my husband honestly was more of a trifle, someone to pass time with and keep the other boys on edge, and vex my parents. He was rough, an orphan who worked as a ranch hand and offered a girl no real prospects.
> The Gulf Breeze suddenly turned exceptionally warm and I leaned out into it, pressing against the railing on the pier so I couldn't see the boats and town behind me, so all I

saw was the vast horizon enveloping me, the limitless water and equally clear sky. The screams of the seagulls flying around me began to soften, lengthen, and change in tone until they sounded like singing, like a Heavenly Chorus. I felt a presence I know now to be the Lord surround me, fill me up. I felt a deep knowledge and wisdom in my heart—I experienced the joy and satisfaction that would come to me if I pursued a life in service to the Lord with this man. It made no sense, but I knew it to be true when a voice spoke to me, "This will be your story." The ribbons of sunlight burning through the clouds suddenly converged into the face of our Lord. Suddenly I was a Woman with a life and mission ahead of her, not a Girl full of whimsical caprice, but a Servant of the Lord with a mission in life, with a special gift and use for the world. I could change things, save souls, have a life beyond raising a fine family and maintaining my good social standing. I could change the world, one soul at a time. It was my duty, my calling. I went home to dinner, strangely aglow. When that King boy came calling that evening, I told him to come back tomorrow morning so he could come to church with my family. I never doubted for a second he'd say yes. He just looked at me strangely for a second, I smiled, and he agreed. I went to sleep that night knowing I had entered into a new life with a purpose for the Lord.

Seeger set the papers down and looked out the sliding glass doors. Lavender and fiery apricot, dawn unfurled across the sky like a divine sigh of relief. Seeger's chest loosened. He leaned back against the couch. He felt as if he were in the final scene of a movie: the camera should pull back from him in a slow dolly shot, turning up to the glorious dawn against which the credits would roll. Or he was the last in a series of paintings: him alone amid the boxes in all the different lights of the past twenty-four hours, like Monet's haystacks. The series would end with this image. If it was a novel, *dawn* would be the last word before *The End*.

He put up the letters, photos, and files he'd pulled out through the night. He took off his clothes. He drew a bath. He sat on the toilet. The churning water echoed in the room that seemed so large now. The cramped masturbation alcove had grown cavernous without Abe and

Rhonda's toiletries filling the countertop and shelves, the matching fuzzy toilet seat cover and rug given away. He sank into the scalding water, closing his eyes. He thought backward, piecing together scenes of his grandparents', his parents', and his life. A clear narrative arc had finally formed, beginning with his grandmother's vision, Abraham's rebellion, Rhonda's matter-of-fact Christianity, through Joan's mysticism, and his own premonitions. Now it was all over. His parents' death and Joan's disappearance concluded the story, a dense period on the page. He was only a minor character in the story, he realized. Like Joan, he had passed through the energies of these families and would carry them with him but, also like her, he was now leaving the stage for an independent life. It was really Abe's story—Abe, who, in a way, had known of his own impending death. Abe, who connected all the major characters. Abe was the focal point. The lines of single-point perspective all converged on Abe. Abe, who was gone. Someone would have to write his story for him.

Seeger looked back on the story with forced detachment. He tried to gauge its content like one of Abe's reading assignments for class or a sample text on a skills-assessment test at school. He tried to distill the narrative, to extract its main idea. His penis shriveled and fingers and toes wrinkled as the water grew cold.

Leaving Texas

Seeger leaned back into his seat on the plane and closed his eyes. His Walkman was in his backpack, *Miscellaneous Marc Faves* cued up to "Torch" (twelve-inch mix) at the start of side one, but there would be plenty of time for that later. He didn't feel his usual anxiety to have constant auditory distraction, enhancement of the mundane. He wanted to be in the moment.

He listened to the murmurs around him, the underlying turbines' roar. The plane banked to the left, then leveled off. The captain announced their cruising altitude and anticipated arrival time at La Guardia.

Seeger pushed up the shade on his window. Farmland quilts slipped by beneath him. The plane pushed forward relentlessly, leaving Seeger's friends and family—Kent and Isaac, Meemaw—far below him in Texas. The jet soared off in the opposite direction of Manifest Destiny and the westward expansion. I'd like to return this Louisiana Purchase, please. You have your receipt?

Seeger's new life was exactly in the opposite direction of Cordelia's, most likely also opposite of Joan's latest camp. At least he and LaTonia would still be in the same time zone, close enough to visit, a short trek from New York to Boston. Abe had once warned Seeger to take his high school friendships with a grain of salt; they rarely survived separate colleges or major moves. Abe said he'd lost touch with all his friends who had left Execution. Distance and transition change people, rewrote their personalities. But maybe he and LaTonia would change in the same direction, since they were moving to sort of the same places: big Yankee cities.

Seeger blinked as the plane broke through clouds into raw sunlight. He squinted at the glare off the thick clouds, a solid blanket below. They looked edible. He peered out at the white below, pure and unblemished like a blank page.

Water vapor, he thought. He blinked.

Angels. He blinked.

Faeries. He closed his eyes, rubbed them. He could hear the squeaking of fluids. He opened his eyes and sighed.

He pulled his backpack from under his seat, holding it in his lap. He leaned down, smelling the sweaty canvas of four years of high school and the melange of scents he distinctly recognized from home. His new life rushed toward him. He held the bag: his present concrete in his hand, his past stored safely in memory.

Seeger stared out the window, remembering idle afternoons with Joan, cloud-gazing on hillside parks in Austin. They would pick out clouds, describe their shapes, and destroy them.

It was one of the first psychic feats she'd taught him. Clouds barely had mass; they were a world without anything solid to grab onto or bounce off. They barely existed. You could easily affect them with your mind. You'd stare at a cloud, relax, will it to disintegrate; and it would. Over the years, he'd tested it back and forth: picked one cloud surrounded by lots of others, so it couldn't be attributed to the wind. His cloud would disappear and no other. He'd pick a big cloud and try to disintegrate only a part of it, only the side of an edge, something that shouldn't happen on its own. It would. Unlike the eye-dust water faeries, the nuclear catastrophes, or global axis shifts, cloud-disintegrating had always worked, had always survived skepticism.

Seeger hadn't tried it in years. He'd nearly forgotten about it. Since it didn't serve any practical purpose, like readings, it felt more like a parlor game, and he'd not bothered with it. It had always worked, though, and didn't require any risky deep meditative states. He looked out at the clouds and thought about trying it. If it flopped, like the seance, maybe he could put all this supernatural crap behind him, leave it with his parents' bodies in Texas. And Joan. Maybe Joan. He wondered where she was, if he'd hear from her again.

Did the seance really flop?

He let the clouds be.

The Black Wedding

Listen to the story I was told once
by the old gravedigger of this county:
there was a lover whose untimely fortune
saw his loved one taken away by death.

Every night he would go to the cemetery
to contemplate the tomb of that lovely woman;
the people would whisper in secret,
"He's a dead man escaped from the grave."

One horrible night he broke
the marble of the abandoned tomb
and dug into the earth, in his arms
he carried away the rigid skeleton of his beloved.

In his sad, dim room,
under the flickering light of a funeral candle
he sat beside the cold bones
and celebrated his wedding with the corpse,
and celebrated his wedding with the corpse.

He tied the naked bones and crowned the empty skull
with a wreath of flowers,
the dry mouth, he covered with kisses,
smiling, he told her of his love.

Then he took his bride to the soft nuptial bed
and lay beside her, full of love,
with the rigid skeleton in his arm,
he fell asleep, never to awaken again.

Traditional Tex-Mex song recorded by Lydia Mendoza. Transcription and translation by Guillermo Hernández and Yolanda Zepeda.